FAST VENGEANCE

DEA FAST SERIES

KAYLEA CROSS

FAST VENGEANCE

Copyright © 2018
by Kaylea Cross

* * * * *

Cover Art & Print Formatting:
Sweet 'N Spicy Designs
Developmental Edits: Deborah Nemeth
Line Edits: Joan Nichols
Digital Formatting: LK Campbell

* * * * *

ISBN: 978-1718841383

Dedication

For my husband, for all the things you do for me and our family that allow me to chase my dreams. I love you for being my steady Eddie. Xo

Author's Note

Well, here we are at Hamilton and Victoria's story. I've been looking forward to writing this one since the beginning of the series, and the words just flew out of my fingers as I wrote it. I hope that's a good sign. I love this story so much, and hope you will too.

Kaylea :)

Prologue

"*Tia* Victoria, do you want some more chicken?"

Seated in the last spot next to the kids' table, Victoria handed off the platter of sautéed green beans and turned her head to smile down at her six-year-old nephew. "No thanks, sweetie, my plate's so full I can't fit another thing on it."

He put the chicken platter down and went back to staring longingly at his own plate, knowing better than to so much as pick up his fork until they were all given the signal. Everyone knew the rules.

She leaned over to whisper to him. "Go ahead and sneak a bite. I'll cover for you."

He grinned and snatched up a bite of cucumber from his salad, doing his best to chew without drawing any notice.

Victoria smiled to herself. Due to her latest whirlwind book tour, it had been a few months since she'd been able to come to Sunday dinner at her parents' house, and she'd missed it. This most recent book about the deadly *Veneno* cartel was her best work yet as an investigative journalist and she was damn proud of it.

The usual suspects were present: her siblings, grandparents, aunts, uncles, cousins and their children. Her father's side of the family, all living right here in Houston, filling the old dining room with life and noise in the way that only a big, extended family could. They always celebrated special occasions together. It was loud and chaotic, but she wouldn't have it any other way.

When all the dishes had been passed around the table and everyone had filled their plates, her father raised his wineglass for a toast to signal that the meal was about to commence. "To the cooks," he said, indicating him and Victoria's mother, his deep voice cutting through the room with ease.

Then he turned to his parents, seated as always side by side to his right. They'd been married for more than fifty years, had risked everything to leave Mexico as teenagers with only the clothes on their backs, and start a new life here in Houston. "And to my father, the patriarch of this family, on his eightieth birthday. This family exists and enjoys a wonderful life because of your bravery and sacrifice. I hope we're all gathered around in this same room in twenty years for your hundredth."

Smiling fondly at her grandfather, Victoria raised her glass in salute. "To *Abuelito*." With a hearty cheers and clinking of glasses all along the two tables set end to end, everyone sipped and then dug in. Conversation and laughter flowed freely along with the wine.

She'd finished her first helping and was reaching for another serving of roasted veggies when tires squealed on the driveway. Victoria and several others turned around to look out the tall windows that overlooked the front of the house. From her vantage point she could just make out the back bumper of a minivan that had pulled up behind her grandparents' car.

"You expecting anyone?" she asked her father.

"No," he said, putting down his napkin and pushing his chair back. "I'll go see who it is. Back in a minute."

He was halfway to the front door when something slammed against it. He jerked to a halt and everyone else went silent, all of them staring at the door, wondering what the hell was going on.

Before anyone could move or say anything, it burst open. Victoria jumped and smothered a gasp as her father stumbled back and three masked men stormed in. They all carried military-style rifles.

A wave of terror broke over her. Cries of alarm rang out from around the table but she couldn't tear her eyes off the intruders. She instinctively grabbed her nephew and turned her body away from the men, shielding the boy while parents gathered up their frightened children and re-treated to the rear of the room. She sat there staring at the men, frozen, her muscles rigid, heart hammering in her throat.

Her father hadn't moved from his spot. He had a gun safe, but it was down in the basement. And even if they used all the guns in it, they didn't have a prayer of fighting off three men armed with automatic rifles.

"Get the hell out of my house," her father snarled, bravely blocking their way.

The masked man in the lead stepped forward and shoved him so hard he crashed into the wall. Then he turned to face them and it seemed to Victoria that his gaze landed on her.

"Victoria Gomez," he said in a tone that sent chills racing down her spine. "My boss has been so looking forward to finally meeting you."

She blanched as realization hit home. Carlos Ruiz, the most vicious *Veneno* lieutenant. He'd come for her.

Her sister-in-law wrenched Victoria's nephew from

her arms and ran to her husband, her entire family now gathered against the far wall at the end of the dining room, the men standing in front of the women. They were trapped in here, the only way out past the armed intruders.

Victoria's entire body was numb as she woodenly pushed to her feet, fear flooding her entire body. But when one of the other men stalked over to grab her father and wrench him to his feet, the anger snapped the band of fear wrapped around her ribcage.

"Let him go," she demanded, taking a step forward. They were here for her, for what she'd uncovered. Her family had nothing to do with it.

The man in front, clearly the one in charge, smiled. A cruel twist of his lips within the hole revealed by the mask. His black eyes glittered like a snake's. "Come here." He held his palm up, crooked his fingers at her. Like she was a dog he expected to come to heel when called.

One of her brothers grabbed her shoulder, tugged her backward. "Vic. Don't," he whispered, his voice tense.

She was afraid to move, but more terrified of what would happen if she didn't. "If I do, you'll let him go?" she said to the man, surprised her voice was working.

The man dropped his hand. Shrugged. "Sure."

Indecision warred inside her. But what choice did she have? She had to protect her family.

"Vic, no," her brother warned.

I have to.

Twisting away from his restraining grip, she ignored the frightened cries behind her and forced her feet to carry her toward the man. Her belly was clamped tight, nausea churning in waves, each step a small eternity. Some of her siblings or their significant others would have their phones in their pockets. One of them would have dialed 911 already. Maybe the dispatcher would figure out something was wrong and send the cops.

They won't get here in time.

When she came within reach, the leader snaked out a hand and grabbed her by the hair. She stifled a cry and stiffened as he hauled her up against him, grabbing his wrist to try and pull free. It was no use. He was too strong. She shuddered at the unforgiving outline of his rifle digging into her right hip.

With a jerk on her hair he wrenched her around to face her family, all huddled around the children against the far wall behind the table, some of them crying, others staring at her with stricken expressions. Victoria stared back at them and met her mother's eyes, panic flooding her system.

The leader spoke to the one holding her father. "Let him go."

Her father immediately rushed over to gather Victoria's mother into his arms and stood with the others, trying to shield his wife. His parents cowered behind him, clinging to one another, their lined faces wet with tears.

Victoria swallowed hard and stood rooted to the spot, her hand wrapped around the powerful wrist holding her hair, not daring to move. Then the man who had been holding her father crossed over to grab her wrists, wrench them behind her and bound them with something tight and hard that bit into her skin. Zip tie.

"Don't hurt them," she blurted, her voice husky as she fought not to cry and beg. She'd spent more than three years tracking the rise of the *Veneno* cartel, and the past nine months using all her contacts to research Carlos Ruiz. She knew what he did to his enemies. And she also knew all the horrific things he did to his female captives.

"We've got to go now," the man said, his mouth right beside her ear, making her cringe. "Say goodbye, Victoria."

Mind working frantically, she swept her gaze over her beloved family. The sight of those frightened faces staring back at her broke her heart. There was nothing she could do to escape. This was the last time she would see them. Ruiz's men would take her to a hideout somewhere off the grid, torture her for days or maybe even weeks before killing her or selling her off, like they had with the other female captives.

Tears flooded her eyes. She couldn't control it. Couldn't stop it. "I love you all," she said hoarsely. "Goodbye."

"No. Victoria, *no!*" her mother cried, her face twisting with grief as she tried to push away from her husband.

Victoria expected the men to haul her away. Instead, the hand in her hair tightened, arching her neck back at a painful angle. Holding her there in front of her family. "Do it," he commanded.

The other two men stepped in front of him, raised their weapons, and opened fire.

"No! Oh my God, *no!*" Victoria's screams of horror were drowned out beneath the thunder of automatic gunfire as it ripped through the room. Her family fell like a field of hay to the sweep of a scythe.

She shut her eyes and tried to twist away but it didn't block out the screams and cries of agony above the noise, the thud of the bullets hitting home.

She kept screaming and fought her captor, trying to wrench free, to stop this somehow. She screamed until her throat was raw, was still screaming after the gunfire had stopped.

The silence finally registered over the roar of blood in her ears. And when she opened her eyes to face the carnage at last, her entire family lay dead or dying on the dining room floor. They lay on top of one another like cordwood stacked at the far end of the room, parents collapsed on top of their children, having desperately tried to shield them with their own bodies.

A high-pitched sound of grief tore from her. From beneath her brother's body protruded her nephew's little leg. It twitched in the rapidly spreading pool of blood staining the tile floor.

He was still alive, but not for long.

Soul-shattering grief slammed into her. She was shaking all over. The pain was unbearable. Searing her lungs, ripping her heart apart. She couldn't breathe. Couldn't bear the agony.

A hood plunged roughly over her head, hurtling her into darkness as the man holding her dragged her from the house. But even in the blackness, all she could see was that horrific tableau of her dead family burned into the backs of her eyelids.

It's my fault. They had been murdered because of her. For however long she had left on this earth, she would have to live with that.

Her captor shoved her onto a seat as an engine roared to life. Doors slammed shut and the tires squealed as the vehicle raced off.

And through the crushing pain of guilt and loss, she was well aware that her suffering had only begun.

Chapter One

An arm wrapped around her throat from behind.

Victoria automatically stepped to the side and turned, throwing her left arm straight out and wrapping it around her attacker's arms, then threw a punch with her right. The moment she was free, she whirled and rammed a knee into her attacker's belly.

An expertly placed forearm whipped out to block it at the last moment. "Good. Very good, you didn't even hesitate this time."

Straightening, Victoria looked at the other woman. "Guess I must have a good teacher, huh?"

Briar DeLuca grinned, her teeth startling white against her dusky skin tone. "Well, you could do worse."

"She could do way worse." Trinity rose from her chair on the other side of the room, cup of coffee in hand. She was sensuality personified as she walked toward them in her red wrap-style dress that came to just below her knees and hugged every curve.

But that magnetic sensuality hid a darker edge.

Underneath all the sleek glamor and sex appeal, Trinity was deadly. Victoria didn't know the details, but both Trinity and Briar had been part of something called The Valkyrie program, a top-secret group run by the government that was now disbanded.

Unlike Briar, who used a sniper rifle for her kills, Victoria got the sense that Trinity had made a career of eliminating her targets by far more…up close and personal means. Both women were fascinating. And they were both survivors themselves, which made Victoria feel more comfortable with them.

"You two done yet?" Trinity asked. "Because there's a bottle of wine chilling in the fridge, and it's been calling my name for the past three hours. You're both lucky it's still in there."

Wearing yoga pants and a tank top that showed off her strong arms, Briar arched a dark eyebrow at Victoria. "Well? Your call."

She nodded and swiped a forearm across her sweaty forehead. They'd been working for nearly an hour at this point. "I'm done."

"Wine it is," Briar announced, spinning around and heading for Trinity's fridge.

"Make yourself at home," Trinity said dryly, following her.

"Always do." She plucked the wine from the fridge. "Oooh, and you've made food for us too?"

"A few nibbles," Trinity answered, bumping her aside with a hip to take out a couple of platters.

Victoria moaned as she took a seat on one of the stools at the island. "Cream puffs?" A whole plate of them, each the size of a golf ball, and all of them covered in dark chocolate.

"And strawberries," Trinity was quick to add. "Also dipped in chocolate, but whatever. Because we all need five to ten servings of fruits and veggies a day, after all."

She popped a puff into her mouth, her pretty blue eyes sparkling as she chewed it.

Victoria grabbed one in each hand, eyeing the berries. She could easily demolish the entire plate.

"Ooh, doubling down right out of the gate. I like it," Briar said, sliding Victoria a glass of wine across the island. "Just make sure you save some for me."

"Not promising anything," Victoria mumbled around her second creampuff, taking the wine.

She was so much more comfortable with these women now than she had been at first. Even to the point that she no longer felt the need to keep the scars around her neck covered. The ones on her wrists and ankles, others scattered over her body didn't bother her as much as the ones on her neck. They were healed but deep in places and ugly. No one looking at them could misunderstand what had caused them.

She resisted the urge to pull her hair forward to hide them. Briar and Trinity knew she was a rape victim who had escaped the *Veneno* cartel. They didn't look at her with pity or treat her like she was fragile. Instead, they had taught her how to fight back.

Victoria had been working out with them once a week for several months now, learning self-defense techniques and basic hand-to-hand combat tactics. Enough for her to feel confident about her ability to defend herself if necessary moving forward. Just one of the ways she was preparing for the next life transition that lay ahead of her when she left the WITSEC facility, looming closer every day. When it would hit exactly she didn't know, but she needed to be prepared for when it did.

Because no matter what her future held, she would never be a victim again.

Taking a final sip, Briar glanced at her empty wineglass for a second, then at her watch. "Eh, we've got time," she announced, and poured herself another glass.

"I love how anal your security team is about time. I could set my watch by them," she said to Victoria. "I know the Marshals Service are the best when it comes to personal protection, but it's been truly impressive to see little bits of how they work."

WITSEC was no joke. "They don't mess around, that's for sure." Yet as good as they were, even the marshals weren't impervious to threats from the *Venenos*. Only a few months back, the marshals had lost a key government asset in the ongoing fight against the cartel. Since that day, they'd tightened measures even more.

"So, where are we meeting next week?" Trinity asked before taking a sip of wine.

"Not sure yet." Today they were at Trinity's place, a high-end, secure penthouse condo where she lived with Brody Colebrook, a sniper for the FBI's elite Hostage Rescue Team.

"We could do it at my place. Matt would love to meet you," Briar said with a grin. She was married to the HRT commander.

"I'd like to meet him too," Victoria said. Their sessions had only ever involved the three of them, so she hadn't met their significant others. "I'll have to run it past my security detail, see what the boss says." The Marshals Service had only allowed these weekly training sessions in amongst the rest of her scheduled activities because of Trinity's and Briar's backgrounds and security clearances. Well, and because Victoria had an insider champion of sorts.

DEA Supervisory Special Agent Brock Hamilton, the team leader for FAST Bravo. He'd set this whole thing up for her, to help give her more confidence and a sense of security while she tried to put the pieces of her life back together.

"When does FAST Bravo get back from their deployment?" Briar asked, sneaking another berry.

"This coming Monday." Victoria had been counting down the days. Beginning on the night she'd escaped Ruiz's clutches, when Brock and his team had stumbled upon her in the woods, he'd become an integral part of her journey on this path to healing. Not healing fully, but enough that she didn't bleed inside every minute of every day.

"If you talk to Brock again, tell him I said hi," Trinity said. Between FAST Bravo and the FBI's Hostage Rescue Team, they were all part of a tightly-knit, slightly dysfunctional and badass family of sorts. They'd brought Victoria into their circle to help her, and she appreciated having that kind of support more than they would ever know, especially since her family was all dead.

"So how are you feeling about next week?" Briar asked her, dark brown eyes delving into hers. "Anxious to get it over with?"

Ruiz's sentencing, she meant. "Yes. I think I'll be relieved when it's done."

"You will," Trinity said with confidence.

"Hope so." Victoria had come a long way to get to this point. She'd endured months of intense therapy, battling her demons and fighting to find a new purpose for her life.

After so many weeks of waiting to learn what the result of her painful testimony would be, Ruiz had finally agreed to a plea deal and sentencing was coming up next week. He wouldn't get the death penalty now, but he likely would die in jail. That was the best Victoria could hope for at this point. It had to be enough. She refused to let him have any more power over her or her thoughts.

"Are you gonna be there?" Briar asked her, topping up Victoria's glass.

"I'm going to wait and see how I feel." Hard as it was to face that monster after what he'd done to her and all that he'd taken from her, she wanted to be there when he received whatever sentence the judge handed down.

Whether or not she could go through with it remained to be seen. Her last interaction with Ruiz had been while she was on the witness stand giving her statement to the judge, and it hadn't been pleasant.

"You given any thought to what you'll do after they release you from the facility?" Trinity asked, slapping Briar's hand out of the way so she could take a strawberry.

Other than start a new life under a new identity in another city? "Some." The one-year mark from the day of the massacre that had taken her family and resulted in her captivity was coming up the week after the sentencing.

It was more than an anniversary; it was a psychological marker, a line she had drawn in the sand. That was the day she had vowed to move forward again.

"The hardest part is going to be finding a purpose after all of this." And losing the few friends she had made here. When she left D.C., she would truly be starting fresh. Right now she was torn between going back to school to earn a psych degree and maybe become a counselor so she could help other trauma victims, or write fiction under a pen name. She already had notes and a partial outline for a book she had in mind that used some of her experiences as a captive.

"Survival," Trinity said flatly, a hard glint in her eyes. "You live your life to the fullest when they let you go, secure in the knowledge that the human pieces of shit responsible for it all are either dead or rotting in jail."

She lowered her gaze to her wine. "It doesn't make the pain go away."

"No," Briar said, sliding a hand over to cover Victoria's, bringing her eyes up to meet that dark stare. "Nothing ever will. But you're so strong. You'll go on because you have to, and because if you don't, then they win. And time will dull the pain eventually." Her tone and the shadows in her too-old eyes told Victoria she spoke from personal experience.

"I hope so. It's true that I feel an obligation to really live after this, and try to find happiness on my family's behalf." They were dead, their dreams and hopes snuffed out within minutes. She swallowed. "The guilt isn't ever going to go away, though."

"We get it," Trinity said. "But eventually I hope you'll live for yourself as well as them. That's something we both struggled with for a long time," she said, glancing at Briar for a second before looking back at Victoria. "When it all comes down to it, moving on and finding happiness really is the best form of revenge."

"Exactly." Briar's smile was sharp as a blade as she raised her glass in a toast. "To sweet revenge."

Victoria's lips curved upward. Revenge had driven her all this time, fueled her and kept her going when all she wanted to do was lie down. It would see her through what came next as well. "I'll drink to that."

"You doing something special to mark the occasion?" Trinity asked, holding up the plate of strawberries to them now that she'd had some. "Anything you might want to do?"

She'd like to be able to go out in public like a regular person, without a security detail or having to look over her shoulder all the time. To go out to eat, or even to a movie. Maybe go away someplace quiet, a cabin in the mountains, and just *be* for a while.

But before any of that, there was something else she had been thinking about...

Her mind immediately latched onto the idea she'd been toying with for several months now. "Not sure. I think it should be something big, something I'll always remember and look back on with a smile." She paused, sipped her wine. "I dunno. Maybe I'll go out on a date."

Trinity's eyes widened in surprise and interest. She lowered her wineglass, her stare never wavering from Victoria's. "You're thinking about dating again?"

Dating, no. Something else entirely, yes. "I'm thinking more along the lines of maybe climbing back into the saddle again, so to speak."

The women stared at her in astonishment, their gazes curious. "Wow," Trinity murmured. "Are you…sure about that?"

Victoria shrugged, unsurprised and unoffended by her reaction. After what Victoria had endured, having sex again seemed like her own personal Everest. A goal she needed to meet and conquer. "Just something I've been contemplating."

"Do you have somebody in mind?" Trinity asked, her expression concerned.

"Maybe."

"Maybe isn't a no, so you obviously do." Briar leaned forward, her expression eager now. "Since your options have been severely limited over the past few months due to your living arrangements and lack of social life, I'll have to assume it's someone we might know." She narrowed her eyes thoughtfully. "Spill."

Trinity chuckled softly. "Give it up, Briar. She's never gonna tell us."

Victoria smiled into her wineglass, keeping the answer to herself.

But yes. As a matter of fact, she did have a specific someone in mind.

Chapter Two

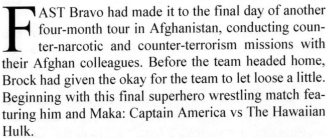

FAST Bravo had made it to the final day of another four-month tour in Afghanistan, conducting counter-narcotic and counter-terrorism missions with their Afghan colleagues. Before the team headed home, Brock had given the okay for the team to let loose a little. Beginning with this final superhero wrestling match featuring him and Maka: Captain America vs The Hawaiian Hulk.

And right now Cap was getting his ass handed to him.

"You gonna make your move, Cap, or what?" one of the guys asked him from somewhere close by as Brock struggled to fight his way out of Maka's scary-powerful hold. Guy was built like a freaking tank.

"Tag me," Granger demanded, crouching next to them. He stretched out his hand, shaking it in front of Brock's face.

It took everything he had, but Brock managed to move enough to slap Granger's palm. Abiding by the rules, Maka let him go and braced himself for his next opponent just as Granger gave a whoop of glee and pounced.

Brock scrambled out of the way just in time as the two men grappled on the floor. Granger somehow was still on top of Maka. Time to end this.

"Hold him down!" Brock shouted. Panting, he rolled to his feet as half the team dog piled on the big guy on the concrete floor. The other half stood by shouting encouragement from the sidelines, waiting for their turn to jump in to this last and epic championship wrestling match.

Desperate to defend his title, Maka struggled to extricate himself and amongst the tangle of limbs Brock's gaze shot to the belt strapped around his teammate's waist. The ugliest damn wrestling championship belt ever made, comprised of paracord, duct tape and the front case of a claymore. But as team leader, it was a matter of pride that Brock take it from him. And besides, after a solid two months of parading it around Bagram while mocking the rest of them for not being able to take him, Maka had this coming.

"Hurry up," Granger growled to Brock, his bearded face now twisted with strain as he did his best to hold onto Maka, who was done playing and trying to throw guys off him amidst guttural snarls.

Brock crouched down just out of range of Maka's big, flailing boots, eyes locked on his target, and waited until his guys had Maka mostly pinned for a moment. Then he seized his moment.

Diving forward, he grabbled hold of the belt with both hands and yanked it free from Maka's waist with a satisfying pop. "Got it!" he shouted, jumping to his feet to hold it over his head in triumph.

Still trapped under a pile of teammates, Maka glowered up at him, one dark brown eye swelling a little. "Doesn't count," he gritted out between clenched teeth, bucking like an enraged bull. "I'm still the champ."

"Brains over brawn, my friend. Can't be champ without the belt," Brock said, enjoying rubbing it in as he wound the belt around his own waist.

Maka let out a roar, the veins standing out in his neck. Hoots and hollers followed. A second later, Prentiss lost his grip on Maka's legs and went flying, crashing back into the folding table leaning against the wall.

"*Get the tables*," Granger called out, grinning like an idiot as he got clear of the writhing mass of bodies and raced around to drag it out and unfold it. Maka swore and fought two more guys off him, but two more jumped in to keep him in place.

They'd already broken three tables during the deployment, but they were leaving base to head home in a couple hours, so what was one more? "Well, if we have to we have to," Brock said with a mock sigh, and started toward Maka with an evil grin.

Maka hit him with a lethal glare, his face barely visible from the midst of the headlock Rodriguez currently had him in. "You bastards, don't you dare—" Whatever else he was going to say was cut off amidst another scuffle.

Two more guys jumped into the fray, laughing like maniacs. Brock waded in, managed to grab Maka around the hips and hold on as they hoisted the big guy off the floor and carted him toward the waiting table. "Get ready," he warned, fighting a laugh. Maka wasn't going quietly, either. Five of them were holding various parts of him, and still the guy wouldn't be subdued.

It took some doing, but together they managed to co-ordinate their movements and hoist Maka above their heads. He stopped fighting, going rigid because he knew what was coming. "You *assholes*," he snarled.

"He's mine." Brock moved into position beneath him, grabbing him by the waistband and planting his other hand between Maka's shoulder blades. "On three," he ordered, ignoring Maka's continued threats. "One. Two... *Three*."

With everyone's help, he shoved Maka higher into the

air and used the momentum to slam his back flat against the tabletop. The hinges shattered, the cheap plywood snapping like a dry twig under the force of Maka's huge frame. A cheer rose up as man and table crashed to the floor with a thud.

Maka grunted, rolling on his side to slay them all with a lethal look.

"And the Hawaiian Hulk is still okay," Granger announced with a laugh.

Breathing hard, face red and covered in sweat, Maka cursed under his breath as he slowly got to his knees. He stayed there for a moment, turned his head to nail Brock with a resentful scowl. "Doesn't count," he panted.

"It totally counts," Brock informed him, sliding his hands over the belt. "Fits me perfectly, too. I think I'll wear it home on the flight."

Maka grunted and struggled to his feet while the team teased him. His expression softened a moment later when someone tossed him a beer. By the time they got on the plane for the first leg of their journey home, Maka merely threw Brock a dirty look before gingerly settling back in his seat.

Time and distance blurred on the trip back to Virginia. By the time they arrived at Quantico at 07:00 local time, everyone was tired but ready for the full day already scheduled.

Back at headquarters that afternoon, Brock groaned and stood on tiptoe to stretch his arms over his head. Commander Taggart hadn't wasted any time in putting them through their paces on their first morning back stateside. They'd done PT together as a team at 08:00 and had been going full out ever since. Even Maka, who was pretending not to be stiff and sore even though they all knew better.

Brock's shirt was soaked with sweat, sticking to his body when he pulled his tactical vest over his head. "Does it feel to anyone else like we never even left?"

To his right, Rodriguez barked out a laugh and kept cleaning his Glock. "I was thinking the same thing."

"Feels good to be back. Home sweet home, boys," Colebrook said with a grin to Brock's left as he packed away his gear into his locker.

"Guess Taggart was worried we might have lost our edge over in our favorite stomping grounds. We're lucky he let us knock off a couple hours early," Brock said. "Personally, I'm looking forward to heading home and catching up on my sleep." His internal clock was all screwed up from the time change. Except for him and Lockhart, the rest of the guys were no doubt anxious to get home to their women.

"Hmm, I dunno, we've been sharing rooms for so long, maybe you guys should bunk together tonight, so Cap doesn't get lonely," Granger called out from the back of the room.

Brock smirked and shook his head at the ribbing. The team could always count on Granger having an endless supply of comebacks and sarcasm. "Had my fill of sleeping next to you guys at Bagram, thanks. And for the record, Granger, you snore like a fucking chainsaw. I don't know how Taylor stands you."

Granger stood up from lacing his boots and gave him a cocky grin. "Because I make up for it in *other* ways that I intend to put to good use tonight." He bounced his auburn eyebrows up and down for emphasis.

Brock huffed out a laugh. "I don't wanna know, man. And now, if you'll all excuse me, and since being team leader has at least a *few* perks, I'm taking first shower." He headed off to the shower room, smiling at the verbal jabs called out after him.

After a hot shower and changing into jeans and a Henley shirt, he opened up his locker and took out his phone. He'd missed one call from his bank, and another from Victoria Gomez. He smiled, pleasantly surprised, and waited to call her back until he was headed home in his truck because he wanted to talk to her in private.

Their history was pretty complex, almost as complex as his feelings toward her. Since the night she'd escaped from the cartel not quite a year ago, he and Victoria had formed a bond of sorts. They'd attended various meetings and briefings pertaining to *Veneno* investigations together over the past twelve months, all strictly business related. But his favorite were the times when they got to meet at the range so he could teach her how to shoot, just the two of them, while her security detail camped out in the lobby.

His background and security clearance were the only reasons it had been allowed. She'd become a pretty decent shot, too. Not exactly the most romantic of settings, but watching her slowly gain her confidence with him while becoming less afraid and far more than proficient with a firearm were rewards in themselves. Those were the only times they'd been alone together, and he wished they'd had more.

The last time he'd seen her was right before they deployed to Afghanistan on this most recent rotation. They'd talked via video chat and emailed or texted back and forth a bit, but always surface stuff and it wasn't the same as seeing her face to face. He'd texted her last night when his team had arrived home, hoping to talk to her. Figure out a way to see her again.

He dialed her number with his hands-free device as he drove away from base, conscious of the tingle of excitement in his gut.

"Hey, I got your text," she said when she answered. "Good to be home?"

Even better to hear your voice. "Yup. Didn't miss the D.C. traffic, though," he added, now stopped on the highway over a mile from his exit.

"I'll bet. Everybody on the team okay?"

He loved that she cared enough to ask. There was so

much he couldn't tell her about what had happened while they were away, but he could tell her that. "All good. Every one of us made it back in one piece." Though Maka would be sore for a few more days.

"I'm glad to hear it." She cleared her throat, signaling she was about to get down to business. If there was one thing he'd learned about her, it was that she spoke her mind. He found it damn refreshing. "Listen, you can totally say no, but I was wondering if I could come over to talk to you about something."

His internal radar pinged. Was something wrong? Outside of the range, the only other place he'd seen her was at a hospital, a lawyer's office or a meeting room in a secure building. "Come over…to my place?"

"Yes. If you're okay with that," she added quickly. "I'd have to get clearance from my security team, but since they all know you, under the circumstances I think they'd probably allow it."

He was still concerned. "Are you okay?"

"Yes, everything's fine."

The tension in his gut eased. What did she want to talk to him about that required them to be face to face at his place? He was definitely intrigued, and wasn't passing up the opportunity to see her. She'd been on his mind constantly while he was away. "Sure, when did you have in mind?"

"I was hoping for tonight, if you're not too tired. It won't take long."

He was bagged, but his tiredness disappeared under a rush of excitement at seeing her again. "Works for me. Have you had dinner?"

"Not yet. Want me to bring something over?"

"I'll grab some groceries on my way home. Does seven work?"

"For me, it does. I'll check with my team and get back to you. Okay?"

"Okay. Talk to you soon." They ended the call, and he found himself smiling despite the traffic as he took the next exit a quarter mile up, diverting to the grocery store. After picking up everything he needed, he headed home on the feeder routes, unpacked everything and tidied up his condo even though he'd had a cleaning service come by a few days before he got home.

He was in the middle of unpacking when Victoria texted that she'd be over at seven. Brock gave her his address, put away his bags and got busy prepping dinner. He was a pretty basic cook and rarely cooked for anyone. Burgers, steaks. Except Victoria didn't eat beef now, because it reminded her of the night her family had been killed.

He blew out a breath, eyed the ingredients laid out on the counter. Really, how bad could he screw up chicken and grilled veggies?

Bad enough.

He could have looked up a recipe online. Except he wasn't much good in the kitchen even with written instructions. So he swallowed his pride, came to his senses and dialed the team's foodie and food inhaler, Maka. Who hopefully wasn't already so deep in homecoming bliss with his girlfriend Abby that he would still answer his damn phone.

"Cap. What's up, *brah*?" his teammate answered.

Thank God. "I need some cooking assistance."

"Yeah?" He sounded surprised. "So, let me get this straight. You pull a stunt like that at Bagram, have the entire team dog pile on me just so you can steal the belt, and now you think you can call me up and ask me for help?"

While at Bagram they'd formed a superhero wrestling league a few weeks in to pass the time. "Yeah. And by the way, it's hanging over my desk in my office right now."

Maka chuckled. "That's cold, man, but fine. I dig that you need my help."

God, maybe he should have just risked burning everything instead of making this call. "Uh huh. So? Yes or no?"

"Of course yes. You want to ask me, or Abby?"

"You'll do. So I'm making chicken and grilled veggies for company. Peppers, zucchini and stuff." Seemed simple enough when he'd seen something similar cooked on the food channel.

"Okay. Whaddya want to know?"

"How do I make it taste good?"

Maka huffed out a laugh. "What kind of seasonings you got?"

"I dunno, some stuff in the cupboard. Basic stuff." He glanced at his watch. "And I gotta be honest, I don't have long to get this done."

"Why, who you having over?"

"A friend."

"A female friend?"

Brock had no trouble picturing the eager expression to match that tone. "Maybe."

Another low laugh. "All right, be all secretive. Here's what you need."

Brock pulled out every single spice he owned from the pantry. All five of them, including salt and pepper. Maka declared the remaining three totally useless and revolting for chicken and veggies. "Yeah, well, that's all I've got. Work with me."

"That is just so sad and wrong," Maka said in disgust. "Man, I'm going with you to the store tomorrow so you can have stuff on hand that will actually make your food *taste* good. Damn, Cap."

He flushed. "I eat out a lot."

"Yeah, I'll bet you do with only that in your pantry."

"Okay, so my seasonings suck. Now what?"

It took some doing, and Brock had to run next door and

ask his elderly neighbor for some basil and balsamic vinegar—which she thankfully had. Once he had all the instructions from Maka figured out, he went into frantic chef mode.

Thirty minutes later, to his surprise the kitchen smelled freaking amazing. He was just basting more of the homemade glazing stuff onto the chicken for the last part of the cooking time when Victoria texted that she was in the underground parking garage. A surge of excitement hit his bloodstream, similar to when he was about to lead the team on an op.

She was still at the WITSEC safe site here in D.C. even though her testimony was over. Maybe the government thought she could still be of help with the ongoing Nieto and Montoya investigations, because they hadn't sent her to her new life yet. The marshals in charge of her security had tightened protocols even more after the breaches with other witnesses pertaining to the *Veneno* cartel six months ago. Her driver would wait in the vehicle while the other marshal came in and checked the building.

Brock met him at the door. They knew each other, so he went back to finishing up dinner while the marshal checked his place.

"Okay, I'll bring her up in a few minutes," he said to Brock when he was done searching. If the marshal wondered what the hell was going on with this visit, he didn't let on with his tone or expression.

"Sounds good." He couldn't wait to see her, had taken the two books she'd written with him to reread at Bagram. Both were about her investigative work on North American drug cartels, mostly about the *Venenos*. Incredible, detailed work he admired, but respected tenfold more now that he had gotten to know her and her story. The cartel had targeted her because of her work, yet even everything she had endured at their hands hadn't crushed her spirit. The woman was a serious badass in her own right.

He'd still been overseas when she'd given her victim impact statement to the judge in front of Ruiz, and he wished like hell he could have been there to support her. They'd talked about it a little afterward, over the phone. Facing down Ruiz after so many months and recounting aloud the things his men had done to her and her family must have been tough.

Tough but awesome, because she had so much strength in her. Maybe more than she realized. She amazed him.

At the knock on the door, more excitement tingled in his gut. He answered it, nodded once at the marshal before allowing his gaze to drink in the sight of Victoria as he stepped back out of the way. "Come on in."

The marshal headed back down the hallway. Victoria aimed a little smile at Brock and walked past into the entryway, her coffee-brown eyes filled with warmth. "It's good to see you."

He put his hands in his pockets to stem the urge to hug her. "Good to see you too." Better than good, although he was careful to hide it.

She took off her coat, revealing a short-sleeve cherry red turtleneck that hugged the lean lines of her torso. Dark, snug jeans made her legs look a mile long. She'd grown out her hair since he'd last seen her, the deep brown waves caressing her shoulders.

She was even more stunning than he remembered.

She glanced around his place. "It smells fantastic in here."

He hoped it tasted decent. If not, he'd order another team dog pile on Maka as punishment. "It'll be ready in a few minutes. Come sit and make yourself comfortable while I finish up."

She followed him into the kitchen and took a seat at the far counter, composed. Contained, as always. It made him wonder what lay beneath that cool exterior. He'd seen glimpses of the fire in her. He wanted to see more of it.

"I bought some wine if you want some," he said.

"Love a glass, although I already had one earlier with Trinity and Briar and I'm a bit of a lightweight."

He raised an eyebrow as he poured the ruby liquid into a glass for her. "How's training going?"

"Good. We've been working on breaking chokeholds and disarming moves. I can give you a demo later if you want to see."

He smiled. "I might." Especially if it gave him an excuse to be close to her. Although after what she'd been through, he was scared to touch her in case it triggered a bad memory.

After making up their plates he carried them over to the counter and paused beside one of the stools, leaving one empty in between him and Victoria. He was always careful about not crowding her or making sudden moves around her, especially when they were alone. "You okay here, or do you want to move to the table?"

"Here's fine."

He lowered himself onto the stool and raised his own wineglass. "To you."

She blinked at him. "Me?"

He nodded. "You."

A startled smile spread across her face, and she touched her glass to his gently. "Well, thank you. And here's to you being home safe and sound."

"Cheers." He deliberately kept the conversation light as they ate, attuned to her body language, her face. She seemed relaxed around him, more so than she was with most other people, but there was definitely something going on in her head. What did she want to talk to him about?

"What rank did you have when you left the army?" she asked, surprising him.

"Captain. I'd just finished off my master's degree in leadership."

"So does your team call you Cap because of that, or because you're a Captain America superfreak?"

He cracked a grin. "The second part."

She studied him a moment, a faint smile playing on her lips. "It suits you. Did you always want to try out for Special Forces?"

Where was she going with this? "Ever since I thought about enlisting." He'd wanted to be part of the tip of the spear, and he'd gotten his wish.

"What made you decide to get out?"

"Constantly being on long deployments. They needed us in so many places, we were lucky if we got to come home once every year." He had to grin, because the irony didn't escape him. "And here I am, winding up in Afghanistan for four months every year."

She smiled then lowered her gaze and forked up a bite of vegetables. "I bet it was hard on your family too. Or your significant other."

Brock analyzed her line of questioning. Was she fishing? "My mom was worried sick every time I deployed. As for significant others, there were only a handful of those and it never lasted." Including his last serious relationship that had ended eighteen months ago. She got sick of him being gone all the time, and moved out while he was deployed.

"You seeing anyone now?"

The question made him glance at her in surprise. It had seemed casual enough, but the way she'd asked it, while avoiding his gaze, made him curious. "No. Just to jog your memory, I've been away for the past four months," he teased.

She shrugged. "That doesn't mean anything."

"Really? Who was I going to get involved with in Afghanistan, even if I'd had the time?" It happened, but as team leader, he took his responsibility to his team and his agency seriously, and tried to lead by example in every way.

She smiled. "Okay, forget I said that."

He leaned back, propping an elbow on the countertop. "Why do you ask?"

Rather than answer, she cleared her throat and reached for her wine, sharpening his interest and attention even more. It was like she was working up the courage to say something, which went against everything he knew about her personality to this point. "No reason."

Beautiful liar. He resumed eating the rest of his meal, watching her out of the corner of his eye. She was definitely nervous. Why?

He finished, forced himself to wait until she had only a bite or two left before asking, "So, what did you want to talk to me about?"

Her fork stopped in the act of spearing the last bit of chicken. She cleared her throat again, still wouldn't look at him. "I have a proposition for you."

All kinds of intrigued now, he pushed his plate away and gave her his full attention. "That sounds interesting." Way too interesting.

She took another sip of wine, almost for courage, then lowered her glass and finally turned her head to meet his gaze. "Once the sentencing happens, if nothing new surfaces about Nieto or Montoya that I could help them with, it probably won't be long until they move me out of D.C. and send me to my new life."

A weird tightening sensation pulled in his chest. Dread. He'd known the time would come when she could leave and start over again somewhere else under a new identity. He just hadn't expected it to happen so soon. He wasn't ready to let her go. Felt certain that he would regret losing her, even though she wasn't his. His feelings made no sense, yet they were there nonetheless. "Right."

She looked away again, began fiddling with the stem of her wineglass. "So, the thing is, I've been working hard to get myself together. Prepare for starting over. For the most part, I feel ready. But there are other things. Areas where I don't feel ready at all."

He stayed quiet, watching her, letting her get to the point in her own time even though he was ready to burst from curiosity.

Drawing a deep breath, she met his eyes again. "I want to reclaim my sexuality again, and it has to be with someone I trust. I was hoping you would consider helping me with that."

Brock barely kept his mouth from falling open in shock. Of all the things she could have said, even though she spoke her mind, this was so unexpected and outside the realm of anything he'd anticipated, he wasn't even sure he'd heard her right. "You want me to sleep with you?" he blurted, needing to make sure he'd understood.

Her cheeks flushed, but to her credit she didn't look away. "If I can go that far. But if it would put you in a bad position or compromise your career in any way, then please pretend I never brought it up," she added quickly.

Brock stared at her in stunned silence for a moment. Was she fucking serious? He'd been harboring secret fantasies about her for months, feeling guilty as hell about it because he knew what she'd been through in those weeks she'd spent as a captive to Ruiz's men. And here she was asking him to take her to bed, but only if he was okay with it?

"Why?" he asked bluntly, refusing to let his little brain take over. This was important. He needed to understand why she needed this, why him, and he needed to hear it in her words.

"Because I want to have a normal life at some point in the future, possibly even a relationship with someone, and sex is going to be a stumbling block for me. When I was held prisoner they took my dignity and my self-image away. I want to reclaim those parts of myself. My femininity and my body, and I need a partner I trust to help me do that. So I thought maybe…" She glanced at him, the first stirrings of uncertainty written in her eyes.

Her answer made all kinds of sense, and yet there were still so many questions he wanted to ask. Starting with the most important one. "You trust me, and I'm glad. But that's not the same thing as wanting me." He paused a beat. "Do you want me?"

Because if she wasn't attracted to him physically, then even discussing this further was a bad idea.

She'd been brutally violated by multiple men. No matter how much he wanted her, no matter how nicely she asked, he refused to add to that trauma. He thought he'd caught a gleam of interest from her a few times over the past year, but hadn't read much into it because he assumed anything between them other than platonic friendship would be impossible.

She blushed harder. "Yes. I want you." It was almost a whisper.

The invisible chains wrapped around his ribcage suddenly released, and a surge of heat swept through him. He drew a deep breath, ordered his heart to slow down. "Good. What did you have in mind?"

"I think a sort of business arrangement would be best. We wouldn't be in a relationship or anything. We like and respect each other, and I think you're attracted to me too." She glanced up at him, almost as though seeking confirmation.

Did she really not know, or had he been that good at hiding it? No point in pretending now. "I am."

Her shoulders relaxed. "Then we'd just…take things one step at a time, hopefully get me over that hurdle. And soon after that, I'll be leaving. So it'll be short term and won't get messy." She said the last part like a sales pitch, as if he needed more convincing.

There was no way he could say no to this, even if he already did have feelings for her. She'd obviously thought this through, felt strongly about it if she'd worked up the guts to come here and ask him to his face. Brave lady. "And when did you want to start?"

She pushed back from the counter and turned on the stool to face him, a nervous smile on her lips. "What about right now?"

Chapter Three

She'd surprised him again, the second time in the past two minutes.

But instead of widening in shock, this time Brock's steel gray eyes heated, darkened, making Victoria's pulse beat double time in her throat as she awaited his response. She'd never been this bold before sexually, but the circumstances called for extreme measures. And she had thought long and hard about this for weeks before asking if she could meet him here tonight, working up her nerve all the while.

It made sense to her. Their time together was limited and would come to an end soon, maybe even in as little as a few days. She needed to do this, to take this part of herself back again. Rediscover what consensual sex was like with a man she actually wanted so she could try to put the nightmare of her past behind her and have the chance to live life fully. Maybe even have a relationship one day after she was put back out into the real world.

But Brock didn't say anything in response. Why wasn't he saying anything? Oh God, what if he'd changed his mind...

Holding her gaze, he slid off the stool, rising to his full height in front of her. Over six feet of powerful, alluring male. Medium brown hair cut short and neat, a little longer in front, wide, powerful shoulders and a sculpted chest.

She curled her fingers around the edge of her stool and tipped her head back to look up at him, nerves buzzing around in the pit of her stomach along with the warm glow of anticipation. She'd all but forgotten what it felt like to have butterflies—the good kind—around a man. Though she was nervous and unsure how she would react to intimate contact, even with him, she wasn't backing out now.

The hush in the room heightened her anticipation, built the tension between them until it was thick as honey and dancing over her skin like electric tingles. She'd missed him while he was away. Even when he'd been in town before that she didn't get to see him all that often, and the thing she'd missed most was having him close by to act as a sounding board while he was deployed.

Since her rescue she'd learned what the FAST teams did, and she had a ton of respect and admiration for them. But she had even more for Brock, and his position as team leader. For the kind of man he was. It was partly why she wanted to do this with him and no one else.

She waited, spellbound, all but holding her breath as he lifted a hand and tucked a lock of hair behind her ear. Even that innocent contact sent her pulse skittering. She'd thought their chemistry would be intense, but now she knew for sure.

"How do you see this working?" he asked her softly, his thumb tracing distracting little patterns over her cheek, creating tendrils of heat that licked across her nerve endings.

Mouth dry, she struggled to find her voice. "We go slow, take things one step at a time and go from there."

Though she'd done a ton of therapy since her rescue, her therapist had cautioned her about rushing into anything physical, worried about how Victoria might react. Only one way to find out, and she'd never backed down from anything in her life. It had cost her everything. Now she wanted to get something back. "If I'm not comfortable with something, I'll let you know."

He nodded once. "Fair enough."

This close, his woodsy, cedar scent wrapped around her, making her want to lean forward and press her nose to his chest, breathe him in. "Okay."

"Scale of one to ten, how nervous are you right now?"

She huffed out a soft laugh. "Honestly? About a twelve. But not because I'm afraid of you."

"That's good. And you don't need to be nervous with me. You know I'll take care of you."

Her insides turned gooey at his intimate tone. "I should mention one other thing," she added quickly, over-whelmed by the powerful and magnetic presence of this man. He dominated whatever space he occupied without even trying, without a single word or action. He radiated a calm confidence that was unbelievably attractive to her. It made her feel safe and heightened her feminine aware-ness of him at the same time.

"What's that?"

"I want you to call me Tori." She couldn't tell him, but it was going to be her new name once she left D.C., so she wanted to practice getting used to it. They'd given her a completely new identity package to memorize, and an in-tricate backstory she'd already learned by heart. It seemed fitting that Brock be the one to call her by it first.

"Tori. I like it." He stopped stroking his thumb over her cheek, suddenly making it easier to breathe. "You sure you're ready for this?" he asked, searching her eyes.

She loved that he'd asked her, that he was checking in to make sure this was what she truly wanted. It solidified

35

that she'd made the right decision in approaching him. Her captivity had stolen so much from her. Ruiz's men had almost broken her. Maybe Brock could help her regain some of her former confidence again. "I'm sure. I want to find out with someone I feel comfortable with and respect, and who I feel respects me."

"I have more respect for you than you know."

His quiet words speared through her. Until that moment she hadn't realized how much she needed to hear them. She trusted him on an intrinsic level, and there was no denying she was attracted to him.

From the moment he'd caught her in the woods and wrapped her up in that blanket, he'd always...been there. In the back of her mind, sometimes in the flesh, but always there and she thought about him constantly. Not sexual attraction at first, given her headspace. Something deeper.

"Thank you." So...now what? She waited there perched on the stool, half-frozen with a combination of anxiety and hope. And maybe even longing.

She let it all flow through her, stopped fighting the need to feel. It wasn't like she was risking her heart or anything. She liked and trusted him, but this was purely a business arrangement. She merely wanted his help in taking this final step back into the land of the living, and wasn't looking for an emotional attachment.

You're already attached, who are you trying to kid? It was true. Except she didn't know how to stop the progression. He made that impossible.

In the quiet his eyes dipped to her mouth and her thoughts scattered. The hand at the side of her face shifted, the edge of it curling around her jaw, warm and gentle. Victoria held her breath, heart thudding, letting her eyes half-close as he leaned down toward her.

But when he got close, something made her plant a

hand on his chest without thinking and push until her elbow locked. Literally keeping him at arm's length.

Brock straightened but didn't move back, staying right where he was. The heat of him all but singed her palm, the thud of his heart steady beneath it, the hard contours of his pectorals a solid ridge.

Realizing what she'd done, she flushed and dropped her hand. "Sorry," she said with a weak laugh. He hadn't made it to first base—hell, he hadn't even made it out of the damn batter's box—and she'd already balked. "It's been a while. When you leaned over me like that I just reacted without thinking," she rushed to explain.

"Don't be sorry." He took a step back, giving her room to breathe, her palm cooling fast without his body heat to warm it. Yet instead of moving away or calling it quits as she'd feared, he held out his hand to her, palm up.

Victoria lowered her gaze to it. She'd studied his hands in secret so many times over the time they had known each other, during meetings or their sessions at the firing range together. She loved his hands. Long fingers, callused at the base. Clean nails cut right to the quick. Hands that were trained to wield a weapon with lethal accuracy, or to incapacitate anyone who posed a risk to him or his teammates.

But whenever he'd touched her, it was to help. To protect. To reassure. She'd imagined what they would feel like on her naked body so many times. Now was her chance to find out.

Reaching out, she met him halfway and placed her hand in his. His fingers curled around hers, his grip sure but gentle. Her heart sped up as he tugged her to her feet and drew her toward him.

She expected him to pull her to his chest and kiss her, gasped when he reached out to wrap those powerful hands around her hips instead. Before she could react he lifted her effortlessly, turning to gently boost her onto the kitchen counter behind him. Putting them almost at eye level, his flat stomach inches from her knees.

"Better?" he murmured, lifting a hand to brush a lock of hair away from her cheek.

The consideration behind his gesture touched her. The tenderness of his touch and the heat in his eyes turned her inside out. *Yeah, you're more than attached, girlfriend. Be careful.* "Much."

Brock smiled a little and lowered his hand, set them both flat on the counter on either side of her hips, his face inches from hers. Victoria slowly reached up to place her palms flat against the hard planes of his chest, a little giddy at finally being able to touch him like this.

God, he was so warm and solid. Beneath her hands his heart beat in a calm, steady rhythm, his breathing slow. Enjoying this slow exploration, she slid her hands up to his wide shoulders. Muscles stood out beneath her palms and fingers, the sheer power of him making something in her abdomen flutter.

Gathering her courage, she raised her eyes to his face. Brock stood absolutely still and stared directly into her eyes, forging an intimate connection that made her heart pound. There was no mistaking the banked hunger in that stare, the masculine interest. This wasn't a sacrifice or obligation for him. He actually wanted her.

Breaking eye contact at last, he leaned forward and settled his lips against the center of her forehead in a warm, lingering kiss. Victoria curled her fingers around his shoulders as her heart did a terrified little backflip, closed her eyes to better absorb the sensation. She'd steeled herself to block out the bad memories he might trigger. But she had no defense whatsoever against this heartfelt tenderness.

His warm exhalations bathed her hairline for a long moment, then his lips skimmed gently over to her temple, paused there a moment before blazing a trail down her cheek to the edge of her jaw where his teeth scraped ever-so-carefully over her skin.

Oh God, he was so much more sensual than she had imagined. And she had imagined his kisses a *lot*. Goose-bumps broke out all over her body, her nipples tightening in a sudden rush. It was a shock to get turned on after suffering so much.

She turned her head slightly to meet his lips, hungry to feel his mouth on hers. He ignored her, taking his sweet time scattering kisses across her jaw to her chin, up the other side of her face before ending with a kiss on the bridge of her nose.

She was dissolving inside, all her anxiety swirling away under the caress of his lips. He wasn't even touching her with his hands, and suddenly she wished he was holding her tight, his thick arms wrapped around her.

Her own crept up to wind around the back of his neck, her fingertips playing with the ends of his soft, brown hair. She sighed and leaned in closer, dying for him to kiss her for real. Those intense gray eyes stared back at her, a mix of silver and gunmetal with a darker charcoal ring around the irises.

His dark lashes lowered as his head finally dipped down once more, the muscles in his shoulders bunching. She tried to meet him part way, made a little sound of confusion and frustration when his lips brushed the corner of her mouth instead of landing flush on hers.

He eased an inch to the right, tenderly caught her upper lip between his before moving to the lower one. Nibbling. Sucking. He did it so slowly she could barely breathe, the sudden rush of yearning taking her off guard.

Unable to stand the slow tease another moment, she gripped his neck tighter, pulled so she could fuse her mouth to his. Brock made a soft, deep sound of either enjoyment or approval and angled his head, parting his lips slightly as he finally kissed her properly.

Heat suffused her entire body, turning the warmth in her belly into a molten need. This huge, sexy man was kissing her with such care and without haste, as though he planned to spend all night doing nothing more than kissing her. It shocked her how much it made her quiver inside. She felt vulnerable yet cherished. Beautiful, even though she was scarred inside and out.

When his tongue touched her lower lip, a tender, sliding caress, Victoria sucked in a breath and opened for him without hesitation. *Touch me.*

Finally, those incredible hands came up to frame her face as he dipped his tongue under her upper lip, between her teeth to stroke the sensitive roof of her mouth. Her head spun. She forgot how to breathe, forgot everything except his endless kiss and what he made her feel, gliding her tongue against his, savoring the sensation of being protected and savored.

She was lost, her entire body alive in a way it hadn't been in more than a year, maybe ever, when he sucked at her lower lip one last time before raising his head. Feeling a little drugged, she opened her eyes and struggled to find her bearings. His eyes glowed with arousal, a faint flush on his cheekbones. She was glad to know she wasn't the only one affected by this.

Running his thumbs across her cheeks one last time, he dropped his hands to his sides and straightened. "You okay?"

Okay? Dizzy, breathless, and wanting more. *Needing* more, her entire body pulsing with arousal. She would have laughed, but she couldn't find the energy and he was dead serious. She licked her lips. "Yes. You?"

He cracked a soft laugh. "Yeah."

Every nerve ending in her body pulsed with heat and...unrelieved need. God, the man could kiss. She'd never experienced anything like it. And when they finally moved on to even more pleasurable things... Something somersaulted deep inside her abdomen at the thought of those hands and wicked mouth on other parts of her body.

But then she thought of her scars, of the look on his face when he saw them, and the heat was doused by ice.

She cleared her throat, checked her watch. God, she'd had no idea so much time had passed. "I should go. I need to call my detail."

Brock didn't argue or try to persuade her for more, simply stepped back and handed over her purse. Her continual awareness of him was heightened to the point of distracting as he stood close by while she spoke to the U.S. Marshal who would come up to get her.

"Okay, see you in a few minutes." Hanging up, she hopped off the counter, a little amazed that her legs were steady enough to hold her up. "He's coming up now."

"Okay." Brock went to the door and got her coat for her, held it out so she could slide her arms into it.

Shrugging it on, she turned to face him, unsure what to say. Thank you? I can't wait to do this again? "Are you still okay with this?" She would have worried that she'd coerced him into this, except Brock wasn't a man who could be coerced into anything he didn't want to do, and the heat she'd seen in his eyes wasn't fake.

The only thing she couldn't deal with was his pity.

He arched a dark eyebrow, the contrast of it and his lashes startling against the unique color of his eyes. "What do you think?"

I think it's a good thing I'll be leaving before I can get any more attached to you than I already am.

She was a little scared, to be honest. It would be way too easy to get emotionally involved with him, even fall in love with him. Good thing the arrangement was finite, and that she would begin a new life in a new city under a new identity once her role as a government witness was over. Soon. "I hope you'd tell me straight out if you weren't."

He nodded. "I would."

She relaxed. "I believe you."

Leaning a shoulder against the wall he crossed his ankles, slid his hands into his jeans pockets, the muscles in his arms flexing with the movement. She could spend hours running her hands over them. "Big day coming up for you later this week. How are you feeling about it?"

He meant Ruiz being sentenced the day after tomorrow. Finally. "I have mixed feelings, but mostly I'm looking forward to it because I just want it all to be over. No matter what sentence he gets, it won't bring my family back."

"No. But after that day, you'll never have to lay eyes on the bastard again."

Relief poured through her at the thought. "Yes." Though she would continue to see him often enough in her nightmares. That part wasn't going away anytime soon.

Blocking that thought before it could take root, she put her hands into her coat pockets to avoid the temptation of touching Brock again. She'd never forget the way he'd kissed her tonight. One taste of him and she already wanted more, could easily become addicted to him if she wasn't careful.

But if she'd learned anything since the night her life was shattered, it was to be cautious and protect herself. "When can we see each other next?"

"What about after the sentencing hearing? Any day where someone like that gets sentenced seems like a good reason to celebrate."

He was right. No matter what the judge decided with the sentence, it was cause for celebration. In a way, it marked her freedom for the first time in a year. And there was no one she would rather share that moment with than Brock. "Okay."

"Then it's a date. Tori," he added with a sexy little

smile that made her heart flip-flop. She liked the way the name sounded coming from him.

An answering smile tugged at her lips, a shiver of anticipation working up her spine as warmth spread through her. She couldn't wait to be alone with him again, see where the time would take them.

A knock at the door signaled the marshal had arrived and Victoria hid her disappointment.

Brock checked the peephole, unlocked the door and looked at her before opening it. "See you soon."

Not soon enough. "I'm looking forward to it." To being alone with him again, but even more, knowing the animal who took her family and dignity away would finally face justice.

Maybe then she could start sleeping at night.

Chapter Four

"**R**uiz."

Carlos sat up stiffly on his bunk and eyed the tray the guard shoved through the slot of his cell in disgust. But it was either eat the shit they called food, or starve.

And…there might be something even more important to be gained from the sorry excuse of a meal than simple nourishment.

Bracing a hand on the edge of the bunk he pushed to his feet, covering a wince as pain forked through his right leg. After lying down for the past few hours it was more stiff than usual. The bastards wouldn't let him use his cane, so he clamped his jaw tight and took the few steps over to the cell door, refusing to show how much it hurt.

They kept him in solitary confinement. He'd always liked time to himself, but the feeling of being trapped got to him more and more each day. They wouldn't allow him contact with the regular guards or other inmates, too afraid that he would be able to continue running his business from inside the walls of the prison.

They didn't realize he'd already found a way.

When Carlos retrieved the Styrofoam tray the guard slammed the small slot shut, whistling some cheery tune as he walked away. The tray contained a lump of some sort of meat covered in what had to be packaged gravy, an ice-cream scoop full of instant mashed potatoes, and those disgusting mixed peas and square carrot bits that came out of a bag in the freezer section of the grocery store.

He painfully shuffled back to his bunk, thinking of the meals he used to eat. Before he'd been locked in this dump, he'd had it all. A huge private estate, a private chef, and his own menagerie of animals in his own private zoo. Now here he was, locked away twenty-three hours every day, eating slop he wouldn't feed to his pet pot-bellied pigs.

The hard mattress barely gave when he sat on it and began forcing the food down his throat. The hot ball of anger burned hotter with each bite. Tomorrow was going to be bad. There was no avoiding it.

His lawyer had begged him months ago to take the plea deal offered to him by the U.S. Attorney's office. He'd refused initially because it was the last fuck you available to him. They had enough evidence to keep him in here the rest of his life anyway. Why not waste their time and force them to prepare for trial?

He'd waited until the last possible moment before the trial began to accept the deal. And only because he faced the death penalty if they went to trial and the jury found him guilty.

The burn in his stomach intensified, turned into a hot coal scorching beneath his ribs. He'd sat in that courtroom day after day as the evidence was brought forth. FBI and DEA agents had testified. Forensics and financial experts. The victim impact statements were what would sway the judge to hand down a severe sentence. Widows and teen-age children of the DEA agents killed by his men in that shootout two years ago.

He set down his tray, stretched his right leg out and rubbed at the stiff muscles, the long-healed bullet wounds still causing him pain every day of his life. All because of a female investigative reporter out on a crusade to expose him and the rest of the *Veneno* cartel.

He suffered daily, but he'd made sure she suffered more. He'd taken away her family. Given her to his men for a few weeks before she was rescued. And while she'd been up there on the witness stand delivering her victim impact statement, looking down at him with that righteous, arrogant expression, she'd talked about what she'd endured, and the things she'd learned during her captivity.

Carlos had been shocked at the things his men had said in front of her. Sensitive, important things about players within the cartel, ongoing and upcoming operations they never should have talked about in front of an outsider, even if they thought she was drugged or unconscious. Of course, all of them had expected her to be shipped off to Asia with the rest of the women they'd captured, where she wouldn't be a threat anymore because she wouldn't survive long.

He'd met Victoria Gomez in person only once, while she was his prisoner. She'd surprised him with her resolve to fight, spitting in his face even while chained to the floor in a shed out back of his property on the Gulf Coast.

Now he realized he'd made a serious mistake in walking away that night, rather than caving her skull in with his cane as he'd wanted to. He should have killed her when he'd had the chance, but he'd been so focused on making her suffer as much as possible.

He pushed his fork through his dinner, didn't detect what he was hoping for. Scooping up a bite of the dubious-looking meat, he thought about the day he'd seen her in the courtroom a month ago. He'd met her hate-filled gaze from across that courtroom and smiled in satisfaction. He may never be a free man again. But what he'd done to her in retaliation for exposing and nearly getting him killed would haunt her the rest of her days.

And as to the man who'd turned him over to the Americans...

Carlos had taken steps to hand over the reins of his old organization. His possible successor had scores of his own to settle. He would carry on the war to end *El Escorpion*—someone Carlos had been loyal to and considered a friend—and take control of the *Veneno* cartel. It was the only revenge Carlos could get now.

His back teeth hit something hard and he immediately stopped chewing, excitement flashing through him.

Yes.

He pulled the small white capsule from between his lips, his heart beating faster. He didn't get news as often these days as he had in the past. Had wondered if maybe the prison officials had become suspicious of his source within the kitchen.

Opening the gel capsule with his teeth, he pulled out the tiny piece of paper and unrolled it. Eagerly scanned the handwritten words.

I accept.

Carlos closed his eyes a moment in thankfulness, then rolled the paper back up, slipped it back into the capsule, and swallowed it with a mouthful of bland, cold mashed potatoes. As he ate the rest of his meal he glanced around his barren cell, the heaviness of his burden now eased. He would likely spend the rest of his days in here or somewhere similar, die an old man between prison walls without ever tasting freedom again.

But the *Venenos* would fall. He had just received confirmation of that.

His only regret was that he wouldn't be there to see it happen in person.

****

Seated in the rear of the armored SUV, Victoria waited in the underground parking garage with her U.S. Marshal security detail, taking slow, deep breaths to manage the anxiety that churned in the pit of her stomach.

She'd done everything she could to help investigators and her legal team to nail Carlos Ruiz to the wall. He'd taken a plea deal to receive a reduced sentence and avoid trial, triggering the sentencing process instead. It had taken her weeks to compose her victim impact statement to read to the judge. To get it just right, and practice it so that she could get through it aloud without her voice cracking.

She was a former investigative journalist and a published author. Words were her best weapon. And she'd used them with the lethal force of the bullets that had struck her family.

Victoria had memorized every word. But on the stand with the monster responsible for turning her life into a waking nightmare seated mere feet away, her brain had gone from fight to flight mode in an instant. So she had ended up reading it instead. Her recounting of the massacre. The things Ruiz's men had done to her. The scars they'd left on her body. In as much detail with as much emotion as she could.

Every word had ripped her apart all over again. Every word had brought back that pain and crawling humiliation because she'd said them to a courtroom of total strangers. And every word had hopefully put another nail in Ruiz's coffin.

After she had finished giving her statement, she'd looked up. Intending to let him see she was undefeated and unafraid after all he'd put her through.

The bastard had been smiling. Fucking *smiling*. Proud

of what he'd done. Smugly enjoying her pain and ongoing torment.

For some reason that smile was the thing that haunted her most now.

She blew out an unsteady breath and tapped her fingers, waiting impatiently for the marshals to take her upstairs to the courtroom. After delivering her statement and seeing Ruiz's reaction, she had decided not to come today. Then she'd thought of her family, the justice they deserved, and she decided she would be nothing but a coward if she didn't attend the sentencing.

A marshal came from the elevators and knocked once on her window, then opened the door. "We're clear," he said, and she followed his partner to the elevator. Both men were dressed in khakis and polo shirts with casual jackets that hid their holsters.

As expected, the courtroom was crowded. She went straight to the back row, purposely kept her gaze lowered as she slid into the last bench set against the wall.

Only when she had her hands clasped tight in her lap and her control wrapped firmly around her did she raise her eyes to the front of the courtroom. Ruiz was seated at the left-hand table in his orange prison jumpsuit with his lawyer and didn't turn around. It was so much easier to stare at the back of his head than have to look into those dark, evil eyes that gleamed with triumph when he looked at her.

She struggled to force the image away, keep her heart rate steady.

"Is this seat taken?"

She snapped her head around, all her anxiety vanishing like a puff of smoke under the surprise of seeing Brock standing there. He wore jeans that hugged his solid thighs and a black button down that hugged his chest and shoulders, a knowing smile on his lips.

Her own lips curved in response. "No. Please, sit." She

scooted over to make room for him, welcoming the distraction of his steady, magnetic presence as he lowered his tall frame to sit next to her. Breathing in his clean, woodsy scent, she felt calmer all of a sudden. More in control.

Brock folded his arms, his shoulder brushing hers. That slight contact grounded her even more. "Wasn't sure if you were going to come," he murmured without looking at her.

"Neither was I." She glanced at his profile. Strong, classic lines, a slight bump on the bridge of his nose. Even here, his posture and bearing radiated authority. "What are you doing here?" He was FAST Bravo's team leader. Their schedule kept them busy all the time, and they rarely got days off. He must have requested special permission to take the time off today.

He turned his head to meet her gaze, and her heart hitched at the look in those steel gray eyes. "I wanted to be here."

For her. He didn't say it, but he didn't have to. His actions spoke a thousand times louder than words ever could have.

He'd met her when she was at her worst, and stayed to stand guard next to her hospital bed that first night. Just so she would feel safe. Now he was here, still lending his support, and she knew him well enough to know that it wasn't because of their arrangement. It meant the world to her.

She broke eye contact and looked down at her clasped hands, blinking at the sting of tears. Damn, she'd been so certain she could keep control of her emotions, but him being here to support her hit the tender spots under the thick armor she'd built around her heart.

"All rise," the bailiff announced from up front.

Victoria rose along with everyone else in the courtroom, her heart thudding and her palms turning clammy.

She was thankful for Brock being beside her as the judge came out of her chambers and took her seat behind the judge's bench.

"Please be seated," the fifty-ish judge said.

Victoria sat, and the rest of the proceedings passed in a blur. Ruiz had rolled the dice and taken the plea bargain. Now he was about to learn his fate for the murder of the DEA agents he'd been involved in a shootout with. For the murder of her entire family. For the aggravated sexual assault she'd endured during her captivity.

Ruiz hadn't raped her, but his men had—on his orders. And he'd *planned* to rape her, had arranged for her to be transported to a hotel in New Orleans for a day or two before he shipped her off to Asia. Except she'd foiled that plan by escaping.

There were other charges too. Human and drug trafficking. Money laundering. Tax evasion.

The judge spoke again. "Having carefully reviewed all of the evidence in this case, I am ready to deliver a sentence on the defendant."

Victoria held her breath, registered the warmth of Brock's hand as he curled his fingers around her cold ones, and squeezed.

"Accordingly, it is the judgment of this court that Carlos Ruiz serve three consecutive life sentences in a federal penitentiary." She removed her glasses and faced Ruiz, holding up a document for him to see, her expression as steely as her eyes. "Mr. Ruiz, for the crimes you have committed, it is my pleasure and privilege to effectively sign your death sentence today. The only way you will ever leave prison is in a body bag."

At those powerfully spoken words, the courtroom erupted into cheers and applause. Victoria didn't join in, a chaotic mix of conflicting emotions roiling inside her.

Instead she rose, caught Brock's look of surprise before he jumped up with her, and followed him out of the courtroom without looking back. It was over. She didn't want to look at Ruiz ever again.

A sense of numbness crept over her as she hurried to the elevators with the marshals flanking her. Ruiz would die in jail. She'd thought the news would make her feel relieved, even happy. It hadn't. Nothing ever could. Even if Ruiz had been sentenced to death by firing squad, it wouldn't erase the grief and pain and loss.

Brock stood close to her as he accompanied them down to the parking garage. She was grateful for the quick escape, and that she would be spared the cameras and crowds assembled outside the courthouse. She just wished she could have had his arm around her.

She felt...disoriented. Maybe even a little numb.

For so long her sole focus had been making sure Ruiz paid for what he'd done. Now that it was done, that chapter of her life was closed forever. She couldn't talk about what had happened to her and her family from now on. And soon she had to become someone else and start a new life elsewhere.

When one of the marshals opened the back door of the SUV for her, she stopped and faced Brock. If they had been alone she would have wrapped her arms around him and laid her cheek on his chest. "Thank you for being here today."

He nodded. "You're welcome. Now move over."

Surprised, she blinked at him.

"Come on, scoot over and let's get the hell out of here. You're free now. Never have to see this place again."

Free. But lost, because the thing that had been motivating her for so long was gone now.

She slid across the seat while Brock jumped into the back with her and shut the door. "What are you doing?" she asked him. This was way outside of normal protocol, so he must have cleared it with her security team first.

"We're going to my place."

She raised her eyebrows. "We are?"

"You okay with that?" the marshal putting his seatbelt on in the front asked.

She looked at Brock. She'd thought she would want to be alone and process everything for a while, but she didn't want to be by herself right now. She wanted to be with him. Needed to. "Yes."

Brock reached across the seat and curled his fingers around her right hand. "Good. Got a surprise for you."

Were they going to be alone? If so...

Got a surprise for you too, Agent Hamilton.

Chapter Five

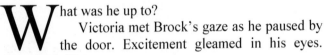

W hat was he up to?

    Victoria met Brock's gaze as he paused by the door. Excitement gleamed in his eyes. "You ready?"

"I think so." A marshal stood behind her as Brock opened the door. But rather than go in ahead of her to check the place, the marshal hung back, against normal protocol. Either they were already relaxing protocol because she was no longer a key witness, or Brock had cooked this whole thing up with them ahead of time.

Taking two steps inside, she stopped, her eyes going wide. Bunches of brightly colored balloons dotted the kitchen, along with a big banner that read *Congratulations!* hanging from the ceiling. A large bouquet of vividly colored flowers sat on the kitchen table, along with platters of food and what looked like a bottle of champagne chilling in a bucket.

"Oh my God, what did you—" She broke off when Oceane came out from behind the wall in the living room with Gabe Lockhart, one of Brock's teammates.

"Surprise!" Oceane said in her Spanish accent. She wore a bright smile on her pretty face, her long, chocolate-brown curls down around her shoulders.

Victoria grinned and went over to hug her friend. "I can't believe it. What are you doing here?" Like her, Oceane was an important asset in the *Veneno* case and rarely left the sanctuary of the WITSEC Safesite and Orientation Center, for her own protection. Their security details must have cooked this up with Brock.

"I wanted to come and celebrate with you." Oceane's blue-gray eyes slid to Brock, and she smiled. "He made it all happen."

Victoria glanced at Brock, her heart squeezing. She couldn't believe he would go to all this trouble for her. Only her family had ever done something like this before. The bittersweet reminder set off a twinge of grief inside her. "Thank you."

His answering smile took her breath away. "You're welcome."

Tearing her attention from him, she turned to Lockhart. "And you got dragged into this too, huh? Lucky you."

The former Ranger's lips twitched in the semblance of a smile, but his pale blue eyes twinkled. "I came willingly."

"Well I'm glad you're both here." She felt much better now than when she'd left the courthouse, lighter and somehow warmer inside to know that these people cared about her this much. "I gather you heard the news?"

Oceane nodded. "My security team got the call about the verdict on our way over here."

"I hear the judge was freaking awesome in the way she worded the sentencing portion," Lockhart said.

Victoria would never forget it, or the goosebumps that had risen all over her skin in reaction to the woman's intensity. "She was."

Oceane reached for one of her hands, squeezed. "How are you feeling?"

Tired. Empty. But less empty and less alone than she had. "I'm not sure, to be honest. Relieved. A lot of other things."

Oceane's eyes filled with empathy. "I can imagine."

Yes. Victoria knew she could.

When they'd first met, she had been determined to hate Oceane on sight because she was Manny Nieto's daughter. Then she'd realized that Oceane was as much a victim as she was. And since the day Oceane's mother had been brutally murdered by *Veneno sicarios* months ago, Victoria had made it her mission to befriend the younger woman. Together they'd formed an invaluable support system for each other.

They were more than just friends; they had become each other's family. Who better to understand than someone who has gone through similar horrors? Their bond would never be broken. Not even when Victoria left D.C. and would never see or hear from her again.

The thought brought a wave of sadness. She shook it off, forced a smile. "I'm glad you came."

"Well, should we eat?" Brock said.

Victoria took in all the food laid out on the oval table in the kitchen. A cheese board, fruit and veggies, finger sandwiches, mini quiches. She arched a brow at him. "Quiches? I'm surprised you're okay with them," she teased.

He shrugged and picked up a plate from the counter, handing it to her. "I'm comfortable enough with my masculinity that I can handle quiche just fine."

More than his words, his tone made warmth bloom in her abdomen. Yes, he was definitely comfortable with his masculinity. And it was sexy as hell. There was so much she wanted to learn about him, so many things she wanted to take the memory of with her when she left D.C. any day now. "Thanks," she said, taking the plate.

"What about you, Lockhart?" Brock asked, handing his teammate a plate. "You okay with mini quiches?"

"It's free food, so yeah, I'm good with it." He handed his plate to Oceane, gently guided her in front of him with a hand on her lower back. "Ladies first."

Victoria caught the flush in Oceane's cheeks as she smiled at him, though Lockhart didn't react. He had originally been assigned to guard Oceane before she and her mother agreed to join WITSEC. He'd been there for her when no one else was the day her mother had been killed. The four of them had met at the orientation center maybe a dozen or so times prior to FAST Bravo deploying overseas, for meetings, briefings and updates about the ongoing manhunt for Oceane's father and his bastard of an enforcer.

With a full plate she sat on the long couch in the living room while Oceane sat across from her on the loveseat. A minute later Lockhart sat beside Oceane, and Brock came over to Victoria with a flute of champagne for her. "It's not exactly Dom Perignon," he said, "but it's wet and it has bubbles."

She took it with a smile. "I'll love it, thank you."

Once Brock handed everyone a flute, he lowered himself beside her and raised his glass. "To new beginnings," he said, looking into her eyes, his words sending a shiver of anticipation up her spine.

"Cheers," Oceane said, smiling at her.

Wanting to deflect the attention off herself, Victoria searched for a safe topic to talk about. "I'm curious. What do you guys do to amuse yourselves while you're over there for four months?"

Brock and Lockhart exchanged a look, and both of them smiled. "It can be dull," Brock admitted. "But never for long. There are always missions or briefings going on, and in our downtime, we've got Granger and Maka to keep us entertained."

"They're the team clowns," Lockhart said, his voice drier than the champagne.

"Why, what sorts of things do they do?" Oceane asked.

"Mostly immature stuff," Brock said. "Practical jokes. Whatever is most annoying to the rest of us. They feed off each other. But I gotta give it to them, when it comes to lip synching, nobody does it better. And board games. Man, those two are something else."

Her family had loved board games. Growing up, they'd spent hours at the kitchen table on Saturday nights playing Risk or Monopoly. Once they'd become old enough to join in, her nieces and nephews had loved it too.

A pang hit her, taking her off guard with its sharpness. She set her plate on her lap and swallowed, the backs of her eyes burning. God, was it ever going to get easier? Would she ever be able to go a day without something triggering a painful memory of them, or a terrifying one of her captivity? And soon she would lose the people with her right now too.

She felt Brock's eyes on her. "You okay?" he asked.

She nodded, put her plate on the coffee table and stood. She needed a minute to herself before she embarrassed herself and made everyone else uncomfortable. "Be right back."

Heading to the bathroom, she shut and locked the door behind her, leaning against it and closing her eyes while she fought back the tears. They wouldn't help. Wouldn't change anything. And she didn't want Brock and the others to know she'd been crying.

Opening her eyes, she stared at her reflection in the mirror. Sunlight streamed in through the bathroom window, illuminating her face. The concealer she'd dotted beneath her eyes couldn't hide the shadows there. Or the ones in her eyes. She looked freaking ancient. Far older than the thirty-two years her birth certificate proclaimed.

And she looked…frightened. Not in the same way she had been. This was deeper, an unsettling sensation like she was standing on the edge of a cliff and knowing the moment was coming when she would be forced to jump.

The deep sadness in her eyes made her heart clench. She had done all she could to avenge her family's deaths. Now what? Although she had no choice but to move forward, she didn't know how. Didn't know if she'd ever be whole again.

All right. Enough.

Giving herself a mental shake, she pushed aside the sadness and the weight pressing on her chest. Brock had gone to all this trouble for her, and she refused to spoil it.

Oceane looked up as Victoria came back to the kitchen. Victoria gave her a smile, then took her seat next to Brock, aware of the way his gaze lingered on her. She didn't want to talk about it. She just wanted to enjoy the time they had left together.

Thankfully, Brock picked the conversation back up. Lockhart interjected here and there with his dry sense of humor, making her and Oceane laugh. "Wrestling?" Victoria asked, shaking her head.

"Superhero wrestling," Brock corrected.

"And let me guess, you were Captain America."

"Of course."

"And who were you?" Oceane asked Lockhart.

"I abstained," he said in a wry tone. "Or more like, stood watch and provided lookout so the rest of these man-children—" He gestured to Brock, "could body slam each other through tables and smash chairs over each other's heads without command overhearing."

Victoria gaped at Brock. "What the heck?"

He shrugged a broad shoulder, a smile playing around the edges of his mouth. "Had to win the belt back from Maka, defend my position as team leader."

"And did you?"

"Sort of," Lockhart interjected. "Cap brought in the rest of the Avengers and they all ganged up on Maka, who was of course the Hulk."

"The Hawaiian Hulk," Brock corrected.

"Yeah. Anyway, they piled on top of him, finally pinned him down, and then Cap stole the belt back. Yay."

"I *took* the belt back," Brock corrected. "And our Hulk did turn a little green after all, in the end. With envy."

Victoria met Oceane's eyes and they both shook their heads. "You guys are ridiculous. If the DEA only knew what you got up to over there."

"Nah, it's good for morale," Brock said, grinning now. "And we only busted a few tables." He chuckled. "Maka's been moving pretty slow since we put him through that last one."

Testosterone. It was a dangerous thing.

Oceane's phone rang, breaking the easy atmosphere. Checking the display, she sighed. "That's my cue to leave," she said, her face falling. "Someone's coming up to get me now."

"I should call my team too," Victoria said, reaching into her purse for her phone. She hadn't spoken to them about this, had no idea what the plan or timeline was, but if Oceane was leaving, then likely Victoria would be too.

"I already cleared it with them for you to stay until six," Brock said, causing her to look up at him. "If you want."

She studied him. More time alone together? She wanted that. But if she stayed, wouldn't word get back to WITSEC and maybe even the DEA that something was going on between her and Brock?

People talked. She didn't care what anyone said about her. She just didn't want to cause any trouble for Brock. "Are you sure it's okay?"

"Positive."

Well… Her other option was to return to the WITSEC

center and spend the rest of the night alone in her room working on the outline for her novel. The thought made her feel lonelier than she expected. "Okay, then." It would give them a couple more hours to further explore her proposition. And time was of the essence, so...

"I'd better head out too," Lockhart said, climbing to his feet. He walked into the kitchen and grabbed his ball cap from the counter, tugged it over his dark blond hair and picked up his leather jacket. "See ya bright and early tomorrow, Cap," he said to Brock.

"You know it," Brock answered, and went to the door. The marshal arrived seconds later and Brock let Oceane and Lockhart out. "Have a good night." Then locked the door and turned to face her, one hand still on the jamb. "How're you doing?"

"Fine." Tired, but glad to have time alone with him. Aching to feel his arms around her. Even if it was only for a little while.

He searched her eyes a moment. Then, without a word, he closed the distance between them and gathered her into a tight hug.

****

There was definitely something going on with those two.

Oceane glanced over at Gabe to drink him in as he walked beside her, both of them following the marshal down the hall toward the staircase entrance. "Is it just me, or did you feel like we were kind of interrupting back there?" she whispered, hoping the marshal couldn't overhear her.

One side of his mouth pulled up, then he hid it and his expression went back to its usual setting of neutral. It was eerie, how he did that. Hiding what he was thinking and feeling. Was he naturally like that, or had he learned it in the military? "Nah."

She frowned at him in annoyance. "Oh, please. You saw it too, you just don't want to admit it." She knew what she'd seen, and there had definitely been sparks flying between Brock and Victoria. Also, her friend was so sad. Oceane wished Victoria's smiles would reach her eyes. Maybe Brock could help her with that.

She glanced at Gabe again, thinking about her own situation. Her experience with men was woefully inadequate. She'd had a few short-term relationships and two lovers, but that was it. Hard to date and keep a guy interested when you had armed bodyguards around you all the time, even on dates.

Harder still when everyone knew she was Manny Nieto's daughter. His *only* child, by his mistress. And worse yet that they had known the truth about him when she hadn't.

Gabe's hands were in the pockets of his leather coat. The scent of it mixed with the fragrance of his soap, something masculine and spicy. She loved the way he smelled. His quiet, thoughtful intensity. They hadn't seen each other since before his deployment, but things had become way easier between them than in the beginning, when he'd temporarily been assigned to guard her. Back then, he'd seen her as a spoiled, naïve cartel princess, as Manny Nieto's entitled and corrupt illegitimate daughter. Now she got the sense that he saw who she truly was.

The one upside of all the tragedy she'd experienced was that it had brought her closer to Victoria, and by extension, Brock and Gabe. Whenever she met with Victoria, Gabe had usually been there too. His four-month-long stint in Afghanistan with the rest of FAST Bravo had seemed to last forever. She thought about him constantly, no matter how often she told herself to stop.

"What will you do now?" she asked him.

"Go back to taking the fight to the bad guys." He

glanced at her as they reached the stairwell. "You?"

"I don't know." She was in limbo for the time being. Not really a federal witness at this point, since neither her father nor Montoya were in custody, so there was nothing more she could give the government on them. She was still under threat, however, since her father seemed to have lost his damn mind and put a bounty of sorts on her head for anyone who could return her to him unharmed. She still needed the government's protection.

Right now, she had no idea what the future held. If the government decided it no longer needed her, it would cut her loose. Might even send her back to Mexico.

Cold seeped through her veins at the thought. She wanted to stay here in the States, become a citizen someday. "I want to feel useful again." Back home, before her life had been reduced to ashes, she'd been a successful financial advisor. She'd managed her mother's sizeable estate and many other large accounts from wealthy clients.

Money and clients she now understood had come from her father. Was anything about her life real? Had she earned anything on her own merit? It was too depressing to think about.

He'd stolen everything from her. Her life, her identity, her trust. But worst of all, her mother, and in a horrific way that was seared deep into her brain forever. Oceane would never forgive him for it. As long as it took, she would see him in hell for that.

"You could start working on your financial advisor certification here while you wait to see what will happen," Gabe suggested.

"Maybe." But what was the point if they were going to boot her out and send her back to Mexico?

"Any new leads on Montoya?"

The mere sound of her godfather's name scraped over her nerve endings like barbed wire. He'd been dispatched to find and bring her back to her father. And while he'd been doing that, his *sicarios* had raped and butchered her mother.

Remembering the things she'd seen that day was like swallowing shards of broken glass, slicing her up inside. Without Gabe to lean on that day, she would have shattered into a thousand pieces. He had seen things, knew things about her that no one else did and didn't judge her for them. Did he know how much that meant to her? She couldn't bear the thought of never seeing him again once she left the city.

"No. They still think he's back in Mexico somewhere," she said.

"Any possibility he's hiding out with your father, wherever he is?"

"Doubt it." She'd been doing everything she could to help investigators track the men down. But she couldn't tell them what she didn't know, and since her parents had deliberately kept her ignorant of her absentee-father's true business involvement, it wasn't much.

It was still so hard to believe everything she had learned since escaping to the States. Until the night armed gunmen had stormed the gated mansion where she and her mother lived in Veracruz, she hadn't fully believed that he was involved with a drug cartel. And certainly not that he'd become one of the *Veneno* bosses.

The man had even gone so far as to pay off her dentist to have a tracking device implanted in a filling. The FBI had removed it the same afternoon they'd found it. Someone within her father's network had taken her mother's body back home and allowed her family to give her a proper burial in the plot her mother had purchased years before. The feds had shown Oceane pictures to confirm it.

Her father, of course, had not attended the funeral, and none of the guests agents had questioned seemed to know where he was. Only that they had heard rumors that he and his wife Elena had separated. Word had it that the funeral and reception had been paid for by an anonymous source. The U.S. authorities were trying to trace it back to the owner, hoping they could link it to her father.

Oceane knew in her heart it was a futile effort. Her father was simply too good at covering his tracks and burying his money.

She and Gabe reached the SUV waiting under the building. She paused, looking at him. He was impossible to read. But he had been good to her in the hour of her greatest need, and she trusted him. Felt something real and powerful for him.

Did he feel anything for her at all beyond obligation and a sense of duty? She had no idea and didn't want to fall for him any more than she already had, in case it was all one-sided. Because it probably was.

"So I guess… I won't be seeing you much now," she said softly, her chest aching.

His pale blue eyes gazed down at her steadily. "I'll be around."

She couldn't think what for, or what might allow their paths to cross again, unless something big came up with her father or Montoya. "Well. I'm glad you're back. It's good to see you."

His lips curved a little. Not exactly a grin, but close. "Good to see you too. You take care of yourself." He opened the back door for her.

When he shut it behind her, the ache in her heart increased tenfold. An overwhelming sense of loneliness crashed over her. Followed immediately by the knowledge that when Victoria left, Oceane would truly be all alone in this world. She would miss her friend terribly.

She blew out an unsteady breath and struggled to get hold of her emotions. She wasn't useless. And she was still here when her mother was not. No matter how bad the guilt got, no matter how heavy the burden she carried became, she couldn't forget that she still had an important purpose to fulfill.

Oceane would find justice for her mother. Her life only had meaning now if she made sure her father paid for what he'd done to them both.

So no matter how long it took, she would do everything in her power to help the DEA capture him.

Chapter Six

All things considered, for the most part Victoria had held it together pretty well until now. But there was something about Brock that reached past all her hard-won defenses and left her a quivering mass of emotion, exposing her tender insides like a raw nerve. Now that they were alone, the yearning to let down the walls she'd erected for the sake of self-preservation grew with each passing second.

The understanding in his eyes as he'd walked toward her just now, the way he pulled her to him and wrapped those solid arms around her, broke something inside her. Resting her cheek to his chest, holding onto him tight, she swallowed and just...*felt*. Allowed herself to accept the silent comfort he offered.

Hitching in a shaky breath, she held on tight. God, she'd missed this. The simple embrace of someone who gave a shit about her. A gesture of comfort and protection when she'd been alone for so long. Her entire extended family had been physically affectionate. She'd been starving for this for almost a year, and worse whenever she was around Brock. But him holding her now made the wait a thousand times sweeter.

"You okay?" he murmured.

"Much better now." He was a good man, committed to serving his country and looking out for the people who counted on him. It had been a long time since she'd known someone like that.

Her heart twisted as she breathed in his scent and savored the feel of his strength surrounding her. Today marked the beginning of the end of their time together unless something important came up that she had insider knowledge about with the *Veneno* cartel in the next few days. She was going to miss Brock like hell when things ended, which of course they had to.

He continued to hold her close for another minute, then held his hand out for her to take. When she did, he led her into the living room. He sank onto the leather couch, drawing her sideways into his lap.

There was no mistaking the feel of his erection growing against her bottom, but thankfully it sparked no fear or dread, only a mild anxiety at the thought of him seeing her body for the first time. Though the scars she bore inside were far worse than the ones marking her skin.

She half expected him to pounce now that he'd moved them here but he merely cradled her to him for a while, seeming in no rush to take things to the next level. Victoria rested her head on his sturdy shoulder, allowing her body to relax. He ran his fingers through her hair, combing through it from her nape to the ends at her shoulder blades in a soothing motion.

It was bliss. She was like a wilted, drought-stricken flower, soaking up every bit of affection and reassurance he offered like rain.

"Tough day for you, huh?" he asked quietly.

She nodded against his shoulder. "I thought maybe I would feel a sense of closure once the verdict came down, but I don't. All I feel is empty." And also sad that she would be torn away from her one source of comfort so soon.

"I think that's pretty normal."

Well it wasn't normal to her. Before Ruiz's attack, she'd had a full, rich life. What she faced ahead looked like a barren wasteland by comparison. "I guess."

"What have you decided to do with the next phase of your life?"

"I want to make a difference." That was all she'd ever wanted, and why she'd gone into journalism.

He made a low sound of acknowledgment. "You will."

He sounded so certain of that. His faith in her buoyed her flagging spirits a little. "I'm not sure what I'm going to do yet. I was thinking either going back to school to become a counselor, or writing a novel."

"You'd be great at both. I read your books when I was at Bagram, by the way."

She smiled. "You did?"

"Yep. And I was damned impressed. I bet you'd write great fiction too."

The praise warmed her. "Thank you." Her therapist thought it was still too soon to be thinking about taking on a new career, but what choice did she have once she left D.C.? She had to find a way to make money and support herself.

"What else, though? Any dreams or bucket list items you want to make happen?"

"Too many to count." A lot of them for her dead family members. Things they'd never had the chance to do. Trips they'd never be able to take. "All that's going to have to wait until I'm settled in my new life." The WITSEC people were going to let her know her destination sometime in the next few days.

He squeezed her tighter, pressed a kiss to the top of her head. "It doesn't matter what you do next, as long as it makes you happy."

She wasn't sure if that was even possible now. Part of her wanted to stay hidden, to remain isolated, while the other craved social interaction again. "Maybe I'll volunteer at a library or something to start." That way she could be surrounded with books and be able to do research for the book she'd been toying with at least. Maybe she could even inspire a new generation of children to be readers.

He chuckled. "Oh, man, now I'm picturing you in sexy librarian mode."

She snorted softly. Sexy? Not anymore, with her physical and mental scars that had left her apprehensive about physical intimacy. Speaking of which…

She curled up closer to him, bit her lip. He was still hard beneath her, but not doing anything about it. His restraint boosted her sense of safety and courage. Her security was coming for her at six. That didn't give them a lot of time to work with, and since he seemed in no hurry to get things going, it was up to her to be the instigator. He was holding himself in check out of respect for her, because of what she'd been through.

Angling her head to nuzzle the edge of his jaw, she breathed in that delicious, clean scent and forced her mind to go blank about everything but him. The bulge under her bottom hardened even more. Again, she wasn't afraid. He made her feel safe and protected and cherished, was nothing like the men who had brutalized her.

Encouraged by both their reactions, she kissed just below his ear, trailed her lips toward the corner of his mouth.

"Tori."

Yeah, she really liked how it sounded when he called her that. "Hmm?" She nibbled at the spot gently, the first tendrils of arousal blooming inside her. Fragile. Hopeful. Like a brand new flower unfurling its tender petals toward the spring sunshine.

His fingers speared into her hair, cupped the back of

her head as he turned to meet her eyes. "Don't force this if you're not ready."

"I'm not." Not forcing. More like jumpstarting. She wanted him, was attracted to him.

Once she got past the insecurity and anxiety, maybe it would be okay. Maybe she could enjoy him like her old self would have, because it wouldn't be just sex. They both cared about each other. She just needed to be careful she didn't let things go farther than that, because her feelings were already leaning toward much more.

Brock didn't answer, merely searched her eyes as if he was trying to decide whether or not she was being truthful, even though she'd already made her intentions plain the other night and granted her consent. She was definitely consenting now, too. And if things had been different, if he didn't have to be so careful of her, she knew without a doubt he would have taken charge from the start. That kind of control and consideration was hot in its own right.

She shifted on his lap, a tiny thrill shooting through her when his body tensed subtly, the slight hitch in his breathing when she rubbed over his erection. She loved knowing that she held the power to turn a sexy man like him on. Sliding her hands up his neck, she wrapped them around his nape and leaned forward to press her lips to his.

He made a low, soft sound and angled his head, taking over the kiss. He nibbled at her top lip, then the lower one before stroking his tongue across it.

She opened immediately, gliding her tongue along his. The sweet, slow caress sparked a fire low in her belly, made her breasts tingle and swell. Awakening her arousal by degrees, her position on his lap giving her a sense of control—because he was giving it to her. And he would stop if she wanted him to.

It made her braver. She couldn't catch her breath, aware of the ache gathering between her thighs. Amazed that she could feel this way again after everything she'd been through. But only because it was Brock's hands on her. His mouth on hers.

"God, you feel good," he murmured, one hand at the back of her head, holding her still for the kiss she had no desire to pull away from. The other smoothed up her spine and down again before dipping low to wrap around her hip and pull her center tighter to his erection. Wanting more, she set her hands on his shoulders and scrambled up to straddle his thighs.

Heat coiled deep inside her the moment her denim-covered core made contact with the hard bulge in his jeans. She moaned into his mouth, letting him know she was into this, how good he was making her feel. This was what she'd needed, been hoping for. To forget everything else for a little while and simply lose herself in him.

Those big hands curved around her hips. Squeezed gently as his tongue teased hers. Testing. Asking.

Yes. More.

"So soft." He kissed the edge of her mouth, working his way across her jaw. She gasped and closed her eyes, let her head fall to the side as his mouth nibbled to the sensitive spot beneath her ear, down her neck to the top of the turtleneck collar.

But when he reached up to pull it down, she froze, her eyes popping open, the spell she'd been under shattering like a crystal vase dropped onto a tile floor.

Out of nowhere, shame and embarrassment swamped her. She grabbed his hand to still it, ducked her chin and shook her head, a tight motion of denial. Her scars were so ugly. Humiliating. A constant reminder of what had been done to her that she would carry with her for the rest of her life.

Brock stayed exactly where he was but didn't push her hand away, the warmth of his breath on her neck sending a wash of goosebumps over her skin. "I've already seen them," he whispered. "I don't want you to hide from me."

Something hard and angry formed in the center of her chest. Bitterness. He *had* seen them, on the night she'd been rescued. But that was different. They'd been strangers then. They were far more than that now. It was bright in here, the late afternoon sunlight streaming through the window to her right. Exposing her scars to him now during this kind of intimacy—especially *this* scar—was distressing.

"I hate them," she whispered back, her pulse hammering in her throat, unsure if she meant the scars themselves or the men who had locked that fucking metal collar around her neck.

She still woke up sometimes with the feel of it there, squeezing, choking her. Holding her prisoner by the chain anchored to the floor in that decaying shed while they'd done whatever they'd wanted to her on that filthy bare mattress.

She shuddered and ducked her head into his neck, clenched her eyes shut as she fought to banish the memories.

"Hey." Brock splayed his hands across the middle of her back and pressed her close once more, angling his chin to murmur against her temple. "They don't define you. You're beautiful and strong and brave. Let me show you. Let me make you feel good."

Victoria kept her eyes shut and sucked in a steadying breath, belatedly realized that she was digging her fingers into his shoulders. With effort she relaxed them, focused on his scent, the way he was holding her. Brock had seen terrible things over the course of his career. He knew about her scars and still wanted her anyway. If she stopped this now, she was admitting defeat and letting those bastards take something else from her. Letting them win.

No. No more.

Though she was afraid of continuing, she was more afraid of letting him go. Of losing this chance with someone who valued and respected her. Someone who would protect her and keep her safe.

Screwing up her courage, she allowed herself to be even more vulnerable and whispered, "Help me through this."

SHE WAS COMPLETELY rigid in his arms as she said it.

Brock stilled, suddenly feeling out of his depth with her and this entire situation. The possessive, protective parts of him howled in outrage and agony at the way she'd been hurt. At not being able to help her let go.

He'd never felt like this about anyone before and he wanted to help give her confidence back, give her pleasure to hopefully begin replacing all the pain. A good memory to take with her into her new life. Far away from him.

The thought of never seeing her again sent an arrow of something uncomfortably close to panic through him, increasing the need to strip her right here and now, cover her and slide deep inside her warmth, claim her in a way no one else ever had or ever would again.

But that would scare the ever-loving shit out of her.

With a mental groan he fought back the hunger and possessiveness raging inside him. Maybe it was better that she not realize how into her he was. He'd meant everything he'd just said. He really did see her as all those things.

She was beautiful to him. He was in awe of her surviving what she had, and still having the strength to help the investigators secure the verdict that ensured Ruiz would die in prison.

Fuck, he wanted her so badly, wanted to erase everything in her head with pleasure. What the hell was he supposed to do? He should stop this, but the rawness of her plea ripped him up inside.

Before he could say anything else, she took him off guard by sitting up and crushing her lips to his. He groaned when she slid her tongue inside to curl around his, sucking on it for a moment before she straightened to stare into his eyes. Her breathing was erratic, a slight flush on her golden skin, her dark eyes blazing with a mixture of desire and determination that made his heart squeeze. But what she wanted was clear.

Okay, angel. He would take it from here.

"Lie down," he managed, stealing one last kiss before wrapping his arms around her back and turning her to lay her lengthwise on the black tufted leather couch.

With one hand he grasped the back of it and pushed down until it was flat, doubling the surface area. Tori lay there watching him, her body language relaxed but her eyes telling a different story.

She was nervous, and it was making him nervous too. He didn't want to fuck this up. Couldn't, without risking further damage to her. And he refused to do that.

His instincts had never led him wrong where sex was concerned, but this was different. More than anything he wanted to unwrap her like a present, lay her out and enjoy every part of her, find out what made her feel good and then give it to her until she shattered in his arms. But damn, he hated the added pressure of working against the clock.

Remembering how she'd reacted when he'd tried to pull the neck of her top down, he got up and crossed to the window to lower the blind. Moments later the room was dim, and he swore he heard her sigh of relief as he went back to her.

Rather than climb onto the couch and cover her with his weight as he was dying to, he went down on one knee beside her instead and ran a reassuring hand over her hair. "Okay?"

"Yes." She gave him a smile and reached up to curl a hand around his neck, tug him toward her. He went willingly, bracing one hand beside her head as he poured himself into the kiss, telling her without words how sexy she was, that he cared and would treat her gently.

When she began moving restlessly on the leather, he risked taking things a little farther and gently cupped the side of her breast in his palm. She gasped against his lips, then arched her back, pushing into his hand.

In answer he reached down and slid that same hand beneath the hem of her top, spreading his fingers out as he glided up her stomach, her sides. With an impatient sound she suddenly twisted up to grab the material and peel it over her head. His eyes locked on the small mounds of her breasts encased in black lace, the nipples pressing against the sheer fabric.

He also saw the marks on her pale golden skin. Most of the scars were round. Small circles scattered over her stomach and the tops of her breasts. Some larger, about the size of a quarter.

A sickening wave of helpless anger crashed through him when he realized what they were. Cigarette burns. The larger ones were no doubt from the Cuban cigars Ruiz supplied his men with.

Masking his response before she could see it, he cradled her breasts in his hands and gently ran his thumbs over the hard tips. A soft, aroused sound came out of her. He gave her more, bending to press a kiss to the shallow valley between her breasts and working his way up to her throat, past the scars ringing that delicate flesh. Wishing he could heal her with his touch.

Tori sighed and tipped her head back, gripped the back of his head when he dragged his tongue against the spot where her neck and shoulder joined. Sucked gently, giving her the faint edge of his teeth and reveled in the shiver that sped through her, the goosebumps that scattered across her skin. He was hard as stone in his jeans, his cock aching for her touch, but he was damn well going to see to her pleasure before even thinking about moving to the next step.

He trailed kisses across her collarbones, down to the tops of her breasts, waited with his lips a breath away from the lace-covered nipple until she made an impatient sound and tugged his head to her breast. Pulling the lace aside, he lowered his head and gently ran his tongue over one hard nub.

"Oh, Brock, yes," she whispered, tugging harder at his head.

Loving the sound of his name on her lips, he obliged, capturing her nipple between his lips and drawing it into his mouth. She moaned and arched into him, demanding more. He was only too happy to give it to her.

He did the same to the other one, followed every cue she gave him, used his instincts to build her arousal higher. Every tiny moan told him what felt best, every arch of her body told him what she wanted more of. And when he slid a hand down to cup between her legs, the sound of need she made sliced through him like a knife.

She helped him undo her jeans, lifted her hips so he could slide them off, leaving her in just a pair of black lace panties. Every muscle in his body tightened as he stared at them, his nostrils flaring as he drew in the sweet scent of her arousal. God he wanted to rip the flimsy material off her and bury his tongue in her folds.

His breathing came faster as he bent back to her breast, teased her nipple while he trailed a hand up and down her silky smooth thighs. Only when she was whimpering and squirming did he slide his fingers under the edge of the lace and lightly trace them over her sex.

Their groans mingled together as he touched soft, wet heat. She gripped his shoulder now, her head tipped to the side as she watched him, her eyes heavy-lidded, lips parted.

Brock stroked lightly through the silky softness of her folds, grazed the edge of her clit on the down stroke. She whimpered and closed her eyes, her hips lifting into his hand.

His heart pounded out of control as he slid back up to circle her most sensitive flesh. Tiny, light circles.

She was panting now, her fingers digging into his upper arm, almost as though she was afraid he would stop. But he was almost beyond that, needing to make her come. And God, he needed to get his mouth on her to finish this properly.

The blood roared in his ears, the need to possess her screaming in his veins. Grasping her hips, he pulled her to the end of the couch and knelt in front of her, pausing to drag her panties down her legs before setting her calves on his shoulders.

She pushed up onto her elbows. "Brock…"

"Shhh," he whispered, dying to go down on her. Make her melt under his tongue. He nipped gently at her inner thigh, stroked his tongue across the spot to soothe the tiny sting as his hands closed around her hips. Holding her in place while he dragged his tongue up—

A solid hand landed in the middle of his chest and pushed. Brock stopped and raised his head to look at her, battling the roar of hunger lashing his body. And then the tension in her thighs registered. The way her other hand was no longer clamped on his shoulder, but braced against it instead.

Fuck. *Fuck.* Taking charge in bed was simply how he was wired, and he hadn't received any complaints yet. But Tori wasn't like anyone he'd been with before.

She'd survived weeks of sexual violence that kept him

up at night thinking about it. She was edging back from giving in because he'd just asserted his dominance without even being aware of it.

He exhaled and sat up on his knees, silently berating himself. *Dumbass.* He'd scared her, pinning her and looming over her like that. God dammit.

Pushing aside the frustration, he set her legs down and straightened. The instant he backed off she curled in on herself, covering her breasts with her arms and tucking her legs up.

No...

Sick at the thought that he'd scared her, he immediately grabbed a throw blanket from the chair beside the couch and handed it to her. Tori wrapped it around her body, covering herself, and sat up, not looking at him.

"Hey." Scooting to his knees in front of her now, he cupped her cheek, bringing her gaze to his. "You all right?"

She huffed out a frustrated breath and nodded. "I'm sorry. I don't know what happened."

"Don't apologize. Hell, I should be the one apologizing."

"No, you didn't do anything wrong." She reached up to grasp his hand, threaded her fingers through his and pressed her cheek to their joined hands. "It all felt really good. I'm not sure what went wrong."

What was wrong was this whole damn setup. Her forcing it before she was ready. The clock being against them. "Tell me what you need." His voice was a deep rasp.

"I think it was the position maybe. Me on my back and you…"

Him acting like a sex-starved guy who couldn't wait to dive between her thighs. God. This hadn't gone at all the way he'd hoped. Worse, he'd let her down. He hated that most of all.

Chiming bells echoed through the room. Tori's head

snapped toward the kitchen. "It's my phone alarm. I set it for ten minutes before six."

They were out of time. God dammit, now he'd left her hanging on top of everything else. "I'm sorry."

Her expression turned sad, tender. "No. Brock, I swear it's not you. Trust me, you did everything right."

If that were true, she would be coming against his tongue right now instead of wrapped up in a blanket trying to explain herself.

"It's me," she whispered. "Maybe I'm…broken."

"You're not broken," he protested, unable to hide the heat in his tone.

"Well. I'd better get dressed." Holding the blanket around her with one hand, she reached down to gather her clothes.

Frustrated, wishing he could do this all over again, he didn't know what to do or say to make it better. So he handed back her panties and jeans and got up to get her a bottle of water. She met him in the kitchen, took it with a murmur of thanks and drained half the bottle.

He gently gathered her into his arms, needing to hold her. "Maybe it's because of the time limit. Too much pressure."

"Maybe." She didn't sound convinced.

Brock hugged her close and kissed her temple, breathing in the scent of her shampoo. The position had triggered something. Her on her back. A feeling of helplessness, likely.

If this was going to work for her, he needed to do something to shift the balance and give her what she needed. She had to be the one calling the shots. Next time—if there was a next time—he was going to have to go way outside of his comfort zone and hand her the reins. She would have to be on top. In control. And shit, with her the idea was insanely hot.

"Hope this hasn't changed your mind," she said finally.

He frowned. "About?"

"About...helping me still."

He closed his eyes, unsure if he really deserved another shot. "You sure you want to do this again?"

"Yes." Her phone chimed in her purse. She glanced at it. "My detail is on the way up." She started for the door.

He stopped her, refrained from caging her against it the way he wanted and settled for grasping her hips. Those dark eyes flashed up to his, and he was relieved to see no fear there. Just a deep loneliness that he ached to erase. "Saturday night. Are you busy?"

She gave a sardonic laugh. "Uh, no."

"Come spend it with me." He pushed a lock of hair away from her face.

"Are you sure that's a good idea?"

"Yes. But the deal is, you have to stay the night with me."

A frown creased her forehead. "I'm not sure they'll allow that."

"I'll handle it." He'd figure out a way to make it happen.

For a moment she looked doubtful, then gave him a little smile that turned his heart inside out. "All right."

The tension in his muscles eased. He lifted a hand, traced his fingertips over the shadows beneath her eyes. "Text me when you arrive safely."

"I will."

"Hope you sleep well tonight, angel."

Surprise flashed in her eyes at the endearment, then the edges of her mouth curved upward. "I'll try."

"When you stay over Saturday night, I'll make sure you sleep like a baby." A knock interrupted the rest of what he was going to say. He checked to verify it was one of the marshals, then stole a soft, quick kiss before opening the door.

She searched his eyes. "Bye."

"Bye." Closing the door behind her, he expelled a long breath and leaned his forehead against the wood. Maybe now that the monster who had caused her so much pain had gotten what was coming to him, she would finally be at peace enough to get a full night's sleep.

Unfortunately, where the *Veneno* cartel was concerned, there were plenty more monsters still out there for him and his team to slay.

Chapter Seven

"I just got word."

Manny Nieto turned from the small table in the tiny cabin kitchen to face his head of security, the only man he trusted to watch his back now. They'd been waiting for this all day. "And?"

"Ruiz is going to die in jail," David said, satellite phone in his hand. "Doubt he'll make it another month, even in max security."

Well, at least that was something. Though it was a better fate than he deserved. Manny would have preferred to learn his nemesis had been tortured, shot full of holes and left to die an agonizing death over a period of days. "He'll appeal. But it won't do him any good."

"No."

"And is there any word on whether he's been in contact with someone in his old network? Or Montoya?"

"Not that we know of."

"Well, find out for sure." Unfortunately, Ruiz being locked up for the rest of his life didn't help Manny much. Even with that headache gone, he had new, equally big ones to deal with. Whatever information his daughter and mistress had given the Americans months back, it had put an unprecedented amount of heat on him and the rest of the cartel. "Anything else?"

"Nothing."

He'd expected as much. Still, each day that went by without any new information about Oceane aged him beyond his fifty-two years. Exhaling a long breath, he leaned back to survey the Spartan hunting cabin he'd been staying in for the past two nights up in the mountains. "Is the perimeter secure?"

"Of course."

"We'll move at first light." Spending another day here was too risky. He had to keep moving, never let his guard down. There were too many enemies out there hunting him now, some of them former friends. That was cartel life. A constant struggle for survival of the fittest.

Manny waved David off, wanting some time to himself. When the front door shut he sank into a chair at the table and put his head in his hand.

Everything had unraveled so fast, blow after blow raining down on him. He'd left his treacherous wife months ago, along with the luxurious existence he'd made for them. Now his life's purpose was twofold: evade the authorities and enemies hunting him, and find his daughter.

He had as many feelers out as he dared, searching for Oceane. But even after all this time and the reward he'd offered via his network, he was no closer to finding her. Last he'd heard, she was somewhere in the D.C. area. Now she could be anywhere, perhaps even on the other side of the globe.

It was hard to believe that even he, with all his money and contacts, had been unable to locate her. The Americans must have found Oceane's tracking device and disposed of it long ago, because he hadn't received a single hit on the beacon since Anya was killed.

He dragged a hand down his unshaven face, the guilt burning under his sternum like a branding iron. He had loved Anya. Would never have ordered her execution if she hadn't betrayed him. Oceane didn't know enough to pose a threat to him or his vast empire.

He'd ordered a clean kill with a bullet Anya would never see coming. Instead the men of his former enforcer, Montoya, had violated her and stabbed her, leaving her to bleed to death in front of Oceane. Manny felt sick every time he thought about it.

It's too late. You've lost Oceane. She'll never forgive you.

Rage and terror blasted through him. He shoved to his feet, began pacing as he did whenever he became agitated. He thought best on his feet, always had. And he was determined to figure out a way past this.

He crossed the small room to push aside the curtain and look out the grimy window. David was fifty yards away checking the property, standing guard as always. It was already getting dark, the sun behind the trees, leaving a brilliant blaze of orange and pink. Soon it would be pitch black here.

He hated the nights the most. That was when his conscience pricked him like merciless needles, making sleep impossible. He always pictured Anya's face. Oceane's face. The terror and hatred in their eyes when they looked at him with identical accusing expressions.

He shook his head, refusing to accept that all was lost. Oceane was his only child. His sole heir. And he'd risked everything, clawing his way through the muck of poverty to get to where he was today.

He'd tried to shield her for too long and it had backfired on him. He needed her at his side. To prepare her for the day when he passed his empire to her. One he'd deliberately kept her ignorant of for her own protection. But it hadn't been enough. And now she'd suffered so much she might hate him forever. Still, he had to try. Get her back and begin the process of repairing everything. She was his legacy.

His jaw tightened as he glanced at the guns laid out for cleaning on the bench by the front door. Neither he nor David went anywhere without having at least two weapons on them. Because the men coming after him were the most dangerous in the entire cartel. Manny should know; they used to be his.

Montoya was a liability as well as a threat and needed to be eliminated immediately. Except so far, he was proving as impossible to find as Oceane. The head of the cartel had promised to help Manny locate him, but the shadowy *El Escorpion* had dropped off the grid last week.

So, for now at least, Manny was on his own.

He should have dealt with Montoya long before now. His former enforcer was a loose end he couldn't afford to leave hanging in the wind. The man was too dangerous. Montoya knew too much about him, about his operations and contingency plans. He was also the most likely person to be able to find Manny.

He stalked over to the bag in the corner and yanked out the bottle of scotch he'd brought, unscrewing the cap and drinking straight from the bottle. He needed to get good and drunk so he would be able to sleep and stop being tortured by all his mistakes.

But alcohol only helped so much. The driving need to find Oceane was always there, burning like a fire in his gut. Before he could look to his future, Manny had to erase his past.

Starting with hunting down Montoya, the man he had asked to be Oceane's godfather.

****

"You got everything you need?"

In the act of spreading out his bedroll on the dirt floor, Juan Montoya looked up at the elderly farmer who was allowing him to crash in his house for the night. One of a series of contacts who made up a safe network he was slowly working his way through across the countryside to stay under the radar. "Yeah, thanks."

"My wife will make breakfast in the morning. I'll bring it to you."

"I appreciate it."

As soon as his host left, Juan got up and checked every corner of the guestroom, searching for any cables, cameras or bugs. Not that he expected to find those things way out here in this tiny village, but he hadn't managed to stay alive this long by being careless. Unlike the men he used to work for, he preferred to work alone. Having men beneath him was useful in some situations, but it was also a pain in the ass when they weren't disciplined and murdered or tortured without his permission. That was all behind him now.

His actions over the past few months had made him one of the most wanted men in North America. Not only was he trying to evade U.S. and Mexican authorities, but the entire and formidable *Veneno* cartel network as well.

There was a million dollar bounty on his head. Damn near four hundred times the annual household income down here in rural Mexico. So yeah, he had to look over his shoulder all the time, because that was a lot of money to a poor man. And the lure of money made even the most morally upstanding people do bad shit. He knew that better than anyone.

The bounty was being offered by the Mexican government, but Juan had a feeling it was likely backed by *El Escorpion* and/or Nieto. There were probably other bosses involved as well, but the head of the cartel and

Nieto were the two most powerful men in the entire organization. Between the two of them, they practically owned half of Mexico, and as much of the government and law enforcement as well.

He sank down onto his bedroll with a weary groan, going over what he needed to do tomorrow. A tip had come in that Nieto was only seventy miles from here. A two or three hour drive in the jeep Juan had rented. Juan would get some sleep, get up before the sun, *then* go after Nieto.

His former boss would have David with him, but that didn't concern Juan. He could get there while it was still dark and be in and out of there before anyone noticed. Two quick kills within a matter of seconds, then be back here in time for that home cooked breakfast the farmer had offered.

He'd already taken steps to mitigate the risk to himself and gain some protection, namely flipping teams and taking over Carlos Ruiz's old network. Juan had been in communication with him through an unnamed source at the prison Ruiz was being held in.

With Ruiz's blessing, he was free to use that network and its materials at his disposal. He would begin by going after his former friend and boss, Nieto. It was business. A matter of self-preservation. Either kill, or be killed. That was how things worked in the narco universe.

Once he had taken over Nieto's sizeable organization and territory, he could set his sights on the big prize: *el Escorpion* himself. He hadn't figured out who the man was yet, but he would eventually. Juan didn't have a personal grudge against him, unlike Ruiz. But with *el Escorpion* out of the way, Juan could make his move.

For a man who had been born into abject poverty in a dusty little farm town in the foothills, the prospect of that much money and control was everything Juan had ever dreamed of and more. Once he eliminated Nieto and *el Escorpion*, he was going take control of what was left of the once untouchable *Veneno* cartel.

Chapter Eight

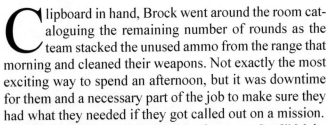

Clipboard in hand, Brock went around the room cataloguing the remaining number of rounds as the team stacked the unused ammo from the range that morning and cleaned their weapons. Not exactly the most exciting way to spend an afternoon, but it was downtime for them and a necessary part of the job to make sure they had what they needed if they got called out on a mission.

"What's on the agenda for this afternoon, Cap?" Maka asked as he took his M4 apart.

"Haven't decided yet."

"Well if there's nothing going on, maybe we could do some more PT and throw a little wrestling in there for fun."

Brock laughed at him. "You just want a rematch because you're a sore loser."

Maka looked up, annoyance stamped all over his bronze face. "Sore loser? That's my belt in your office. You didn't win it or earn it, you ganged up on me and forcibly took it from me. Big difference."

"Can we do a lip sync battle instead?" Granger asked,

busy stripping his Glock. "I don't think Taggart would be too impressed if we started breaking tables here."

"He's got a point," Prentiss said, reassembling his rifle. Then to Maka, "You sure you want more of that punishment and humiliation?"

Maka turned an incredulous look on his teammate. "I had like, six of you on top of me and you put me through a freaking *table*."

"A flimsy collapsing table. Come on."

"Whatever. I held my head as high as my neck would allow afterward."

Lockhart was as quiet as always, methodically taking apart his sniper rifle. "What about you?" Brock asked him. "Any suggestions for how we should spend this afternoon?" He wasn't really asking, since he already had things to review with the team per Taggart's request, but it was fun to get the banter rolling.

"We should rent an actual wrestling ring at a gym," Lockhart said without looking up from cleaning his scope. "Make it real."

"Hell yeah, we should," Maka piped up, looking excited by the prospect.

"Only if we dress up in costume for the matches," Granger said.

"In leotards," Khan put in with a smirk. "I'd pay money to see that."

Brock burst out laughing at the mental image.

"They wear *bodysuits*, dumbass, not leotards," Granger said to Khan. "Deadpool is badass in his. And what are you laughing at, Cap?"

"Oh, nothing," Brock said. "Just picturing a human tank like Maka wearing a leotard—if we could find one to fit him."

Now Maka looked offended. "I would so rock a leotard."

"We need to make this happen," Colebrook said, all

enthusiasm.

The guys all started jawing at each other, trash talking and making bets about who would have the best shot against Maka in the ring one on one. Brock took advantage of the opportunity to squat next to Lockhart, who had now bowed out of the conversation.

"Hey, you heard anything about Oceane? About whether they're going to keep her here for a while longer?" His teammate checked in with her pretty regularly.

"Last I talked to her, that was the plan. What about Victoria?"

He kept his expression impassive even though the mere mention of her name stirred up all kinds of emotions. "She'll be leaving early next week, unless something else comes up in the meantime." It was driving him nuts to stay away from her, but with his schedule it couldn't be helped.

Three days had passed since that not-so-perfect ending at his place. He'd talked to her on the phone each night to catch up on each other's day, mostly just to hear her voice. Damn, he hated how things had gone the other day. And with the deadline of her impending departure speeding toward them, tomorrow couldn't come soon enough.

Hoping to shake things up and make her more relaxed, he'd arranged for them to meet at a fancy hotel downtown. He'd gone to the Marshals Service about it and they'd agreed because of her situation, and because they were familiar with the security protocols of the hotel since it was frequently used by political figures.

"She know where she's going?" Lockhart asked.

"Not yet." A heaviness settled in his chest. She hadn't even left the city yet and he already missed her. She was so deep under his skin at this point, the idea of never seeing her again was hard to deal with. But he wanted her safe, and he wanted her happy. So if he had to let her go, then he would find a way to live with it.

A musical ring tone cut through the banter and trash talk going on in the room. Brock glanced at Rodriguez as he leaned over to grab his phone, looked at it and answered. A second later he shot to his feet, his expression taut as he put one finger in his ear to block out the noise. "What?"

The room went silent, all eyes on him.

Rodriguez was intent on whatever the caller was saying, his eyebrows drawn together in a deep frown. "God."

From his reaction, Brock knew exactly what the call was about. Rodriguez's mother.

Fuck. Brock pushed to his feet, stood watching Rodriguez as his teammate dragged a hand through his hair in agitation and took in a shaky breath, his jaw tight, a haunted look on his face.

"When?" Rodriguez said quietly, the word brittle. Then he closed his eyes and exhaled a hard breath. "Okay, I… *Dammit*." His voice shredded. Colebrook popped up beside him, laid a hand on his friend's shoulder. "Look, I'll call you back," Rodriguez said hoarsely, and ended the call.

Colebrook threw Brock a questioning look. Brock hustled over and together they walked Rodriguez out into the hall to Brock's office for some privacy. He shut the door as Colebrook steered the other man toward a chair.

Rodriguez dropped into it and dragged a hand down his face, looking shell-shocked. "My mom died an hour ago. Everything was fine. Well, as fine as it has been for the last few months. My dad went down to get something from the cafeteria. She went into cardiac arrest while he was down there. They called him right away but by the time he got back, she was gone."

Brock sat on the corner of his desk and leaned his elbows on his thighs. "I'm so sorry."

"I was flying out in the morning to see her," he said in

a wooden tone, staring at the carpet. "Christ, if I'd known I would have taken the red eye last night." He raised haunted golden brown eyes to Brock. "I should have been there. God dammit, I should have fucking *been* there."

"I'll call Charlie," Colebrook murmured from beside him, pulling out his phone to dial his sister, who was Rodriguez's fiancée.

Rodriguez didn't argue, just put his head in his hands and pulled in an unsteady breath. His mom had been battling MS for a long time now, and the whole family had been on an emotional roller coaster for more than a year. But it was such a cruel twist of fate to take her while she was alone, a day before her son could be with her. With FAST Bravo's last deployment, Rodriguez had gone more than four months without seeing her except on Skype.

"Want me to change your flight?" Brock offered. "I can get you on the first one available this afternoon."

"No. Thanks. I'll figure it out." He sat up and slumped back in the chair. "I don't know how long I'll be gone. Funeral arrangements were all decided by her months ago, but it'll still take a few days to get everything organized. Not sure when the service will be."

"Don't worry about any of that. You just take care of your family. That's all that's important right now."

Rodriguez nodded once, swallowed. "I can't believe she's gone," he croaked out.

Colebrook lowered his phone. "Charlie's on the way. She'll be here to pick you up in fifteen."

Another nod as Rodriguez buried his head back in his hands and made a valiant effort to fight the tears in his eyes.

"Be right back," Brock murmured, and left to inform Taggart what had happened. They would have to find a temporary replacement for Rodriguez while he was away, in case FAST Bravo was called out for something. When he was done and stepped out into the hall, Charlie Colebrook swept into the building. Her dark brown gaze locked on Brock in concern.

"Hey. He's in my office," he told her before she could say anything, gesturing down the hall.

"How is he?" she asked worriedly, hurrying toward him.

"Not good."

She made an empathetic sound and walked to the office with him. Brock opened the door for her and stood back. Colebrook stepped outside with him to give the couple privacy.

Rodriguez stood and turned toward the door. The instant he saw Charlie his face crumpled. She went straight to him without a word. Rodriguez wrapped his arms around her and buried his face in her neck, a sob ripping out of him as Brock swung the door shut.

Out in the hallway with him, Colebrook let out a harsh sigh. "I feel so fucking bad for him."

He nodded. "The timing's just plain mean."

"Yeah." He rubbed the back of his neck, shook his head, visibly upset. "We were a lot younger than him when we lost our mom. But I think it always hurts the same, no matter how old we are."

"Yeah." Damn, Brock was calling his mom the first chance he got. He hadn't seen his family since last fall and needed to plan a trip home to Illinois soon.

"Just another reminder about how short life really is. None of us know how long we have left on this earth," Colebrook murmured, his gaze on his sister and best friend as they held each other on the other side of the glass.

Yeah, it goddamn was short.

Brock's jaw tightened, a rush of desperation flashing through him. Tomorrow was likely the last time he would ever get to see Tori. He was going to take full advantage of the little time he had left with her.

As he headed out the door, he dialed his mom's number.

"Well hello, stranger," she answered good-naturedly with her typical wry humor.

Brock deserved the slight dig under it. He hadn't spoken to her in over two weeks, though he'd texted the night they arrived home from Afghanistan so she would stop worrying. "Hey."

"To what do I owe the pleasure?"

"I was just thinking about you, wanted to call and hear your voice."

****

Life was so precious and fragile.

Fernando Diaz swallowed twice to get the bite of pineapple past the invisible restriction in his throat as he watched his young children playing on the living room rug after their lunch. He would do literally anything to protect them and the rest of his family. And could partly understand why Nieto had gone to such lengths to keep his daughter ignorant of his activities, even as an adult. Fernando was guilty of being overprotective too.

Given the recent turn of events and the splintering of two rival factions of the cartel, he had to do more than ever to protect his family.

"You know what this castle needs?" His mother, Maria, leaned forward on her hands and knees to choose another handful of Lego bricks, his children busy adding their architectural efforts to the lopsided plastic castle they were working on together.

"A library," his five-year-old daughter said in her sweet little voice. "A big one, with a ladder in it. Like the one Beast gives Belle."

"An excellent idea," his mother said. "But what about

a secret escape route?"

"Like a tunnel?" his seven-year-old son asked, intrigued.

"Exactly." His mother beamed in approval and leaned down to point inside the castle. "See right there? What if we pretend to build a secret staircase from the library that goes beneath the castle?"

"Oh! From a secret door! You have to pull on a certain book on the shelf to get the door to open. So only we would know how to get inside," his daughter said excitedly.

"You are so clever, *mi corazón*," she praised. "And where should we have this tunnel lead to? Say, if we wanted to escape an attacking army."

"Of pirates?" his son piped up.

"Pirates, or maybe soldiers. Where would be a good place for this tunnel to go?"

Pedro thought about it a moment. "The water?"

His mother smiled. "I think that's a very smart choice. Then we could get away by boat if we need to."

"Like *Papá's* yacht," Isa said.

"Perhaps. But maybe something even faster, in case we needed to get away in a hurry."

"One of his helicopters, then. Or his speed boat," Pedro said.

"Yes." She wrapped an arm around each of the children and pulled them close for a kiss on the end of their noses. "My smart little angels."

Pedro and Isa beamed up at her, and Fernando couldn't help but smile. His mother truly was amazing. Just as she had with him, she educated the children about necessary survival skills in such a subtle, fun way that they had no idea that they were in fact being indoctrinated into the ways of protecting themselves in the vicious cartel world they unwittingly lived in.

On the heels of that thought, guilt settled in the middle

of his chest. "*Papá* has an important call to make," he announced, getting up from the couch. He'd put this off as long as possible, but there was no more time to waste with the added dangers they faced now. His wife was in the bedroom busy packing the last of their necessary items right now. "Keep building. I'd like to hear more about the tunnel when I get back."

"We won't be long," his mother said, and kissed his children on the top of their heads before rising and following him down the hall.

Fernando pressed his hand to the biometric scanner beside the door, then bent to activate the retinal scanner. His mother stepped in after him and shut the door. Steel bars slid home across it, sealing them in and keeping everyone else out.

The secure landline sat on the antique oak desk in the corner, brought over from Spain by one of his ancestors two centuries ago. Without looking at his mother he picked up the phone and called the number of the government official best positioned to help with this situation.

When the woman on the other end answered, Fernando spoke the words he had prepared ahead of time. The phone would automatically turn his voice into a digital one that no computer system could identify.

"I have a tip on the whereabouts of Manuel Nieto. He's currently in Chihuahua, near this location." He gave the coordinates of a remote cabin where Nieto had last been sighted by a villager eager to accept the reward money for information that might lead to Nieto's capture. "He is armed and has his bodyguard with him." He glanced over at his mother, who nodded in approval. Then he ended the call.

"Well," he said to her, settling the receiver back into its cradle. "I guess that's it. Time to go."

"I'll get the children. You check on Sophia."

He found his wife in their bedroom, standing at the

window that overlooked the back of the house, gazing out at the pool and the immaculate grounds surrounding it. Wrapping an arm around her waist from behind, he kissed her temple. "It's time. Ready?"

She nodded and pressed her lips together, her eyes shimmering with tears.

He hugged her tighter. "I'm sorry, *mi amor*," he murmured. "You know we don't have a choice." Authorities were getting too close for comfort, both Mexican and American.

Taking her hand, he led her downstairs to where his mother was helping the children put their backpacks on. Everything had been prepared long ago, every detail well rehearsed. Including the game they had devised for the children. As far as they were concerned that was all this would be: a wonderful game.

Life was all about games, after all. Except in this case, only the winners survived.

"*Abuela* has a surprise for you," his mother told them, and Fernando's heart ached at the excitement on those precious little faces as they gazed so trustingly up at her. "Remember the tunnel we talked about? Well, we're going on an adventure down a secret one right here in our house."

Isa's dark eyes widened. "We have a secret tunnel?"

"Oh, yes. It's very special." She held out a hand to each of them, gave a confident smile. Maria Diaz never showed fear or any other weakness, no matter what was happening. Not even when her husband had been murdered in front of her more than two decades ago. She was the strongest person Fernando had ever known, and his role model throughout his life. "Are you ready?"

"Yes!" they both squealed, reaching for her hands.

Together as a family they headed down to the safe room in the basement, their head of security following discreetly behind them. Others were already stationed at the tunnel exit, ensuring the area was secure.

The safe room was state of the art, no expense spared. In the luxuriously appointed bathroom in the downstairs suite, he opened up the shower door.

"Watch this," he said to the children, and pressed what looked like a button for the steam shower on the wall. The tile floor slid open, revealing a tunnel lit with lanterns set into the ceiling.

Isa's eyes went wide and Pedro gasped. "Wow!"

Fernando smiled and turned to his wife. "After you."

Sophia put on a brave face. As his wife she had known this day might come. Sad as she was to leave this house they loved, their fortress was no longer safe. "Come on, let's go," she said, even managing to put some enthusiasm into her voice. She took the children's hands and started down the concrete steps. His mother went next.

Before following them, Fernando looked back over his shoulder to his head of security. "Destroy the entrance when I signal you."

"Of course."

Taking the heavy duffel bag from him, packed with supplies and cash, Fernando followed his family into the staircase. Leaving now would buy them some time and relieve the pressure. Authorities would launch a manhunt for Nieto soon. He would take care of Montoya later, once he and his family were settled.

One problem at a time, one step at a time, he told himself as the trap door slid shut above him. Locking them in this subterranean labyrinth that led to the waiting boat. They had planned for this. Thought of everything.

El Escorpion always had a plan ready for every possible contingency.

Chapter Nine

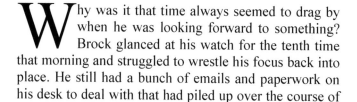

Why was it that time always seemed to drag by when he was looking forward to something? Brock glanced at his watch for the tenth time that morning and struggled to wrestle his focus back into place. He still had a bunch of emails and paperwork on his desk to deal with that had piled up over the course of the team's deployment.

He looked up at a knock on his door to find Commander Taggart there. "You busy?"

"No, please. Save me from myself." He gestured to the files waiting on his desk.

Grinning, Taggart stepped in and shut the door. "Yeah, being stuck back behind a desk sucks, doesn't it? Welcome to my world." He put his hands in his pockets and rocked back onto his heels. "Just got a call from the Mexican Attorney General."

Oh? "What about?"

"Apparently they got a tip that generated a solid lead on a possible location for *El Escorpion* yesterday afternoon. SF raided the mansion but there was no one there and the place had been totally cleaned out. As in *gutted*. The office had been blown up, and so had the safe room. All the computers were charred beyond saving, and they'd shredded and burned all the paperwork in the place, too.

"They found a tunnel entrance, but whatever blew it up filled the first section full of concrete and rock so they can't get in there and no one's sure yet where it lets out. Somewhere close to the water, though. They're still searching for it. I'm told they were close, missed him by a matter of hours."

"If it was him," Brock pointed out.

"Right. But whoever it was went to a whole hell of a lot of trouble to cover his tracks, so it was someone from the cartel. And judging by the look of the estate, they weren't hurting for cash, so they were high up in the organization."

"Nieto?"

"Maybe. They've got another possible lead to follow up on, but this time they want the DEA's assistance when they execute the search warrant."

Brock's eyebrows went up. "Damn, they must be desperate if they're finally allowing us down there." The only reason the U.S. government had caught Carlos Ruiz in its net was because of a tip they believed had come directly from *el Escorpion*. The only way to get the head of the cartel, Nieto, or even that sadistic son of a bitch Montoya, was to go into Mexico and get boots on the ground. Something the Mexican government had never allowed until now.

"We likely won't be kicking in any doors down there," Taggart said dryly.

"Yeah, no. That would be too much to hope for."

His commander's aqua eyes twinkled. "At any rate, they want FAST Bravo down there to advise and support them in this upcoming op. Command's given us the green light."

Oh yeah. FAST Bravo could only operate down there with the Mexican government's permission, and it had to be a joint mission with Mexican forces. No FAST team could operate unilaterally in a foreign country. "When do we head out?"

"I'm arranging a flight for 05:00 tomorrow."

The turn of events stunned him, but they'd been wanting into Mexico for freaking ever, so he wasn't complaining, except it meant his time with Tori would be cut short. *Damn.* He'd have to find a way to fix that. Although no amount of time with her would be enough. "What about Rodriguez? He won't be back until next week. Probably late next week."

"I don't want to find a replacement for him just yet. I'd rather get down there, get a feel for what's happening and make sure they're serious and not dicking us around before we think about going operational. I'll make the call then."

Good enough. "All right. I'll alert the boys."

After calling the team he stared at his phone, debating what to do about Tori. He would likely have to report to base by 04:00, which meant the leisurely morning he'd planned for them to spend together in bed with room service wasn't going to happen. It sucked, and though he wished like hell he could have those hours with her, Fate wasn't cooperating.

She was such a bitch sometimes.

He dialed Tori's cell, and the sound of her voice when she answered hit him square in the heart. "Hey, been thinking about you," she said, a smile in her words.

"Yeah? I'm glad to hear that, because I've been thinking about you nonstop since the other day."

"Well that's nice to hear. You at home?"

"No, the office."

"It's Saturday and you guys just got back from deployment. They couldn't give you the weekend off?" she asked wryly.

"Nah, they like to keep us busy. Get their money's worth out of us." He leaned back in his chair, tapped his fingers on his desk. "Any chance you can talk to your security detail and meet me earlier tonight?" They had arranged for her to arrive at seven.

"Maybe. Why, did something come up?"

"Yes. I can't go into detail, but we're wheels up at 05:00 tomorrow."

"Oh."

That was definitely disappointment in her voice, and maybe he was a bad person for admitting it but he was glad to hear it. "I want as much time with you as I can get. I thought we could add a couple hours on the front end instead to make up the difference."

"I'll make it happen. Can you be there by four?"

He smiled. "I'll be there. Text me once you get confirmation?"

"I will. See you soon. And Brock?"

"Yeah?"

"I can't wait to see you." She hung up.

Brock lowered the phone to his lap, his whole chest tightening until it felt like his heart might explode.

****

Three minutes to four.

Brock wasn't here yet. Victoria paused outside the hotel room and waited while one of the marshals swept it. He reappeared a few moments later. "All clear. We'll be here to get you at five."

"All right. Thanks." He and the others knew why she was meeting Brock here, and she wasn't even embarrassed because she didn't care what they thought. She shut and locked the door, then looked around the room. It was on the eleventh floor with a view of the river.

A king-size bed dominated the space, covered in a thick white duvet and fluffy pillows. Staring at it, nerves buzzed around in her belly. The other day at Brock's place hadn't exactly gone according to plan for either of them.

For whatever reason, at the critical moment her body had just…shut down. She hadn't even had a flashback, which was what she'd been most worried about. Hopefully tonight would be different, because she wasn't going to get another chance to do this. At least not with him, and right now she couldn't imagine ever wanting to do it with anyone else.

Tonight was their goodbye.

Not wanting to think about that because it brought too many painful emotions with it, she carried her overnight bag to the dresser and set it on top. She'd packed light, just toiletries and a change of clothes. Then she paused to check her reflection in the mirror above it.

She looked pretty good, all things considered, her royal blue wrap dress flattering her figure that hadn't quite filled out to her pre-captivity weight yet. She'd left her hair down and used a curling iron to give some body to the ends where they bounced along her shoulder blades. A light blue decorative scarf concealed her most hated scar and finished off the outfit with an elegant touch.

Someone knocked on the door and her heart jumped. "It's me," a deep, delicious voice said from the other side.

A smile curved her mouth, the nerves in her belly changing to excited flutters as she went to check the peephole before opening it. Brock stood there in dark jeans and a black T-shirt that stretched across his muscles, and the smile he gave her made her heart flip-flop.

"Hi," he said, stepping inside with a bag in hand, his gaze roving over her body. "Wow, look at you."

"I haven't dressed up for anything in a long time. It felt nice to put on a dress again," she said, her heart flip-flopping all over the place. She'd ached in places she hadn't even known she had over the past two days, waiting to see him again, never sure if she would be sent from D.C. at a moment's notice. Now they were finally together again and she was going to make the most of it.

Brock set his bag down next to the door and stared at her. "You're so beautiful."

Her cheeks heated. "Thanks." She wanted to hug him so bad, but didn't want to seem needy or desperate so she stayed where she was, hesitating.

Thankfully he made the first move, closing the small distance between them and wrapping his arms around her. Victoria sighed and let herself cling for a long moment, breathing in his scent, trying to memorize everything about this moment so she could carry it with her for the rest of her life. "I missed you," she murmured.

"Missed you too." He squeezed her tighter, kissed the top of her head, her temple. "Feels like forever since I got to do this."

To her, too. "They told me today where I'm going." Bellingham, Washington. An hour or two drive north of Seattle.

He stilled. "Oh?"

She couldn't tell him where, even though she wanted to. "It's far away."

He made a low sound. "When?"

"Tuesday." She pressed her lips together as something close to grief welled up inside her. No, damn it, she was not going to spoil this and cry all over him. She was going to enjoy every last minute of their time together, and hopefully now that they didn't have such a tight deadline, things would go better. "Do you think you'll be back before then?"

"No."

She nodded, smothering the disappointment. "So this is it, then."

He sighed, his breath stirring her hair. "Looks like."

Pushing back to look at him, she gave him a bright smile. "Well then, let's not waste any of it." Taking his face in her hands, she kissed him.

Brock groaned and slid one hand into her hair, the other splaying over her lower back to pull her into his body. But after a moment, he pulled back. "I was going to ask if you were hungry. We could order something up to the room first."

"Not for food." She didn't want to wait, didn't need to ease into this. They only had hours left together. After two days of anticipation, he was finally here and the change of setting made it feel like she had a clean slate to work with.

He gave a low laugh. "Okay then." His eyes gleamed with an odd mixture of hunger and tenderness that turned her heart over. "But wait, I brought some things." He gently disengaged from her arms.

Curious, she watched as he picked up his bag and walked over to set it on the bed. Then he went over to the windows and pulled the curtains shut before coming back to unzip his bag and start laying things out on the bed.

Candles, she realized with a sappy smile. He'd brought candles.

He looked over at her, his sensuous lips curving up at the corners. "I wanted this to be special. Thought it would help set the mood better if we turned off the lights and made it more romantic in here."

She had a feeling there was more to it than him making a romantic gesture. She suspected he'd planned this because he somehow knew she would feel more comfortable with him seeing her body by flattering candlelight rather than by something harsher.

A squeezing sensation constricted her ribcage. "I love it, thank you."

"You're welcome." Smiling to himself, he set the candles on the night table to the left of the bed and began lighting them one by one. "Can you hit the lights?"

She reached behind her and flicked the switch. The closed curtains blocked out all the daylight, leaving the room bathed in the soft glow of the flickering candles. Not too bright. Soft. Inviting.

Intimate.

And suddenly it was all she could do not to run across the room and tackle him to the bed, the mix of joy and sadness warring inside her.

A giggle shot out of her at the mental image, surprising her so much she put a hand to her mouth. Brock looked over at her, grinned. "What?"

She shook her head, grinned back. The thought of her trying to tackle the wall of muscle standing beside the bed was ridiculous. "I don't know. But that felt good."

He set the lighter down, cocked his head slightly and crooked a finger at her, the motion confident. Full of authority. Sexy as hell. "Come here."

His low voice stroked over her senses like velvet. Her heart thumped as she closed the distance between them. No anxiety now. Nothing but joy and anticipation, her body heating, softening. A smile tugged at her lips.

"God I love it when you smile," he murmured, wrapping one solid arm around her waist to draw her close, his free hand threading through her hair.

"Been a long time since I had anything to smile about. Thank you for that." She was happier in that moment than she had been in forever. Even though her heart was breaking at knowing she was about to lose him.

His eyes darkened, then he kissed her.

Hungry to feel him, all of him, Victoria plastered herself to the front of his body and ran her hands over his shoulders. She skimmed them across the width of his back, savoring the feel of the powerful muscles beneath the soft cotton of his shirt, the possessive way he held her. The way she felt in his arms.

Sexy. Desirable, even with her scars.

Her body pulsed, her nipples hardening and an empty ache forming between her thighs. She wanted to touch his skin. Feel it against hers. She slipped her hands beneath the hem of his shirt, raked her fingers gently down his back. Imagined doing the same when he was buried inside her.

Brock groaned into her mouth and released her to reach up and grab the back of his shirt with one fist, dragging it up and over his head. As he let it drop to the floor and lowered his arms to his sides, her breath caught at the sight of him. Every dip and hollow of his muscles were bathed in the warm yellow glow of the candlelight. Her mouth went dry. Her brain stopped functioning.

With a hungry sound she set her hands on his chest, the heat of him all but searing her palms. She pressed her mouth to his breastbone between the ridges of his pecs, let her fingers wander while she rubbed her cheek against the chest, kissed his hot skin and flicked her tongue out to taste him.

His hand tangled in her hair, fingers caressing her scalp as she nuzzled and explored, the hard bulge at the front of his jeans pressing into her abdomen. Heat gathered inside her, a steady pulse of arousal. She gripped his hard butt, lifted her head to kiss him, her tongue tangling with his.

Those big hands slid up and down her back, followed the curve of her hips before reversing. They paused on her shoulder blades. He nipped at her lower lip, sucked it, his fingertips gliding over her jaw, down her neck to the scarf.

He found the knot, deftly freed it as he nibbled and teased her lips. She was distracted by the threat of him removing the scarf, barely stemmed the urge to grab his hand, stop him.

With effort, she shut her brain off. Let her eyes drift closed and allowed herself to focus on the gentle caress of the light fabric as it whispered across her skin when he pulled it free. He made a low sound of either approval or encouragement and kissed her deeper, his tongue delving in to stroke, tease.

His head lifted. She blinked dreamily, slowly coming out of her trance to find him watching her. He took a step back, the light blue scarf still in his hands, that powerful torso and arms that would fuel her fantasies for years to come on display for her.

Holding her gaze, Brock began winding the fabric around his wrists.

At first she didn't understand what he was doing.

She watched, stunned, as he reached past her to yank the comforter down, then got on the bed. Stretched out on his back before her, still watching her, he raised his arms over his head to grasp the headboard.

Victoria stopped breathing as she realized what he was doing, the sight of him too erotic for words.

His eyes were like molten steel as he gazed at her, the bulge of his erection pushing against his jeans. This powerful, heart-stoppingly sexy man was surrendering himself to her. Offering himself to her so she could have full control over what happened next.

She wasn't sure whether she was terrified or more turned on than she ever had been in her life.

He didn't smile, his expression intense. That magnificent chest rising and falling with each breath he took. "Tie this good and tight, angel, because if you don't, there's no way I'll be able to keep my hands off you."

Chapter Ten

The shock on Tori's face transformed into a look of enthrallment, and the heat in her eyes as she stared at him made Brock's heart pound. He'd decided on this well before coming here, and was going with his gut. She'd had all control stripped from her when she was taken captive. She needed to take it back.

She stepped closer to the bed, the candlelight flickering over her golden skin. "Are you sure about this?" she whispered, glancing at the scarf wound around his wrists.

Yes. He curled his fingers around the bottom rung of the iron headboard and nodded once, about to come out of his skin. Surrendering control this way wasn't even remotely in the realm of his comfort zone, but he would gladly do it for her. "Do it."

The look on her face, like she'd been starving and suddenly given access to an all you can eat buffet and didn't know where to begin, made him go hard all over. Her dark brown eyes glowed with arousal as she climbed up to kneel beside him in that sexy as hell dress and reach up to secure the scarf to the headboard.

He had a moment's unease as she tugged the fabric taut around his wrists, his dominant nature rebelling at the idea of being rendered helpless when all he wanted was to grab her, strip her and pin her beneath him on this bed. But there was something so fucking hot about the act of laying himself out like this for her.

Giving the fabric one last tug to secure the ends around the iron rung, she slipped her fingers under the fabric at his wrists to check it, her eyes flicking down to his. "Not too tight?"

"No." Snug, but not cutting off his circulation. And fuck, if she didn't touch him soon he might lose his mind.

A slight smile curved her mouth as she settled on one hip beside him, sweeping that dark, hungry gaze over the length of his body. "I think I like having you at my mercy."

His fingers flexed restlessly. "So touch me." His voice was rough, his body on edge. Because he was dying for her touch. To see what she would do to him.

Her eyes snapped back to his, and the feminine hunger and power there made the breath back up in his lungs. Setting one hand beside his head, she leaned down to hover her lips inches above his. Brock bit back a growl, his breathing coming faster. *God, kiss me. Touch me.*

Her lips settled on his, light as a sigh, and her tongue grazed his lower lip. He opened, lifted his head to increase the contact, needing more. She gave it to him, capturing his head in her hands and kissing him hard and deep. When she stopped a minute later they were both breathing fast and her pupils were dilated.

She stood, faced him as she trailed her fingers down her neck. Teasing him. Brock followed every single movement of those graceful fingers as they traced the edge of the dress down to her cleavage, down to her waist where the tie on her dress was.

She pulled it slowly, never looking away from him.

One panel of the fabric slipped open, revealing the upper swell of her breasts for a moment before she reached inside and undid the other tie. She pushed her shoulders back, letting the deep blue fabric slither to a puddle at her feet.

Brock groaned at the sight of her standing there in nothing but a red bra and matching panties. Proud. Strong. His heart thudded, trying to beat out of his chest. "Come here," he rasped out, glad he was tied up because there was no goddamn way he would've been able to keep from touching her now.

She prowled toward him, there was no other word for it, and climbed up to straddle his hips. They both sucked in a breath as she made contact with his erection. Tori leaned her weight on her hands and bent forward to kiss him, rubbing her core against him. He groaned into her mouth, his hips lifting to ease the ache between his legs.

She kissed her way down his chin, nibbled down his neck to his chest, pausing to dart her tongue across his nipple, suck lightly. Brock made a low sound of pleasure and watched her, riveted, while those sweet, soft lips trailed lower. Tracing the ridges of his abs, pausing at his navel before she scooted down his legs to rub her cheek over his confined erection.

He closed his eyes. Swallowed. Wondered how the hell he was going to survive this. He bit back the words on his tongue, the demand that he wanted to see her naked. Kiss and suck her everywhere. Make her crazy. This was her show. He had to let this all unfold in her time.

Her fingers slipped just under the top of his waistband. His eyes popped open to watch as she undid the button, slowly slide the zipper down, the metallic rasp loud in the hushed silence.

She dragged the denim and his underwear over his hips. He lifted to assist her, his cock springing free, the feel of her hands grazing the insides of his thighs as she peeled his jeans and underwear off making the muscles there twitch. He was so fucking hard for her. Aching.

Sitting back on her heels to stare at him, she made a low, hungry sound and coasted her palms up over his thighs. Inch by torturous inch, her fingers caressing as they eased higher, higher, sliding inward…

His entire body contracted when her hand curled around him, the air leaving his lungs in a rush. She bent down, kissed his rigid abdomen, rubbed her cheek against him, the silky fall of her hair trailing over his hyper-sensitized skin. Then she gave him a stroke, the caress of her palm like fire against the swollen head of his cock. Her tongue darted out to lick just below his navel.

Fuck.

Brock held his breath, clenched his fingers around the iron bar, imagining they were clenching in her hair instead. Guiding her mouth lower to his straining flesh.

And then those soft, warm lips brushed the head of his cock. Parted to slide it between them.

He groaned in sweet agony and fought the need to push deeper into her mouth, his eyes slamming closed. The wet glide of her tongue made him shudder, his entire body rigid as she sucked gently. "Christ," he bit out, being restrained somehow making him a hundred times more sensitive than normal.

"Hmmm," she murmured, and when he pried his eyes open to look down at her, the arousal in her gaze as she peered up at him with his cock between her lips made the burn so much worse.

Sweat popped out along his spine as he watched her. He hadn't expected this. For her to want this. He had thought this would be all about her pleasure, about her using his body to take what she wanted. But it sure as hell looked like torturing him like this turned her on.

God.

She sucked him harder, swirled her tongue around

him. Watching his face while she waged a brute assault against his control. He gasped when she released him with a soft popping sound, his whole body aching, dying for the release that hovered tantalizingly out of reach.

But all that faded away the moment she sat up and reached back to undo her bra. Watching him, she slid one strap down her shoulder, then the other before baring her breasts to his ravenous gaze and tossing the lace aside.

He swallowed a groan as she cupped them, her thumbs sweeping across the hardened tips. Then she crawled forward up the length of his body and he cursed his bound hands as she straddled his hips and leaned down, dangling her breasts like ripe fruit above his waiting mouth.

He lifted his head to take what she offered. Closing his lips around one tight nipple, a bolt of possessive hunger ripped through him at the soft whimper that spilled from her lips. She slid her hand beneath his head, cradling it, holding him close as he suckled, teased just as she had him. Her hips moved, rubbing her core against his cock as she offered him her other breast, panting softly.

With a gasp she sat up abruptly, the candlelight glowing on her skin, her cheeks flushed, eyes heavy-lidded with arousal. He worried for a moment that something had triggered a bad memory for her, but then she reached down and shimmied out of her panties, skimming them down her legs and off. And when she turned to face him once more, his ravenous gaze went straight to the exposed folds between her thighs, glistening in the flickering light.

He made a low sound of need when she slowly slid a hand down the center of her body, pausing to hover over that tender flesh, her teeth sinking into her plump lower lip. Her lashes fluttered as she caressed herself, her back arching. "You make me so wet," she moaned shakily.

Brock couldn't tear his eyes away from her caressing fingertips. He swallowed and licked his lips, dying to taste her, every muscle in his body strung taut.

"Come up here," he rasped out. He needed to taste her. Right now.

Her eyes lifted to his. She slid her hand from between her thighs and reached her glistening fingertips toward his mouth. Brock moaned and sucked them eagerly, licking the pads of her fingers, the intense arousal in her eyes killing him.

He wrenched his head to the side so he could speak. "Come up here," he repeated, a husky command instead of a plea this time. He wanted to worship her with his mouth. Give her what she needed.

Her cheeks flushed darker. She hesitated a moment, then eased her way up, finally straddling his face. Still too far away for him to get his mouth where he was dying to put it, the scent and sight of her arousal making his head spin.

"Closer," he ground out.

Letting out a shaky exhale, she reached up to grasp the top of the headboard and slowly splayed her legs farther apart. A low, dark sound came out of him as he settled his mouth against her parted folds. She gasped, her thighs tensing, but didn't pull away.

"Stay right there, angel," he murmured against her, and eased his tongue along her softness.

"Brock," she moaned, a slight tremor in her thighs as he licked and sucked, pausing to focus on the swollen, rosy bud of her clit.

He growled and went to work on driving her out of her mind. Soft flutters. Slow, licking caresses that delved inside her. And finally, gentle suction around that tender bud at the top of her sex, his tongue rubbing soft and sweet.

Tori mewled, panting, her hips rocking against his mouth, head tossed back.

That's right, angel. Let me make you come. He was on fire, totally focused on her, barely managed to bite back a protest when she suddenly lifted away and scrambled to the side.

But this time, it wasn't because she was scared. No, that was pure, electric heat in her eyes as she slid off the bed and stood before him, her breasts rising and falling with each excited breath. "Condoms?"

Thank you God. "In my bag."

She practically dove for it, came up with a packet and tore it open. He was hard as fucking stone, his cock flexing, reaching for her when she smoothed the latex over him. He drank in every detail of her as she moved to straddle his hips and paused, setting her hands on his chest before meeting his gaze.

"Slide down on me," he told her, barely managing to get the words out. His heart hammered at his ribs, all his muscles coiled tight.

One side of her mouth curled up in a sensual smile as she reached down to position him. Her teeth sank into her lower lip as she pressed downward with her hips. Engulfing the head of him in warm, wet heat.

Her swift intake of breath sliced through the haze of pleasure swamping his brain long enough for him to focus on her face. She wasn't afraid though. Her eyes were closed, her lips parted now as she sank down more, one hand caressing her clit. She looked like a woman totally abandoning herself to sensual pleasure.

As long as he lived, he would never forget the sight of her like that.

Brock swallowed and gripped the rung of the headboard until his knuckles ached, fighting the need to surge upward and impale himself. Tori eased up him a few inches, slid back down, taking more, more, until he was finally buried inside her. He stopped breathing, a shudder ripping through his body.

She sighed, shifted to lean more of her weight on the hand planted on his chest, right over his thundering heart, and began to move. Each slow glide of her sex over the length of him made fire lick up his spine. Every tiny gasp and moan of pleasure from her lips drew his muscles tighter, until he was ready to beg for her to ride him until he came.

The expression on her face was pure, erotic enjoyment, eyes closed, face flushed as she took her pleasure from his body. She was so fucking gorgeous like that, lost to sensation, it almost broke his control.

Heat sizzled along his nerve endings, his cock swelling as he approached the point of no return. And when she leaned down to offer him her breasts once more, his control snapped.

"Untie me," he growled, no longer caring about the power dynamic, needing only to touch her, hold her and make sure she came before he did.

Her eyes flew open. She stared at him for a heartbeat, hesitating, then reached up to undo the binding with unsteady fingers. Relief slammed through him.

The moment his hands were free, he levered up to grasp her around the back and drew her torso higher so he could suck her nipples properly. A loud, sweet moan rolled out of her throat. She curled her fingers around his shoulder to anchor herself and rocked faster on his cock, her fingers still caressing her clit.

Fuck. Fuck, it was so intense. He reached down to grasp her hip, hold her steady as he lifted into her rhythm, helping her with the angle, his mouth busy teasing her nipple.

"Ah, Brock, *ahhh…*"

Yeah. Like that.

Just like that.

He gripped her tighter, fought the urge to surge into her, forced himself to keep his thrusts to an easy glide. Her sex squeezed him with each slick stroke, dragging guttural moans out of him that mixed with her plaintive ones.

"Oh, God," she cried a moment later, her spine arching, fingernails digging into his shoulder as she peaked, her core clenching around him.

Brock was lost.

She rode him through her orgasm, the sounds of her pleasure snapping the last threads of his control. His free hand clamped down on her other hip, his grip desperate as he thrust deep one last time and started to come.

His strangled roar was muffled by her lips as she bent to claim his mouth, her tongue twining with his. Ecstasy tore through him, shockwaves of sensation that obliterated everything else. Finally he sagged back against the mattress, gasping for air. Tori laughed softly and covered his lips with hers, dropped tender kisses all over his face.

Brock groaned and tilted his face up for more, releasing her hips to wind his arms around her back and pull her in tight to his chest. With a sigh she rested her head on his shoulder, her fingers drifting lightly over his right pec.

He closed his eyes and tightened his hold, absorbing the weight and warmth of her snuggled up so trustingly in his arms. He'd never felt this way before, like he'd just had his chest carved open and his heart torn out. And now that twisted bitch Fate was going to take her from him.

The desperation in his grip reflected the emotional turmoil inside him. His mind spun, trying to figure out a way to stave off the inevitable. Anything that would allow Tori to stay in D.C.

But that was so fucking selfish of him. He wouldn't endanger her life for anything, not even to keep her with him. Although he would make sacrifices for her if it would enable them to stay together. He would consider going with her if she asked him to.

She kissed his jaw and pushed up. "I need to go to the bathroom."

Reluctantly he let her go, cleaned himself up while she

was in the bathroom. When she came out a minute later she paused there in the doorway, an almost shy smile on her face, the candlelight bathing her naked body.

The scars were hardly noticeable now, except the ones around her neck, wrists and ankles. And while he hated them because of what they signified, of the suffering she had endured, they were also physical evidence of that steely inner strength of hers he loved and admired so much.

She seemed surprisingly hesitant as she stood there in the doorway. He reached out a hand. "C'mere."

Relief flashed across her face and she came to him, her slender curves riveting his attention. He pulled her flush to his body before tucking her head into his shoulder and pulling the covers over them.

Letting the quiet surround them, he ran a hand up and down her back. She was so warm and soft. He felt completely at peace with her. But there was no point in giving her the words crowding the back of his throat. They would only bring pain, not happiness. "You hungry now?"

She tipped her head back to smile at him. "I believe I have worked up an appetite, yes."

He ordered them room service. They sat cross-legged, facing each other on the bed in the hotel robes. Feeding each other bits of fruit and cheese and chocolate cake by candlelight, talking about their childhoods, politics and the state of the world.

Anything and everything except to acknowledge the fast approaching deadline when they would be separated forever.

After they were done he set the room service tray on the floor and reached for her, unwrapped the robe from her body like he was unwrapping a treasured Christmas gift, and made love to her again. This time he had full use of his hands and put them to good use, pushing her to the brink before stretching out on his back and letting her ride him again. He wanted to take control so badly, roll her over and pin her under him, but he didn't want to push and it was so damn good this way too.

Tori fell asleep after midnight with her back to his chest, his arm wrapped securely around her ribs. He'd intended to stay awake the rest of the night, not wanting to lose a moment with her, but he was so content he drifted off too.

His phone alarm woke him at four.

No.

His eyes snapped open and he rolled away from Tori to shut it off. When he turned back she was sitting up, the outline of her barely visible in the darkness. "Is it time already?" she mumbled sleepily.

"Yeah."

She wound her arms around him and crawled into his lap, naked. She didn't say a word, but the almost frantic way she held him said it all.

Brock closed his eyes and clenched his jaw, holding her tight. It felt like someone was cleaving his chest open, his heart aching so bad he could barely breathe.

"How long do we have?" she finally asked a minute later.

"Five minutes, maybe."

She made a distressed sound and clung harder, burying her face in his neck.

Pain sliced through him, tightening his throat. They sat there in silence, holding each other, not knowing what the hell to do. He'd known there was a risk of devastating them both when he'd agreed to this, but no matter how fucking much it hurt he would never regret it. And he would never, never forget her.

More than five minutes passed before he could gather the strength to do what had to be done. "I gotta go, angel."

She nodded against his shoulder, her breath hitching, the jerk of her shoulders making his heart split wide open.

"Don't cry," he begged, the backs of his eyes burning.

"S-sorry," she whispered. "I can't help it."

Fuck. Just...*fuck*.

He kissed the crown of her head and made himself let her go.

It was like peeling his skin away with a dull knife.

He went to the bathroom, flipped on the light and quickly got dressed, the crushing pressure in his chest getting worse with every second. After washing his face and brushing his teeth, he steeled himself and went back out into the bedroom.

Tori stood before him in a hotel robe, looking impossibly young and fragile, her dark hair loose around her shoulders, her feet bare. And the brave smile she gave him that wobbled around the edges all but killed him where he stood.

As if drawn to her by an invisible wire, he wrapped her up in his arms and crushed her to him. Covered her face in fervent kisses before fusing their mouths together one last time.

It wasn't enough. Would never be enough and he wasn't sure how he was supposed to cope with this pain, or knowing that he couldn't protect her from it either.

His phone chimed again. 04:30. He'd barely get to base on time if he left right this instant.

He lifted his head, brushed a lock of hair back from her cheek and searched her eyes. "I have to go," he whispered.

She nodded, her eyes bright with tears. "I know." One hand gripped the back of his neck, the other one of his wrists. She squeezed it, her voice shaky as she said, "Thank you for everything. I'll never forget you. Ever."

"Don't thank me." He didn't want thanks for anything that had transpired between them. The burn at the back of his throat turned into a full-on fire, the lump there all but choking him. "Won't ever forget you either." He crushed her to him again. Needing one last moment of holding her.

Then he took her face in his hands, gazed deep into those beautiful eyes that would haunt him for the rest of his life. How was he supposed to walk out of here knowing he would never see her again? "You be careful."

"I will."

"And...be happy." He swallowed, fought back the undertow of emotion so he could continue. "I need to know you'll be happy."

The pain in her eyes slayed him. "I'll try."

You're hurting her more by dragging this out. Go. "I..." *I love you. I'm here if you ever need me.* "Take care of yourself, angel."

"You too."

One last kiss, then he grabbed his bag and walked out, leaving his bleeding heart behind him on the hotel room floor.

Chapter Eleven

---◈◇◈◇◈---

"Manny. Phone call for you."

Manny looked up as David came in through the back door of the rental house, bringing a breath of salt-scented air with him. "Who is it?"

"Ortega."

His contact within the Mexican Customs Authority. He took the secure, encrypted phone from David, answered as he walked through the kitchen to stand at the windows overlooking the garden. "Ortega. You have news?"

"Yes. The DEA team arrived in Mexico City an hour ago."

His eyebrows rose in surprise. That had been quicker than expected. They must be acting on fresh intelligence. No matter. Manny could easily adjust his own timeline and be ready for them if they were indeed down here for him. "How many men?"

"Twenty-six. Including one of its FAST teams."

Okay, they must have a credible tip then. A solid lead

to hunt with. "Who are they working with?"

"I heard they're with our special forces."

As he'd suspected. "And I'm the target?"

"One of them. Apparently they have several active operations in the works."

So they would also be targeting *El Escorpion* and Montoya. "Where are they heading next?"

"Veracruz."

A long way from here. "When?"

"No one knows. Soon, I would think."

Someone knew. "Find out. I need to know where they are at *all* times, and know where they're going *before* they move. Understood?" His entire plan depended on that insider knowledge.

"Yes. Of course."

In the meantime, he would have David keep working their contacts until they got an answer and confirmed all of this. "Anything else?"

"No."

It was enough for now. "Update me immediately when you hear something more."

"I will."

Yes, he would. Because if he didn't, Ortega's family would suffer for it. That's the way this game was played, and though Manny didn't love the violence the way some of his kind did, he certainly wasn't bluffing. He would use whatever weapon available to him to get what he wanted.

His daughter. At any cost.

He ended the call and handed David back the phone. "They're in Mexico City with a FAST team, coming to Veracruz. He didn't know when they're arriving."

David's calm expression never faltered, and Manny was strangely calm as well. They had both prepared as much as possible for what would happen next. All they could do now was see it through. "Everything's ready. The place is secure and the last chatter we picked up said you were still in Chihuahua," David said.

So then Manny still might have some time to get everything finalized. Though he wasn't counting on it. "And Montoya?" The reward money Manny had offered for him should have turned up something by now.

David shook his head, his lips curling in disgust. "No one's seen him."

Well he was out there. And every day he kept breathing, the greater the threat he posed became. "Keep working our channels. Put pressure on people, find out where he is and keep on top of the Americans." Everything depended on advance warning of their arrival.

"I will."

Manny turned to look out at the balcony. God, he hated being on the run and looking over his shoulder every step of the way. It could be worse, though. He also had time and distance in his favor, since the taskforce hunting him would still be thirteen hundred kilometers away once they reached Veracruz. "When do we move?"

"Tonight. I've got men at the house setting everything up for us."

Manny nodded and turned away to walk through the sliding glass door onto the balcony. Standing at the railing, he gazed at the horizon. The landscape here was lush and green, a tropical paradise he'd missed so much.

Between the tall cypress trees that edged the rear of the secluded backyard of this safehouse, sunlight glittered off the azure surface of the Caribbean Sea. Only a few miles from his final destination, a place he had spent so many happy weeks at with Oceane and Anya over the years.

His daughter had not been there since she was a child, the last time when she was eleven or twelve. Maybe there, if everything worked out, he and Oceane could begin to mend their broken relationship. One baby step at a time.

He would tell her the lies he had carefully crafted, convince her that he had nothing to do with her mother's death. Show her the fake evidence he had obtained to prove that Montoya had been behind the murder all along. Convince her that as her father, he had sent Arturo there to guard her and her mother, and Montoya was supposed to be there in case they needed to fight their way out.

But then Montoya had allowed his men to do the unthinkable. The man was so vicious and unpredictable, Oceane might believe it once Manny told her about her godfather's true nature.

She would believe him. She had to.

If not, he would be forced to take more extreme measures to make her stay. Either way, she was staying with him so he could monitor her and eventually show her the true scope of what she would inherit.

David stepped out onto the balcony to join him and took a deep breath of the fresh air. "Feels good to be back here."

"Yes." Manny was more at ease now than he had been in months. He was safe here. He had David, the most loyal of his men with him at all times, constantly monitoring the security situation and keeping an ear out for anything about Oceane and the men hunting him.

"They're distracted," he murmured to David, gazing out at that speck of blue in the distance. The government, he meant. "Too many targets to hunt." With any luck, it would take a while longer for them to realize he wasn't in Veracruz. That should buy him enough time to put his plan into action.

"No one has heard from *El Escorpion* since the raid on the estate."

"That's to be expected." A man like him, with unlimited money and resources after nearly four years at the helm of the cartel, could be literally anywhere now.

"You think he's gone to ground? Or is it because you've been blacklisted and he's cut all ties with you?"

"Both." Manny wasn't stupid. He had caused the cartel

and its leader a lot of inconvenience with Oceane and Anya's disappearance, and then the bungled op with Montoya.

But all was not yet lost. After an exhaustive and incredibly expensive investigation of his own, Manny was certain he finally knew who the mysterious head of the *Veneno* cartel was. He had even sent in an anonymous tip to get authorities to act and take some of the heat off him. Looked like it had worked.

"If it's actually him, no one has seen or heard from his family either."

Manny shrugged. "Because he's taken them with him. They'll surface eventually. At least this gives me something to barter with." Both with *el Escorpion* and the rest of the cartel, but also the Mexican and U.S. governments. "Let's just make sure we're ready for anything."

"Of course."

Manny didn't want to die or be captured. But desperation had driven him to this decision. He was going forward with his plan, no matter what the risk.

This was Mexico. They were on his turf now, and things worked differently here than they did north of the border. If he couldn't find his daughter, he would force the Americans' hand here and make them bring her to him.

****

"Man, it's like we're back in Mississippi again," Granger muttered, wiping his forearm over his sweaty forehead as he tossed his boots to the linoleum floor of the barracks they were staying in. Part of an old military base where they were housed with their new Mexican Special Forces friends. "Muggy as hell. I can practically wring out my shirt and I only got out of the air conditioned vehicle two minutes ago."

"Beats winter in Afghanistan," Brock said from the next bunk over.

Granger grinned. "Yeah, okay, I'll give you that one."

They had been in Mexico two full days now, and had landed here in Veracruz last night. The government had sent them here based on the tip they had received, and because it was the state where Oceane and her mother had lived. Where Nieto had based extensive operations out of over the years.

From the moment they arrived, Brock and the rest of the team had been getting the lay of the land, monitoring new intel and working all the sources available to them.

"I'm usually right," he said. "I don't know why you guys don't realize that by now."

Something pinged off the back of his head.

Whirling around, he found Maka grinning at him from the bunk across the aisle from his, his precious Nerf gun in hand. "You gotta be shitting me," Brock said. "You seriously packed that thing?"

"I'm always packin', Cap," he said, and fired off another round. "Consider this payback."

Brock managed to block it before it hit him in the chest, the rubber-tipped foam bullet bouncing off his forearm instead. "You're a pain in my ass, you know that?"

That smug face split into a wide grin, his teeth a startling white against his deep bronze skin. "Nah, you love me. And hey, I brought one for you too."

Brock eyed him. "Yeah? You wanna have a shootout with me?"

Maka shrugged his wide shoulders and bent over his bunk to rummage through the duffel on the floor. "I'm down with that. Been working on this one for a while. You're gonna love it."

Brock grunted, set his hands on his hips and waited.

Sitting up, Maka turned to him with a blue Nerf gun in his hand. "Happy belated birthday."

His birthday was last month. Brock blinked and crossed over to take it from him, couldn't help but grin when he saw it up close. "Aww, you made me a Captain America gun." He'd even painted it bright blue and added the iconic star shield on the sides of it.

"I did. And I made some modifications to it, too. Now it fires semi-auto. And yours has blue bullets, so we can tell who shot the shit out of the other easier."

He barked out a laugh as he examined the modified barrel. "I take it back. I do love it. Now where's my ammo?"

A mischievous glint entered Maka's gaze. "Can't remember. Maybe I left it at home." He raised his weapon and pulled the trigger.

Brock shouted with laughter and grabbed his pillow to act as a shield as he ran at Maka, catching him across the body. The two of them bounced off the old mattress and hit the floor.

"Hey, Cap needs help taking the Hawaiian Hulk!" someone shouted.

Pinned beneath the human tank on top of him, Brock gasped for breath as he tried to get out of the headlock Maka put him in, his face turning color from the pressure at his throat. "Do not!" he managed to wheeze out.

Shouts and whoops filled the barracks as the team came rushing to his rescue. Maka got in one good noogie, hard enough to make Brock's scalp burn, then the team attacked him. This time Maka was laughing like a maniac as he struggled to escape the mass of humanity piled on top of him.

Brock wiggled free and climbed to his feet, grinning like an idiot. They'd all needed to blow off some steam, and this was good harmless fun. Well, mostly harmless.

Colebrook had his legs wrapped around Maka's waist from behind, his arms around that wide chest. Prentiss was twined around Maka's legs like a living snake.

Granger was lying on top of them all, clinging to whomever he could get a grip on.

Even Khan ran over to throw himself on top of Granger, eliciting a yell from everybody under him, and looked up at Brock, his expression exactly like a little kid on Christmas morning. "Get him, Cap! Now's your chance!"

"What should I do to him?" Brock mused.

"Whatever, but do it fast, this fucker's gonna Hulk out any second," Colebrook grated out, his face turning purple from the strain of keeping Maka subdued.

"All right, hold him still."

"Easy for you to say," Prentiss panted, still holding on for dear life.

Next to them, Freeman had his phone out, videoing the spectacle. "Wait, I'm switching to photo now. Okay, say cheese."

"Smile, Maka," Colebrook wheezed, red-faced as he grinned up at the phone.

Brock turned toward his bunk to retrieve his new weapon but Lockhart was already standing behind him, holding out the Captain America gun, now fully loaded. "Give him a taste of his own medicine, Cap."

"Good idea," he muttered. Spinning around, Brock aimed it at the back of Maka's head, just visible in a gap between Granger and Khan, and pulled the trigger.

A flurry of foam darts bounced off three of the other guys before he finally hit Maka, and he didn't stop until he ran out of ammo.

"Hey, it works pretty well," he called out to Maka, who was still battling. The big guy's face was set, his nostrils flared as he fought his way free of his teammates, one by one.

Movement to the right caught Brock's attention. Commander Taggart stopped in the barracks doorway, his eyebrows rising as he took in the scene. "Good to see you boys enjoying yourselves. Do me a favor and not break any tables in here, huh?"

"Nah, we're good," Brock said as Maka shoved to his feet, grinning again, a bruise forming on his cheek. God, he loved serving with these crazy bastards. "You need us?" he asked Taggart.

"Just you. Got another meeting."

Brock followed him out into the late afternoon heat and across the base to the building where they would hold their briefings. For the past three days they had searched for a solid lead on Nieto, Montoya or the slippery *El Escorpion*. So far nothing had led to much.

"Anything solid to go on yet?" New tips seemed to come in all the time, though most of them turned out to be useless.

"Maybe. They've got something else for us to check out with another source tonight."

He nodded. Both he and Taggart had accompanied Mexican officials and SF guys to a handful of meetings with informants and contacts since arriving in country. Brock knew a little Spanish, understood slightly more than he could speak, but was far from fluent and native speakers spoke way too fast for him. It was a pain in the ass, but at least that way they were in on everything and got to observe firsthand how things worked down here.

When they walked into the building, their Mexican counterparts were already assembled around a table in the briefing room. The head of the taskforce spoke in heavily accented but good English about the latest intel. Nieto was rumored to be somewhere here in Veracruz with his head of security and a handful of men.

"When's Rodriguez due in?" Brock murmured to Taggart during a lull in the briefing.

The native Spanish speaker was joining the team sometime today, now that his mother's service was over. Brock and Taggart had both told him to stay in California with his family, but due to the situation unfolding here, Rodriguez had insisted on coming down to assist with the op.

Losing a loved one was a hell of a thing to go through, and Brock fully understood why his teammate would want to work right now, since he was going through something similar with Tori. In a way it was like a death too, because even though she was alive, she was still gone forever. He needed to keep busy, otherwise the heartache might kill him.

"Not until twenty-two hundred," Taggart answered.

Damn. Would sure make Brock feel better to have one of their own here to listen in and translate during the meeting.

Taggart's phone rang. He answered, spoke to someone for a minute, too low for Brock to overhear. As soon as he hung up, it rang again. Looking at the number, Taggart sighed and answered, giving Brock a look he recognized all too well. The irritation there was loud and clear. His commander had way too much to do and only one of him to do it. And now he was supposed to go meet this informant tonight as well.

"I'll take this one," Brock offered when Taggart got off the call, nodding at the folder on the table.

Pure relief flashed in his commander's eyes. "You sure?"

"Yeah, I got this."

"I owe you. Report in when you're on your way back to base." Taggart slapped him on the shoulder and walked out, already on another call.

After finding out that he and the Mexican feds were leaving in ten minutes to meet the contact, Brock ran back to the barracks to grab his sidearm and holster. The guys were all quiet now, napping or reading or playing cards.

"Got an informant meeting," he told them as he gathered his stuff. "Won't be back until after chow, so grab something for me. Rodriguez is due in late tonight."

"Will do," Khan said with a wave without looking up, his brow furrowed in concentration as he stared at his cards, Maka and Prentiss across from him.

Brock snorted a laugh. "Yeah. Try not to miss me too much."

"We won't," Granger called out.

Back outside, Brock jogged out to meet his two counterparts—both Mexican Federal Police—and climbed into a waiting SUV. The drive gave him time to think more about Tori. How he regretted not telling her he loved her. He hadn't said it because he'd thought it would hurt her more, but now he wasn't so sure. At least if he'd told her she would know without a doubt how much she meant to him.

By the time they reached the meeting location an hour away, the sun was setting, the sky ablaze in a wash of orange and blood red, the trees throwing long shadows onto the road.

The driver pulled into an empty gravel parking lot off the road that led to some hiking trails through the hills. Next to him, the other cop was on the phone to someone else, presumably the informant. Brock only caught a word here and there, his Spanish limited and the speed of the conversation too fast.

The guy up front swiveled in his seat to look back at him. "He'll be here in five minutes," he said in English.

"You know him?" Brock asked. He only knew what he'd been told in the briefing. Apparently this informant had a tip on one of their HVTs he wanted to give them in exchange for cash.

"Yes. We've met him several times for things in the past month."

All right then. Nothing to do now but wait.

Contain, disrupt, dismantle. That was FAST's motto, and it was never more appropriate than now, when they were finally down here going after the heart of the cartel they had been battling for years.

The guys up front chattered away in Spanish until a car approached from the east. They waited until the driver exited the car. Brock couldn't see anyone else in the back. "It's him," the driver said, and stepped out.

Brock hopped out and scanned the surrounding area. He didn't like the feeling of exposure here or the brush in the background where anyone could hide, but the cops didn't seem concerned and they had built a sort of rapport with the informant.

The driver of the car stepped forward. "*Hola.*"

"Alejandro," the older cop said in a jovial tone. "*¿Qué pasa?*"

Alejandro held up his hands and did a slow circle to show that he had no weapon hidden beneath his shirt. He answered the cop in rapid Spanish and the conversation went back and forth for a bit.

Brock glanced at the informant's car, still didn't see anyone in it. He scanned the trees again, picking up the odd word here and there as the cops talked to the guy.

"Hamilton," the younger one said to Alejandro.

Brock swung around at the mention of his name.

The informant nodded at him, his gaze assessing. "You American?" He had a pronounced accent.

You think? He stuck out here like a freaking sore thumb. "Yeah."

"There's a bag in the back," the younger cop said to Brock, nodding at their SUV. "Can you get it? He's giving us intel on Nieto."

Which Brock would have to ask to have translated on the way back to base, because he hadn't understood a thing they'd been talking about. "Yeah. Gimme a sec."

He walked back to the SUV, his Glock in its holster on his thigh, and grabbed the small plastic bag of cash from the trunk area. As he eased out of the back seat and straightened beside the vehicle, a car door popped open behind him.

Brock whirled and dropped the bag as he drew his weapon. Something sharp hit him in the ribs. He went down, his body jerked like a marionette as the voltage coursed through him. He hit the gravel hard, spasming like a landed fish, dimly aware of shouting and gunshots in the background.

Finally the voltage stopped.

Before his limp muscles could recover enough for him to move, someone was coming toward him. He pried his eyes open just in time to make out the blurry shape of a man crouching beside him, a hood in his hands.

Adrenaline and rage blasted through him. *Fight.*

His lax muscles refused to obey.

The hood was coming toward him.

Fight, goddamn you.

Blackness engulfed him as the hood came over his head. A second later his arms were yanked behind him and secured.

Brock gritted his teeth. Managed to lash out with his boot, connected with something hard enough to draw a grunt from his attacker. But it was no use. Something stabbed the side of his neck, a sharp sting spreading under his skin. His head swam, all the sounds around him becoming distorted.

Something bound his ankles. Then he was being dragged backward, the heels of his boots scraping across the gravel. The man grunted as he hoisted Brock up and tossed him onto something hard.

His limp body grew even heavier. He started to fade out.

A thud sounded overhead, making his eyes open a fraction, though all he could see was blackness.

A trunk, he realized with a sinking sensation.

An engine roared to life. Gravel sprayed as the tires

spun, then hit pavement and the car took off.

Brock fought the inescapable pull toward unconsciousness as long as he could. Struggled to think. To move.

His phone. Did he still have it on him? Maybe his team could track his phone and get a location on him.

It was his last thought before the darkness swallowed him.

Chapter Twelve

Gabe Lockhart jackknifed up in his bunk from a dead sleep when Taggart burst into the barracks, his face and posture tense. "Listen up," his commander barked, scanning the room. "The meeting with the informant was a setup. Both Mexican cops are dead, and Hamilton's missing."

What? Gabe threw his legs over the side of his bunk and reached for his gear as the room exploded into questions and exclamations.

"Who was the informant?" Rodriguez demanded, having just arrived, his duffel still open because he'd been in the process of unpacking.

"Some local they've worked with before. We don't know if he's the kidnapper, or if he was just the setup man."

Holy fuck.

Gabe was on his feet with his weapon in hand and heading to the door without even being conscious of moving. The team all rushed to the briefing center to find out what was going on.

They walked into chaos. People were scrambling around the room, talking on top of one another. The police commander was arguing with the SF commander, both of them shouting at the other.

Taggart shouldered his way through to the center of the room. "Somebody tell me what the fuck is going on *right now*," he bellowed. Everyone shut up and looked at him. "Rodriguez," he snapped. "Get over here and get me a damn sitrep on Hamilton."

The team stayed together near the back of the room while Rodriguez and Taggart battled to find out what the hell was going on. Nobody seemed to know anything, so finally Taggart demanded to be taken to the meeting location, motioning to the others to follow as he headed for the door. The whole team piled into two SUVs and raced for the meeting site while Rodriguez stayed behind to monitor the Mexican search effort.

"Can you fucking believe this shit?" Maka said from the driver's seat as he tore after the vehicle Taggart was riding in.

"No," answered Granger, in the back next to Gabe. "*Venenos* gotta be behind this."

"One of the HVTs," Gabe said. "Question is, which one?"

"Nieto or Montoya," Prentiss said from the shotgun seat. "Has to be."

It took way too damn long to get to the meeting site. Mexican Federal Police had everything cordoned off by the time they arrived. Two cops lay dead on the gravel parking lot a few yards from their vehicle sprawled on their stomachs, weapons drawn.

From their positioning it looked like they'd been running for cover behind the vehicle when they were shot down. The SUV's front quarter panel had bullet holes in it and the rear driver's side door was open.

Gabe's stomach was tight as a drum. Hamilton was

likely still alive. But this was a race against time to find him before he was butchered.

The dinner he'd wolfed down sat like a congealed lump in his gut as he thought of the *Veneno* victims they'd come across before. Including Anya, who was essentially one of their own.

She had been raped and brutally murdered by Montoya's men. If they could do that to her, what the hell would they do to Hamilton?

"Why take Hamilton and kill both the others?" Gabe said to Freeman as they waited for Taggart to get up to speed with the cop in charge.

"To make a statement to the DEA and the U.S. government."

Maybe. But Gabe had a feeling there was more to it than that. "So they had to have known one of us was coming to this meeting."

"Yup. Would have been Taggart if Hamilton hadn't stepped in." Freeman's jaw flexed as he stared at the scene, hands on hips, frustration coming off him in waves. "Motherfuckers."

The seven of them stood there waiting, precious minutes ticking past until Taggart finally stalked back to them, his face like a thundercloud. "Basically, nobody knows dick all. Obviously there are no CCTVs out here, and they don't have a satellite feed on the area. Only thing they've got so far is the SUV's dashboard cam video, and that only shows the suspect car approaching the lot, then leaving in the opposite direction. No footage of the attacker."

He paused, drew in a frustrated breath. "They've got roadblocks up in the surrounding area, but who the hell knows how tight they are, and there were no witnesses to give any additional intel."

This wasn't good. At all.

"What can we do? We can't just sit here," Granger protested.

"We can't do shit," Taggart bit out. "They won't let us assist with the search, say it's not our jurisdiction." He thumped a finger into his chest. "Hamilton is one of *ours*, and that sure as fuck makes this my jurisdiction. I've already contacted the CIA to see if they have any satellite feed of the area during the attack."

"That's BS," Maka growled, taking a step forward as if he was going to charge over there to the Mexican cops and start knocking heads together.

Taggart planted a hand in the middle of the big man's chest. "Stop. Last thing I need is to have you arrested right now." He scanned the team. "We're heading back to base. I'll raise more hell from there."

Grumbles and protests erupted, but everyone did as they were told.

The drive back to base was tense and silent. As soon as they arrived they went into the command center. By this point more than two hours had passed since Hamilton had been taken.

He could well be dead by now. Although Gabe's gut said they wouldn't kill him, at least not yet. It didn't make sense for the kidnappers to go to the trouble and risk of taking him if all they wanted to do was kill him. They could have done that back in the parking lot.

Rodriguez was over to one side of the room having an intense conversation with two officials. The moment he saw them, he waved Taggart over, his expression urgent. Taggart rushed to him as Gabe and the others hung back and held their breaths.

Gabe watched them closely as they talked, tried to figure out what was going on.

Don't be dead. Don't be dead, he prayed silently, thinking of Cap.

They'd been through countless ops together and multiple deployments to one of the most hostile regions on the planet. To lose Cap like this would be a devastating blow to them all.

After what seemed like an eternity, Taggart came back over to them, his eyes cold, jaw tight. "It was someone working for Nieto."

Gabe hissed out a breath. *Knew it.* Son of a *bitch.* And the bastard would do something this fucked-up to try and get Oceane back. "Someone ID'd him?"

"No. A message came in from one of Nieto's lackeys. Nieto's holding Hamilton in exchange for his daughter. The lackey left a contact number of a go-between for any further communication."

"Fucking hell," Gabe muttered, and spun away. He had to walk it off. Couldn't stand still one more second with this helpless rage tearing through him. Behind him, the rest of his teammates peppered Taggart with questions but Gabe only half-listened.

"No idea on a location for Hamilton yet," Taggart said. "No timeline either. The message was sent by text from a burner phone ten minutes ago. They're trying to find out where the signal originated from but it cut off almost immediately."

"So basically we still have no freaking idea where Cap is," Granger said.

"No," Taggart muttered. Then he sighed. "All right. You guys go back to the barracks for now. I'll monitor this with Rodriguez and come update you if anything happens. Be ready to move. The second I find a possible location on Cap, we're going, and I don't care how much Mexican red tape I have to slash to make it happen."

Damn right.

With no other option open to them, the team returned to barracks and went over their gear again. Everyone was quiet and pissed off. Scared as hell about what was happening to Cap right now. Because sure as shit, wherever they were holding him, Cap wasn't going to be treated like Nieto's guest.

Another eighty minutes passed before Taggart walked in with Rodriguez. Gabe set aside his sidearm and turned on his bunk to face them. "Anything?"

"Nope." Taggart sat on Cap's bunk, glanced down at the Captain America Nerf gun sitting on top of the unrolled sleeping bag. "The good news is, he's probably alive. The bad news is…"

He wouldn't be for long. Taggart didn't have to say it, it was clear.

Maka heaved out a heavy breath and scrubbed his hands over his head, his agitation mirroring the mood of the entire team. "So that's it? Nothing more we can do?"

"I've got half of headquarters back home working on it, in addition to every asset we have down here," Taggart replied in a tired voice. "But for now…no."

"There's gotta be something," Granger protested. "Something those guys aren't doing that we can," he said, pointing toward the command building.

Taggart nodded slowly. "Yeah, there is."

Everyone went still, the room becoming eerily silent as they stared at their commander. Gabe's pulse picked up, something warning him that whatever Taggart was about to say, Gabe wouldn't like it.

"There's one sure way to guarantee we can draw Nieto out of hiding," Taggart said, his cool aqua gaze landing on Gabe.

Gabe's heart stopped beating. *Oceane.* Taggart didn't say it, but that's what he meant. That they could basically dangle her as bait in front of Nieto to try and get Hamilton back. A human bartering chip.

"No," he rasped out, shaking his head, hating even the thought of it. He wanted Cap back as bad as anyone, but not at her expense. She'd been through way to fucking much already.

"At this point it might be our only option to get him back alive." Taggart stood and skirted the end of Cap's bunk, heading for the door. "I'll update you all when I hear something."

As soon as he left, everyone looked at Gabe. "You think she'd do it? Come down here and do a staged exchange for Cap or whatever?" Freeman asked.

Gabe clenched his jaw, fighting to keep his emotions in check. It was crazy and he fucking loathed the mere idea of her coming down here and exposing herself to further danger in the middle of cartel country. But would she do it if they asked her?

"Yeah. Yeah, she would." Because she wanted to put her father away. Get justice for her and her mother. For Victoria. And she would want to save Hamilton as well.

The rest of the guys all started talking at once. Gabe's chest was too tight, he couldn't breathe in here. He pushed past them to fish his phone from his gear, then walked outside, pissed as hell that his commander would even ask this of her.

He dialed Oceane's number, needing to talk to her. To warn her.

It rang and rang and rang, but no one picked up, not even voicemail. He hung up, his mind racing.

Victoria. She deserved to know what had happened to Cap, and maybe she could talk to Oceane about this. No doubt Taggart already had the WITSEC people meeting with DEA officials to propose a plan to get Hamilton back.

Gabe wanted his team leader back alive, of course he did. But Cap was trained and knew the risks of the job. Oceane was an innocent civilian. Putting her life on the line to do it made it feel like someone had dropped an anvil on his heart.

His mind was made up. He was probably breaking a dozen agency rules by doing this, but he didn't give a fuck at the moment.

He dialed Victoria's number, his heart thudding as it rang in his ear. *Come on, pick up. Pick up...*

"Hello?"

"Victoria, it's Gabe."

"Gabe? What's... Is everything okay?"

By her tone she already knew it wasn't, and he wouldn't lie to her. Oceane had been right the other day; there was definitely something going on between Cap and Victoria. "No. Listen, I don't have much time, but I wanted you to hear this from me before the news breaks. Cap's been taken prisoner by Nieto."

Her sharp gasp hissed in his ear. *"What?"*

He closed his eyes at the horror and shock in her voice. "A few hours ago, during a routine meeting with an informant."

"Oh my God, is he—"

"We don't know where he is. But we think he's still alive. Nieto has claimed responsibility. And there's one more thing."

"What?" she asked urgently.

"The agency and WITSEC are going to want to meet with Oceane about this. I need you to talk to her before that happens. In person, if you can. Tell her..." *That I don't want her risking herself for this. That I would do anything to protect her and spare her any more pain.* "Just tell her she's not obligated to do anything they ask."

"All right. I'll go find her right now. Will you let me know if there's any word about Brock?"

"If I can."

Gabe ended the call and closed his eyes, feeling like he was being torn in two. He already knew how this was going to play out. They were going to ask Oceane to come down here and involve her in some way, as a front to an operation that would hopefully save Hamilton.

Coming down here would mean risking her life. Period.

But if she didn't, Hamilton was almost certainly dead.

So no matter how he sliced it, this thing was a shit sandwich.

****

Victoria choked back tears as she rushed down the hall to the stairwell and ran the three flights to the floor where Oceane's room was. Her friend hadn't answered her phone when Victoria had called a few minutes ago.

The hallway was empty. She was out of breath, trembling as she knocked on the door. Seconds passed. She knocked again, hard enough to hurt her knuckles. "Oceane. Open up."

No answer.

"Dammit." Where was she? At this time of night Oceane was usually curled up in bed either reading or watching TV.

She couldn't believe Brock had been taken hostage, let alone by Nieto. When she thought of what he must be enduring right now at the hands of those animals Nieto and the others used as *sicarios*…

Violent, vivid images bombarded her. Memories of what had been done to her and the other girls during her captivity. The way her family had been massacred. The countless other *Veneno* victims she had seen photographs of during her research for her books.

"Oh, God, Brock," she whispered, her shoulders hitching as her voice crumbled. She couldn't bear it. Couldn't stand to think of him being tortured and eventually killed, and it was worse that she knew exactly what that kind of fear and pain felt like.

He owned her, heart, soul and body. Leaving him behind when she flew out of D.C. tomorrow was unbearable enough, but this? Leaving when he was in peril and she would never know what had happened to him?

Her stomach pitched. The muscles beneath her jaw tightened, saliva pooling in her mouth. She sank to the floor and swallowed repeatedly, willing the nausea to pass. *Think, Victoria, think.*

If Nieto had taken him, then it meant he planned to use Brock for something. Torturing and killing him as a fuck you to the DEA and the rest of the government proved nothing. He wanted something. He wanted—

His daughter.

Victoria put a hand to her mouth. "Oh, no." Gabe's message was now all too clear. She had to find Oceane, explain what had happened and then…

God, it was so selfish of her, but she wanted Oceane to do whatever it was they asked. What kind of horrible human being was she, to want her friend to endanger herself for Brock?

But I love him.

A tear slipped down her cheek. She quickly wiped it away with the side of her hand and stood, intending to call one of the marshals on her security detail. Her thumb was poised above the button when her phone buzzed in her hand.

The marshal she'd been about to call. "Hey, I was just—"

"Where are you?"

"On my way back from Oceane's room."

"Commander Taggart has called a remote emergency meeting. They want you in the third-floor conference room in five minutes."

Her stomach sank like a brick. She stopped, set her free hand on the wall to hold her up. Because if Taggart was calling them together to announce that Brock was dead…

"Is Brock dead?" She could barely force the words out of her tight throat.

"No." He paused, and she could breathe again. "I hadn't realized you'd heard about him already."

She ignored the second part and hurried for the elevator, praying Nieto hadn't hurt Brock. She would do anything to save him. "Meet you at the conference room in five."

Chapter Thirteen

"**W**hat's happened? Something about my father?" Oceane asked as one of the marshals assigned to her security detail hustled her down the hall to the conference room. He'd tracked her down in the WITSEC Safesite library where she'd been looking for a book.

"Yes."

Her stomach knotted. What had he done now? "Why does Commander Taggart want to talk to me?"

"There's a situation unfolding," was all he said, and opened the door for her.

DEA and WITSEC officials filled the room. Across the long, rectangular table in the center of the room, she spotted Victoria. Her friend looked up at her, face pale, her dark eyes haunted.

The knots pulled tighter. What the hell was happening? She headed straight for the table, concerned for her friend. "Are you all right?"

"Honestly?" Victoria shook her head. "No. Brock's been taken hostage."

Oceane gasped and stopped in her tracks. "How is that even possible?"

"FAST Bravo is in Veracruz to help with an op. He was taken there."

No. "When?"

"A few hours ago."

She swallowed, her pulse thudding in her throat. "My father is behind it?"

The pity on Victoria's face gave her the answer.

"No. Damn it, *no!*" Why was he doing this? She spun to face the officials at the far end of the room just as Taggart's face appeared on the large screen mounted on the wall.

"Commander," one of the DEA agents said. "We're all here, including Miss Nieto and Miss Gomez."

Oceane scowled. She couldn't wait until WITSEC gave her a new surname. She hated being affiliated with her father even on that level.

Needing the support of a friend, she rounded the table and sat beside Victoria. The other woman reached for her hand, held on tight as the meeting began. Oceane fought tears of rage and frustration as she listened to what had happened, and how her father had claimed responsibility before making his outrageous demand. The threat was clear: bring her to him, or Hamilton would die.

Although he would likely die no matter what they did. That was how monsters like her father operated.

As she listened to the possible responses and actions being discussed in the room, all the betrayal rushed back. All the pain and despair. The grief she was still trying to figure out how to deal with.

She had been chased from her home by her father's rivals because he had wanted to take over Ruiz's territory and claim his place within the cartel. When she had fled as she had been taught, choosing to come to the U.S., he had done everything in his power to drag her back to Mexico—even going so far as to have the tracker planted on her.

Then the worst of all. After his attempts to locate and bring them home failed, her mother had been brutally raped and murdered.

Oceane couldn't grasp it. Still refused to believe that her father had ordered the murder. He was an accomplished liar, yes. But he had loved her mother. No matter what other lies he had told her or hidden by omission, Oceane was sure of that much.

She had seen them together many times, though not often as an adult. After she graduated high school he had become an absentee parent, seeing her only rarely, maybe once or twice a year. But without a doubt, her parents had loved each other, no matter how screwed up or unconventional their relationship was.

Evil as her father was, she couldn't accept that he would order the murder of the woman he'd loved for nearly three decades.

But now this. Taking the FAST Bravo team leader hostage to force the American government to turn her over to him. He was clearly desperate or crazy. Or both.

She struggled to get out of her head and listen to what was being said now. They were talking about flying her down to Mexico tonight, to assist in the case going forward. The thought of stepping foot on Mexican soil again scared the hell out of her.

The U.S. government had kept her here under 24/7 protection because of the reward her father had offered for her capture and safe return to him, and in case they needed her help with the investigation on her father or Montoya. Now the time had come.

She wasn't stupid. They wanted to use her as a lure to draw her father out. This wasn't even about saving Hamilton. For Commander Taggart and Victoria it was, but for the DEA and FBI, involving Oceane was part of the bigger picture. To get her father.

In a lull between suggestions that ranged from the ridiculous to the impossible, Commander Taggart stopped and spoke to her directly. "Do you have anything to add, Miss Nieto?"

"Oceane," she corrected, hating that damn name. "I've been in the U.S. for too long. He'd never trust me now, even if I showed up on his doorstep pretending I wanted to reconcile." Which she didn't. She would sooner shoot him in his lying face, spit on him, then tell him what she truly thought of him before walking away and leaving him to die on the floor.

"We're not suggesting you actually meet him."

She didn't see any other way to pull this off. "He won't hurt me." Not physically. He might be crazy and evil, but no, he wouldn't harm her. The lengths he had gone to in order to recover her showed that.

"Regardless, we're not going to hand you over to anyone. We can work out the logistics of our next step once I get the green light, but to make this work your call to your father's contact has to come from within Mexico, in case they trace it. They need to know we're serious and not playing games. And we don't have much time to give you to think this over. Brock Hamilton's life is hanging in the balance, and this also might be our only shot at arresting your father."

He paused, his pale aqua eyes holding hers. "Will you help us?"

Oceane looked over at Victoria. Her friend's dark eyes searched hers. Full of pain. Fear. Because Brock's life was in danger. Because Oceane's father was a raging psychopath who thought he could get away with anything simply because he was rich and powerful.

"Gabe called me earlier," Victoria said to her. "He asked me to tell you that you don't have to do this."

Oceane absorbed the words for a moment, warmth spreading inside her to know that Gabe would try to protect her, attempt to ease her conscience if she said no. Victoria had done her duty in passing on the message. But beneath the words, Oceane heard the plea in her friend's voice.

And she understood. Because if their positions were reversed and it was Gabe's life in danger, Oceane would want Victoria to do everything in her power to free him.

Oceane's choice was clear. Brock was Gabe's team leader. He meant a great deal to Victoria. And to Oceane as well. She considered him a friend. She couldn't be a coward, sit here at the WITSEC site where it was safe and just let him die simply because she was afraid.

"Yes I do," she murmured, and squeezed her friend's hand as she turned her attention to the front of the room. "Commander Taggart."

All eyes swung to her, the room going quiet. Brock didn't have much time, if he was still alive. Oceane wanted to save him. She wanted justice for her and her mother. She wanted all of this to be over with and behind her so she could move forward. Or at least try to.

The only way that would ever happen was if she helped them catch her father. Because she was the only bait that could lure this particular shark.

"I'll do it," she said, her voice clear and steady in spite of the way she shook inside. She'd come a long way in terms of being able to mask her fear during her time here. Maybe she'd even managed to fool everyone in the room just now.

Taggart gave her a tight, relieved smile. "Thank you. I'll start making arrangements on my end now and confirm everything with you once you arrive."

"All right."

She walked out of the meeting in a daze, trailing behind one of her marshals. Her phone rang. She pulled it out, her heart tripping when she saw Gabe's number, and ducked around the corner for a moment's privacy. The marshal continued on another dozen or so paces before stopping, giving her some room. "Hi," she said on a sigh, aching to hear his voice.

"You don't have to do this. It's dangerous. Maybe more dangerous than anything you've faced so far because we can't control what happens down here," he said in a clipped tone.

He must have been in the room with Taggart and overheard everything. "It's a plane ride and a few phone calls. It's the least I can do for Brock."

"It's way more than that, and you know it."

Yes. So much could go wrong between now and then. Her father had eyes and ears everywhere throughout Mexico, even in the government and law enforcement. Money and threats against family members helped keep corruption strong in her homeland.

There was even a chance that someone in the room with Taggart right now could leak her impending arrival and she might walk into a trap when she arrived back on Mexican soil. But what was the alternative? Letting Brock be tortured to death?

"I have to do it." Oceane thought of Victoria and what she must be going through right now, knowing Brock had been taken captive by the cartel that had cost her so much.

It was so unfair. And sad. Victoria had suffered so much. Even more than Oceane had. She couldn't imagine ever recovering from the kind of loss and abuse her friend had suffered. Why shouldn't Victoria be able to find some happiness after all she'd been through? Why couldn't people like them have a happily ever after?

The sins of the fathers shall be visited upon the sons.

Or in her case, daughters.

"You *don't* have to," Gabe argued.

"Gabe, please. I need to do this. Don't you see? I owe

it to Brock. My mother. To Victoria. And I owe it to my-self. I want to save Brock if I can. I want to help put my father away. It's time for me to be brave. If I walk away from this chance I'll never be able to live with myself going forward."

His hard sigh came through the line, full of frustration. "Dammit, I *knew* you'd say that."

She gave a wobbly smile, even though he couldn't see her. "You know me so well. And also, it's really good to hear your voice right now."

He was silent a moment. "There's nothing I can say to change your mind?"

She put a hand to her bubbling stomach, blew out a shaky breath. She was scared to death. But this was the right thing to do. If she wanted to be able to live with herself, then she had to see this thing through. "No. But I'm going to have you and the rest of FAST Bravo there to have my back, right?" She waited a beat and when he didn't answer right away the fear grew. *Right?*

"Yeah. We'll have your back every step of the way."

The twisting in her gut eased a little, and her heart squeezed at the intensity in his voice. He cared about her. A lot more than he'd let on whenever they spent time together. It touched her deeply, because she was falling for him and was glad to know she might not have done it alone. "Good. I'll see you in a few hours."

"Okay. Be safe."

"I will." She sighed and lowered the phone.

It was finally time to go home. Face her demons head on.

And slay them if she got the chance.

****

"Miss Gomez, will you stay a minute?" Taggart asked her as Oceane and a few others left the room.

Victoria paused in the act of pushing up from her chair and sat back down again. "Of course."

Taggart waited until it was just her, her security and a few other officials. "Would you be willing to accompany Oceane down here?"

She hid her surprise, her pulse jumping. "Yes, absolutely."

"I know you two are close, and I think she'd feel better if you came with her. Also, in terms of intel, you're the best insider source on the *Veneno* players we're after. There might be something you know that could give us a lead. It would mean postponing your move tomorrow, but I feel you would be a valuable asset in this case. Your insight might mean the difference for us being able to locate and recover Agent Hamilton in time."

Did he suspect that she and Brock were involved? Whether he did or not, it didn't matter now. "I'll do whatever I can to assist you in finding Agent Hamilton."

He gave a tight smile. "Thank you. I realize this puts you at risk. Rest assured, we'll make sure you have adequate protection the entire time."

She nodded, appreciating the reassurance, but she was only concerned about Brock right now. Even with all she'd suffered from the cartel, she was absolutely going to Mexico. "I'm ready." Ready to go into enemy territory and do whatever was necessary to save Brock.

"Good. I'll get you the flight info as soon as I've got it."

Victoria's heart pounded as she left the room and headed for the elevator. She hoped the plane would be ready soon, because she couldn't stand waiting when Brock was being held captive.

Rounding the corner, she stopped when she saw Oceane standing there with her cell in hand, looking sad. "You all right?"

"Yes. No. I'm not sure."

156

Victoria pulled her into a hug, squeezed her fiercely. "Thank you. I know it's a totally inadequate thing to say in light of the risks you're taking to do this, but...*thank you*."

Oceane nodded, returning the embrace. "You love him."

"Yes." She didn't even consider pretending otherwise with Oceane.

"Even though you're leaving tomorrow."

"I'm not leaving tomorrow," Victoria said as she pulled back.

Those pretty blue-gray eyes focused on her. "You're not?"

She shook her head. "I'm flying down to Veracruz with you tonight."

Oceane's eyes widened. "Really?"

"Yes. They want me to assist with the investigation from there, because of my background." Her lips curved in a humorless smile. "I'm considered a bona fide insider expert on the *Veneno* cartel because of my investigative work and my insider knowledge gained during captivity. They also thought you'd be more comfortable if I went along, plus it'll only cost them a plane ticket. But I don't care about why they're sending me. I just want to help Brock any way I can."

A relieved smile spread across her friend's face. "I'm so glad you're coming."

"Me too. I just wish we were on the flight down there already. For Brock, every minute counts."

"Yes." She reached out for Victoria's hand, squeezed. "We'll get him back. I swear it."

Victoria prayed it was true. Because the alternative would destroy what was left of her soul.

****

Brock's teeth chattered as he came to in complete darkness. His head pounded and there was a bitter, metallic taste in his mouth.

Whatever they had injected him with was wearing off, but he was groggy as hell and his hands and feet were bound to the chair he was on. He was shirtless. They had removed the hood but he still couldn't see anything.

Snippets of what had happened came back to him. The Taser. The sting of the needle. Being locked in the trunk.

Jesus, he was freezing, his entire body wracked with uncontrollable shivers. Did they have him in a damn freezer?

A door opened, letting in a tiny amount of light. Quiet footsteps sounded outside the room, then three silhouettes appeared, backlit in the doorway.

Brock sat up straight and steeled himself for what happened next, fighting the lingering fuzziness in his brain. But maybe it would be a blessing. Maybe it would help numb whatever they planned to do to him.

The blinding beam of a flashlight seared his retinas. He slammed his eyes shut and turned his face away from the light, but just as quickly forced them open and squinted at the man holding it. At first the image was blurry, then it slowly took form and came into focus.

His heart sank like a block of concrete.

Manny Nieto stood in front of him, flanked by two big men, one of them his head of security.

Nieto stepped forward and folded his arms across his chest. "Awake at last," he said with only the barest trace of an accent. "Now you can answer my question. Where is my daughter?"

He was so fucked. His SERE training had taught him how to take a beating, but he wasn't looking forward to that part, and he'd seen firsthand what these bastards did to their captives. His teeth clacked together despite every effort to stop shivering. He didn't want these assholes to think he was afraid.

"S-safe in the U.S." *Where you'll never get your filthy fucking hands on her again.*

Nieto stared at him for a long moment, his expression and stance calm but his eyes fierce. An underground volcano ready to blow. "There's not much in this world that is of any real value to me anymore, Agent Hamilton. But my daughter is the one thing I would take on hell itself to get back. Now. Where is she?"

"How the hell would I know? I'm not a fucking U.S. Marshal." He didn't know the WITSEC Safesite location, and even if he did, he wouldn't tell this fuckwad where it was, not even under torture. Oceane and Tori were both there. He would rather die than jeopardize their safety in any way.

The man drew in a breath and released it on an impatient sigh. "I'm only going to give you one more chance to tell me what I need to know, and then this is going to get ugly for you. *Where. Is. My. Daughter.*"

Brock was pissed off enough that he wanted to stare into those cold eyes in defiance, but that was stupid. He settled for staring at the collar of Nieto's shirt instead. There was nothing he could do to stop this next part. Nothing except bear it as best he could before they broke him. Because based on what Brock knew about them, they *would* keep going until they broke him.

His heart slammed against his sternum as the silence stretched out, part of him wishing they'd just get on with it already.

Nieto made a soft, scoffing sound. "Maybe you'll feel differently after you spend some time alone with my associate here." He said something in Spanish to the others, then spun around and walked out.

The head of security spoke to the other man in English, wanting Brock to hear it. "Don't kill him. Yet." He stopped at the door to flick a switch. A dim light flickered on overhead. Then he walked out too, shutting the steel door behind them with a clang that echoed up Brock's spine.

His breathing increased as the remaining man stepped toward him. Big son of a bitch, around Brock's size and build. He had the eyes of a killer, the gleam of anticipation in them telling Brock he fucking loved his work.

This is gonna suck. He held his body rigid, put on his game face and prayed he had the strength to take what was coming.

The man stepped around behind him. Brock's senses were on full alert, every single sound amplified over the panting of his shallow breaths, his muscles shuddering in the freezing room.

Something metallic rattled behind him.

Chains.

A chill raced up his backbone, having nothing to do with the cold. Fuck, this was gonna be bad.

Something sliced through the bindings on his wrists. Before he even had a chance to bring his arms up, steel manacles clamped around his wrists. Ice cold. Heavy. Biting into his skin.

His heart stuttered. Broke a little as he thought of Tori in this same situation. Manacles around her wrists and ankles, cutting into her skin so deeply they had left scars. The one around her throat—

A soft clanking sound came from behind him. Rhythmic. Almost like something was being cranked or ratcheted.

The manacles tugged on his wrists, pulling them out to the sides. He resisted, but it was no use.

His arms began to rise. He immediately unlocked his fists to grip the chains, his fingers wrapping around the icy metal links.

Sucking in a deep breath, he fought to empty his mind as the mechanism raised his arms above shoulder level, extending them into the air in a V shape. Then his body began to lift from the chair as well.

He gritted his teeth and shut his eyes, fought back the wave of fear assaulting him as the manacles bit into his wrists. In SERE school he'd been taught to vocalize his pain in order to get his captors to go easier on him. He didn't bother now, because it wouldn't do him any good.

It didn't matter how much he screamed in here. He couldn't give them the information they wanted, because he didn't know it, so their only goal was to break him. Inflict as much pain as they could and then either kill him or leave him to die as a statement to the DEA and the U.S. government.

Taggart and the others will come for you.

Even if it was just his body. That brought him a small measure of comfort. They would find him and take him home, no matter what.

God, he was glad Tori was starting her new life in the morning. He didn't want her to ever know what had happened to him, it would rip her wide open. She'd been through enough without adding that to her burden.

The chains continued to lift him.

His ass came off the chair. His feet bore his weight for a few more precious moments. He stretched up onto his toes to prolong it, buy himself a few more seconds before the pain hit, dreading the moment when his arms would bear the full brunt of his two-hundred-ten-pound frame.

He locked his jaw as his toes left the ground and tightened his grip on the chains. He was strong, but sparing his shoulders and arms was only a temporary reprieve. In this cold, within minutes the strength in his hands and forearms would be gone, leaving only his wrists and shoulders to hold his weight.

He held on as long as he could. Long past the moment when his hands and fingers froze to the metal and turned so numb he could no longer feel them. But finally, the inevitable happened.

The burn in his shoulders was immediate as his grip gave way, the freezing, unforgiving metal clamped around his wrists biting into his flesh as they held him prisoner. All the while the chain cranked higher, higher, raising him toward the ceiling. Dangling him a couple of feet off the floor.

His whole body shook in the cold, the shivers making the pain worse, the muscles in his shoulders and arms now stretched to the breaking point. He squeezed his eyes shut, clenched his teeth to keep from making any sound, refusing to give this sadistic asshole the satisfaction.

The chain stopped moving. Brock swung back and forth a little, bound and helpless for whatever this asshole wanted to do to him. Terror and dread were like a dark tidal wave growing inside him, rising higher with every heartbeat. He choked it down. Used all his mental strength to make his mind go blank.

Go somewhere else in your head.

"I'll be back in a while to get started on you," the man said with a heavy accent, breaking through his concentration. "Don't go anywhere." Laughing under his breath, he paused to flick off the light before walking out, plunging Brock back into total darkness.

The sound of the door closing echoed with terrifying finality, the darkness seeming to make the temperature drop another ten degrees.

Hanging there in complete blackness, Brock tipped his head back and prayed. His wrists and shoulders were on fire, the unforgiving metal cutting into his skin as gravity did its job and slowly began to rip his joints and muscles apart.

How long was he going to be held like this? Until he froze to death?

Desperate to escape the only way he could, he closed

his eyes, cleared his mind and thought of the only person who could bring him a measure of comfort right now.

Tori. And if he could go back in time, he would have told her he loved her before walking out that door.

Chapter Fourteen

The muggy, tropical air hit Oceane as soon as the aircraft door opened, flooding her with a thousand bittersweet memories. After so many months, she was finally home.

Except this didn't feel like home anymore. Not after everything that had happened, and especially not with her mother gone.

She followed one of her marshals down the metal staircase they had wheeled up beside the plane, with Victoria right behind her. Security was tight, a mix of DEA and Mexican military personnel on hand to ensure their safety, everyone heavily armed.

She prayed all of them were with the good guys in this scenario, and not planted here by her father's network. Given what had happened to Brock, however, she wasn't hopeful on that count.

Taggart was at the base of the stairs waiting for them, a powerful, commanding figure in camouflage tactical pants and a black T-shirt that hugged his muscular frame. "Good to see you both," he said, shaking hands with her and Victoria. "Thanks for coming."

"Any word on Brock?" Victoria asked, her voice urgent.

Oceane glanced at her. The question and worry on her friend's face made it plain that something significant had happened between her and FAST Bravo's team leader, and at this point Oceane figured Victoria didn't care if everyone knew it. All she cared about was getting him out of this alive.

"A few tips, but nothing solid yet. No trace of the hostage takers. We traced Hamilton's phone. Got a signal early on when he was first taken, but they must have disabled it soon after because there's been nothing since. Mexican police have roadblocks up and they're monitoring all airports, marinas, train and bus stations. CCTV footage located the getaway vehicle, but it was ditched and they transferred to a new one in a blind spot. Based on the intel we have, we think Hamilton is probably still somewhere in Veracruz city itself, or close by."

Oceane's heart sank. So much time had passed since he had been captured, and Veracruz itself was hardly small. How would they ever find him now?

"I'm taking you straight to HQ. I'll bring you both up to speed on the latest during the drive there," he said, gesturing to the SUV idling near the small terminal building.

She slid into the backseat with Victoria and a marshal, while Taggart got into the front passenger seat. Her heart leapt when she glanced up to see Gabe turning to look back at her from the driver's seat.

"Hi," she breathed, unable to hide her smile and relief. Had he driven Taggart here because he wanted to see her?

For the most part she was getting better at masking her emotions, except around him. He was always contained and hard to read, but now she knew there was far more going on under that calm surface, so she didn't want to hide her feelings. She *wanted* him to know what he made her feel.

Protected. Alive. More female than she ever had in her life.

His pale blue eyes warmed, the barest hint of a smile tugging one side of his mouth up. "Hi. Flight okay?"

"Yes, fine."

"Good." He turned back around and put the vehicle into gear.

She fastened her seatbelt, still smiling a little. The entire flight down here she'd begun to question everything about her decision to do this. Knowing she might possibly save Brock's life helped ease her panic. It didn't matter how afraid she was, she had to do whatever she could to help him. Her life wasn't in jeopardy with her father. Even if she was taken by him somehow, she could attempt an escape later.

Ten minutes later they arrived at the base where they had set up headquarters. Everything became far too real as she followed Taggart and Victoria to the main building. She hung back to walk beside Gabe, his solid presence helping to calm her nerves. If Taggart hadn't been right there, she would have reached for Gabe's hand to bolster her courage.

He glanced over at her, kept his voice low. "You doing okay?"

It felt good just to be beside him like this. "Yes." Terrified she would screw something up and dreading the moment when she heard her father's voice again, but otherwise not too bad. "This is going to work, right?"

"Sure as hell hope so."

Headquarters was a hive of activity and noise. She faltered at the threshold, momentarily overwhelmed.

Gabe stepped forward and set a hand on her lower back, his touch warm, reassuring. "We've got your back," he reminded her in a murmur, his fingers curling against

her spine, the gesture protective, even a little bit possessive.

It calmed and centered her. Helped stem the tide of
alarm threatening to overwhelm her.

Taking a deep breath, she walked over to where Taggart stood with Agent Rodriguez and a group of Mexican
law enforcement officials. After introductions, she and
Rodriguez translated back and forth for both sides as the
taskforce laid out the potential plan they had devised during her transport. Everything they said made sense to her.

Taggart turned to her. "You ready to do this?"

She stole a glance at Gabe out of the corner of her eye.
He hadn't said much during the discussion, but he'd been
watching and listening carefully. If he had concerns about
the plan, he would have said so. So that made her feel a
little better.

"Yes," she said to Taggart.

He nodded once. "Get her a phone," he said to no one
in particular.

One of the Mexican officials brought over a cell phone
she assumed was secured with some kind of encryption
and ushered her to a private room. Taggart followed, and
so did Gabe.

Standing next to the desk when Taggart shut the door
behind them, enveloping the four of them in blessed quiet,
she shoved aside the anxiety swelling inside her. "What
do I say?"

Taggart handed her a piece of paper with a number for
the contact on it. "Tell him what we talked about in there.
We need proof of life on Hamilton first, or there's nothing
further. Once we get that, we go from there," he finished,
his cryptic words sending a shiver down her spine.

In all honesty, the less she knew about the operational
side of things, the easier this would be. She didn't want to
know what they had planned. Better for her to be totally
ignorant of that part, so she couldn't accidentally screw

up by giving something away to her father or his men.

Staring at the number in her hand, Oceane drew in a deep breath. She prayed this would work, that Taggart and the team could somehow get a lock on the signal of the phone she was about to call.

Once they got proof of life, hopefully she could figure out a way to help them get the location where Brock was. If she could save him by doing this, then it would all be worth it, even if it meant never getting the answers from her father or the closure she was looking for.

She reached for the phone, heart pounding, palms clammy, aware of Gabe's eyes on her from his position beside the door. But he couldn't take this next step for her. She had to find the courage to face this on her own.

"Okay," she murmured as she began dialing the number. "Let's do this."

****

Manny looked up from the latest spreadsheet from his accountant when David walked into the kitchen. His head of security smiled. "She's here."

Manny slapped the laptop shut and swiveled to face him, his heart beating faster. "In Mexico?"

He nodded. "Veracruz."

"You're certain?"

"Yes. I just got a heads up from Sanchez. She called the number we gave them. She's with the DEA contingent."

So fast. Incredible to think she was finally here, back where she belonged. He hadn't spoken to her personally for security reasons. "And? What did she say?"

"She said she wants proof of life on Hamilton before we go any further with the negotiations. A video. That was it."

Negotiations. He snorted in irritation. It infuriated and

insulted him that he should have to *negotiate* to get his own daughter back. Was this Oceane's demand, or the DEA's? He would make them pay for turning her into their puppet.

It also angered him that she would make such a demand of him, dictate that he had to prove the enemy was still alive, even if he had been expecting something like this. But he'd been praying for this chance for so long, and his daughter had a soft heart. He could use that to his advantage.

"Get the video. Send it to them and name the place where I get to pick up my daughter. If they try to stall or pull anything, he dies, and my men attack their location to get her back."

"Of course. I'll call the men and alert them to what's going on, get the video started. Once the proof is sent, you and I can go over everything, make sure we've covered all the contingencies before we hear back from the Americans. Also…"

"Yes?"

"Victoria Gomez is with her."

Manny processed that in silence for a moment. "Why would they bring her down here?"

"I'm not sure. I've got people tracking her movements, just in case we want to use her for something."

"Good." Manny dismissed him by turning back to the laptop, wanting to be alone with his thoughts. He opened it, a huge lump in his throat, the backs of his eyes burning.

His little girl. At last.

After all this time he was finally going to see her again, and hopefully begin the long process of reconciliation he'd been dreaming of these past months. It wasn't going to be easy, but the most important things in life never came easy. Manny was used to battling for everything that mattered to him. Now he would fight for Oceane, the only thing pure left in his life. She was his future.

The spreadsheet on screen before him listing the profits of his latest investments blurred before his eyes. He wiped an impatient hand over them, cleared his throat and tried to focus on the numbers.

He'd already begun the transition process and finalized his will. Elena was no longer a beneficiary, having been paid out a settlement in cash when their separation had been finalized. She was too smart to try and drag anything out in court. Smart enough that she would take the money and start over somewhere.

Now he was free.

Tomorrow marked a new dawn. Tomorrow when they finally met face to face again, both he and Oceane could turn the page and begin their lives anew.

Together.

****

Brock jerked awake with a gasp when a bucket of icy water hit him in the face, drenching the front of him. As soon as he came to, he wished he hadn't.

He was still hanging from the chains attached to the ceiling, his entire upper body in agony. His right eye was swollen shut. Both arms were totally numb except for the constant, biting pain in his wrists and shoulders.

Every single breath was its own separate agony, the places where the thin metal rod had struck leaving welts and bruises, maybe even cracked a couple of ribs. He must have passed out at some point during the beating because he'd been completely under when that water hit him.

Hard shudders ripped through him now that he was awake, his exhausted, beaten body reacting once again to the cold. But he was sluggish now, the prolonged exposure to the freezing air having taken its toll on him.

Brock's good eye focused on the lone figure in the dim room. The man responsible for torturing him stood in front of Brock with a smirk on his face. "Rise and shine," he said in a singsong voice.

He caught only a flash of movement, barely had time to flinch as the rod swung out and smashed across his face. His roar echoed throughout the room as the bridge of his nose split open, pain exploding through his face.

He struggled through the fog of agony, fought to clear his head. Blood dripped down his face, running off his lips and chin in a thin rivulet that dripped onto his bare, bruised chest and onto the concrete floor below.

Another blow lit up a stripe of anguish across the left side of his ribs, in the spot where even his tensed muscles couldn't protect him. He closed his eyes, not wanting to see where the next blow would land, and forced his mind to go empty, not even trying to stay quiet anymore.

Pain wouldn't kill him. Pain was shitty, but it was a reminder that he was still alive. He had to hold onto that.

With effort he let his body go slack and drifted in between blows, concentrating on thoughts of Tori. He clung to an image of her face. On the night she'd come to meet him at the hotel. Her nervous smile at the beginning. The stunned look on her face when he'd wound the scarf around his wrists, offering his body to her.

He'd never given himself that way to anyone. Only her. In return she'd let down all her walls that night. They both had.

That night had changed him forever, and he would never be the same again. Not that he was likely to live much longer to prove that theory. But if he did survive this he was going to find Tori and consider giving up his career for her.

The bastard hit him across the back now. Brock clung to Tori's image, drew strength from it. A resolve to hold on through the blows that rained down on his defenseless, suspended body.

He fought for breath, struggled to let the pain wash

over him. Tears slipped down his face, mixing with the blood, his soul crying out in agony, his hoarse voice echoing in his ears.

You can take this. Suck it up and take it.

Tori had endured worse than this and survived. He would hold on for as long as it took, or until he gave his last breath.

Don't let them break you.

His team would be searching for him, along with other American and Mexican agencies. If he could just stay alive long enough, he had a chance of making it out of here.

Providing this sadistic son of a bitch didn't kill him first.

He tensed, anticipating another blow. Then the sharp notes of a ring tone cut through the room.

The beating stopped abruptly.

Letting out a painful, cautious breath, Brock sagged and opened his good eye to find his tormentor staring at the cell phone in his hand, frowning. The man answered, watching him.

Brock only caught little bits of his response to whoever it was. Then he hung up and gave Brock another smirk that made him long to break the cruel fucker's neck.

"Need to take a video of you," he said, holding up the camera. "So smile nice."

Brock glared down at him with his one eye, refusing to respond in any other way. The bastard was loving every moment of this.

"Say your name."

He gathered his strength inward. If they were recording him, there was a reason. Were they sending proof of life to Taggart and the others? Or just so they could kill him and send this to the U.S. government after as a giant fuck you?

It's Taggart.

He had to believe that. Had to, for his sanity.

Drawing in a shallow, painful breath, he tried to ease the shaking but his teeth continued to chatter, blood dripping down his face and chest. "S-supervisory Special Agent B-Brock Hamilton," he rasped out.

"And what agency do you work for?"

"DEA."

"Okay. Now smile."

Brock longed to break his neck. Fantasized about it as he hung there. *Fuck. You.*

Chuckling, the man tapped out a message to someone, then lowered his phone and tucked it back into his pocket. Picking the rod back up, he faced Brock and grinned, his eyes gleaming with an unholy enjoyment. "Now. Where were we?"

Chapter Fifteen

———◇◇◇◇———

"**D**oes anyone here look familiar at all to you?"
Victoria scooted her chair closer to the
table and carefully examined the photos
Taggart slid in front of her. Members of the taskforce
were trying desperately to trace the number Oceane had
called, but they hadn't been able to get a lock on the signal
yet. The battery had likely been removed or the phone destroyed.

"Are these all cartel members?" she asked.

"Most of them. We're hoping you can identify a few,"
he said.

It was so damn hard to focus on this when they didn't
know what was happening to Brock. Oceane had called
her father's contact three hours ago demanding a proof of
life video, and still nothing.

Victoria supposed she should be grateful that they
were involving her with the investigation at all because
without something to keep her busy right now she would
be losing her mind with worry. It tore her up, made her
physically ill to think of Brock being beaten. Tortured.

Worse.

"Commander Taggart."

They both looked up as a Mexican official hurried toward them from the other end of the room. "We just received a call from the local police. Someone called them with a possible tip on Agent Hamilton's location."

Victoria's heart beat faster as the man reached the table they were working at and set a folder down in front of Taggart to open it.

"What's the tip?" Taggart asked, leaning forward to read the contents.

"The anonymous caller said he had a location on the American hostage. Not an address, but he texted this picture." He flipped the page to show a photograph of a house. It was grainy and dark, not the best quality, but the house was distinctive. More of a mansion, at least from the looks of it through the tall wrought iron gates at the end of the long driveway.

"Anyone recognize it?" Taggart asked.

The man shook his head. "We've got analysts trying to identify it and the location of the cellular signal now."

"Do you have a recording of the call?"

"Yes. This way."

Victoria rushed after Taggart into a private office off the main room. The man excused two other people working at the desk, waited until the door shut behind them before pulling up something on his laptop. "Here." He hit play.

"I know where the American hostage is," the man said in flawless Spanish.

Victoria looked up from the photograph of the house to stare at the laptop screen, focusing on the voice. There was something familiar about it that nagged at her.

"I took a picture of where he's being held. If you want more information, it'll cost you. Ten thousand U.S."

She knew that voice. Maybe from her captivity.

Her heart began to pound as the dark memories she battled daily began to surface. Taking her back to that dark time and place when she had been used in ways that would always make her feel unclean. Tainted.

Fear and pain intertwined in her mind. Her body. Her throat worked as she swallowed, sifting through those seemingly endless days and nights of darkness while various men had defiled her.

For Brock. You have to do this for Brock.

She closed her eyes and concentrated. Battled through the panic tightening her throat. Forced herself to dredge up the horrors she had sworn to bury forever.

Shadows. The menacing, oily feel of fear coating her skin, her tongue.

The shape of the men's silhouettes, outlined against the daylight outside the shed as they stood in the doorway. Coming to defile her.

Faces. Some of them clear as a photograph, others blurry and indistinct.

Smells. Cigars, the reek of cigarette smoke that made her shudder, her flesh cringing at the threat of those glowing ends searing her naked skin.

Beer. Whiskey. Stale sweat and cologne.

And voices.

Whispering cruel, terrifying things as a man's body pinned her to the filthy mattress. Laughter when she couldn't keep her cries of pain and fear locked inside.

Like the voice speaking now. Straight out of her nightmares, making her flesh prickle. But who? She fought to sift through the images in her head.

The man named an account that she would bet anything was offshore someplace, then continued. "Text me at this number when the transfer is done." He cleared his throat just before the recording stopped.

Victoria sucked in a ragged breath and opened her eyes as recognition hit with sudden clarity.

Everything stilled. The blood drained from her face, her fingers clenching around the folder as a face became clear.

"Stop." It was barely a whisper. But Taggart and the other man looked at her sharply.

Her heart hammered in her ears. "Play it back again." She needed to be sure.

Nausea twisted her stomach but she forced her eyes shut as the recording played again. That distinctive voice rolled over her, taking her back to that hellish prison at Ruiz's hideout.

The same voice that had taunted her as he raped her.

He'd visited her in the shed out back half a dozen times. Each time he'd finished with her he'd yanked his pants back up and delivered a verbal barb as he stood towering over her, smug in his power over her.

We own you, filthy whore. You're gonna die a slut, just like you deserve for what you did to Ruiz. You are nothing.

He'd laughed. Then cleared his throat exactly like on the recording as he walked out. Leaving her trembling in pain and humiliation, crying silent, scalding tears in the darkness.

"You know him?" Taggart finally asked, his voice taut.

She opened her eyes and nodded. "Not his name. But his voice and his face." She rubbed her hands over her upper arms, trying to warm herself. Taggart draped a jacket over her. "He was one of Ruiz's *sicarios*. Likely one of the men rumored to be working for Montoya the past few months."

Taggart's eyes searched hers. "Can you look through the rest of the pictures, see if you can find him in there? If not, we'll try an online database."

"Yes." If it helped them find Brock, she would do anything. Even confront the ghosts that haunted her.

Back at the table in the main room, she searched

177

through the pictures with renewed urgency. She was half-way through the stack when the Mexican official returned.

"Our analysts traced the origin of the call from the out-skirts of Cancún."

She blinked. "Cancún?" That was over eight hundred miles away from here. How did the caller know about Brock? Unless Brock wasn't in Veracruz at all, as they'd assumed?

She tuned the men out, letting them worry about that as they discussed the latest development. A minute later, her heart stuttered in her chest when she came across a photo of a man she recognized.

"This is him," she said, tapping the man on the far right of the picture. It wasn't a clear shot of him but the image still made her stomach roil.

"You're sure?" Taggart asked.

"Yes. He's got hazel eyes and a slight gap between his upper front teeth. And a snake tattoo on his left forearm that winds up his wrist. The head is on the back of his hand." She had become all too familiar with it in the glow-ing light from his cigars as he took his time burning her with them. She shook the memory away, focused on the men standing beside her.

The Mexican official leaned over, his expression dark-ening as he looked at the image. "Javier Sanchez. One of Ruiz's most wanted *sicarios*."

Javier Sanchez. She'd heard both those names during her captivity but had never been able to put them to a face until now.

"How would he know about Hamilton?" Taggart asked. "Was he in on this? Was he the one who attacked him and took him hostage?"

"It's possible."

"Call your contacts in Cancún," Taggart commanded, turning away and pulling out his cell phone.

"Taggart."

Taggart and Victoria both looked over their shoulders as Agent Rodriguez strode toward them, his face set. "What is it?" Taggart asked.

"We got it."

Taggart tensed. "The video?"

"Yeah."

Fear spread up Victoria's spine like the caress of icy fingers. Whatever the video showed, the look on Rodriguez's face told her it wasn't good.

"Is he alive?" she blurted out, unable to stand it.

"Yes. At least when it was taken."

"I wanna see it," Taggart said.

"Over there." Rodriguez motioned to the far end of the room where a group of agents were gathered around a large monitor. The rest of FAST Bravo were there as well, riveted to what was on the screen, their expressions ranging from horrified to lethal.

Victoria headed for them, barely aware of her feet moving as she crossed the room with Taggart. Agent Freeman glanced up, saw her coming and stepped away from the group to block her path, holding up a hand as he shook his head. "No. You don't want to see this, trust me," he said.

Get the fuck out of my way.

She managed to hold it back and shoved his restraining arm aside instead. Heart thudding, she stepped around him to look at the screen.

The instant she did, she came to an immediate halt, the soles of her shoes suddenly glued to the floor. She covered her mouth with one hand, tears flooding her eyes as she took in the horrific image before her.

Oh my God, no. Please, no...

Rodriguez leaned forward, hit a button to start the video. A chilling voice came from behind the camera.

"Say your name."

They'd beaten Brock to a pulp. He was covered in blood. And they'd included proof of the date by showing the front page of a newspaper.

She bit her lips together, blinked back tears as she watched in horror.

It took a long moment for him to respond, and when he did his voice was so hoarse with pain that she died a little inside on hearing it. "S-supervisory Special Agent B-Brock Hamilton."

"Did it come?"

At the question from behind her, Victoria tore her eyes away from the horrible image and spun to face Oceane, who rushed into the room with an anxious expression on her face.

She locked eyes with Victoria. "Did they send the video? Is he alive?"

This time Victoria was the one to step forward and try to block her friend from seeing the monitor. But it was too late. Oceane had already looked at it.

She froze, her blue-gray eyes widening in shock, then horror. She twisted away with a cry, covering her eyes too late in a futile effort to block out what she'd just seen.

SHE HAD ONLY seen the screen for a split second, and that sickening image was already burned into her memory forever.

Oceane struggled to breathe, tried to make sense of what she'd just seen, couldn't control the horror and outrage swamping her.

They'd chained him. By the wrists. Left him hanging from the ceiling in some sick reproduction of Jesus on the cross, his arms spread out and his legs dangling beneath him.

He'd been covered in blood, his face split open. And he was shaking, a combination of pain and cold, judging from the blue tinge around his bloody mouth.

Her father had done this. Ordered for Brock to be tortured and then had one of his men film the aftermath.

Oh God, she was going to be sick. She swallowed, her stomach pitching. She took a stumbling step forward, blindly reached for something to steady herself with.

A low curse sounded from somewhere in the background, then strong arms banded around her from behind, holding her upright.

Gabe. His familiar, comforting scent surrounded her, but as reassuring as his presence usually was, it didn't help the nausea. She gagged, tried to push free before she got sick on him.

Someone shoved a trash container in front of her. She reached for it, latched onto the sides as her stomach heaved, bringing up the tiny amount of dinner she'd forced down her throat earlier on the plane. Acid burned up her esophagus, her eyes watering as she retched until it was empty.

Someone took the bucket from her. Gabe scooped her up in his arms, lifting her off her feet. She made a sound of protest and weakly pushed at his shoulder, but he wouldn't be swayed. In moments he'd carried her outside into the muggy night air. Victoria was there, holding the trash can.

"Put me down," she whispered to Gabe, pushing harder on his chest. As good as it felt to have him hold her, she didn't want him to see her as weak. And God, he and the others must all hate her guts for what her father had done to Brock.

He set her on her feet gently. "Sit down, then," he ordered softly. Someone must have brought him a water bottle because he unscrewed the cap and handed it to her.

She took it, rinsed her mouth out several times, spitting into the bushes that lined the concrete sidewalk that led to the main building's entrance. How had she been fathered by a man who could do such a thing to another human being? How had she lived for so many years without ever seeing the true monster inside the man?

"Here," Gabe said, holding out a silver wrapper. A stick of gum.

She unwrapped it and stuck it in her mouth, her stomach quivering. Victoria knelt down next to her, set a comforting arm around her shoulders, her dark eyes worried.

Oceane shook her head, tears clogging her throat. "I'm sorry. So, so sorry," she whispered, her chest hitching.

"No." Victoria dragged her into a hug and Oceane's control nearly broke. She didn't deserve Victoria's concern. Not when Manny Nieto's blood ran through her veins. "You have nothing to be sorry about. This isn't your fault."

"Yes, it is. My father did this to get me back." She shuddered, unable to grasp the depths of his depravity. The level of cruelty he could have inflicted on someone.

A big, gentle hand settled on the top of her head. "This is on him. Not you. He's the monster and he makes his own choices." Gabe.

She didn't deserve his understanding or support either. This entire situation was because of her and her father. Her jaw trembled, shock finally hitting her. "Brock was still alive on the video?" she made herself ask.

"Yes," Victoria answered.

But might not be now. "When was it taken?"

"We're not sure. Maybe a few minutes ago," Gabe said.

As the shock and anguish began to recede, something stronger began to form in their place.

Anger. A deep, burning resolve to do something about this.

For vengeance. To make sure her father could never hurt anyone ever again.

She stood, locked her knees and wiped at her face impatiently with the heels of her hands. The peppermint gum

helped freshen her mouth, the queasiness subsiding a little. "Do they know where he is?"

"Somewhere near Cancún, we think," Victoria said.

Cancún? Her attention sharpened on her friend. "What
makes you think that?"

"One of Ruiz's *sicarios* called in a tip, thinking he was
being anonymous. They traced the call to there. And he
sent a picture of a house where he claimed Brock was being held."

"Show me."

Gabe curled a hand around her waist as he guided her
back inside to a desk where a folder was laid out. The moment she saw the photo of the house, her heart stuttered.
My God...

"I've been there," she said, her heartbeat quickening.

"When?" Gabe asked, turning to wave Taggart and the
others over before looking down at her again.

"When I was young. We used to stay there on vacation
sometimes. My fath—" No. She wouldn't call him that
any longer. Not one damn time more. "Nieto would come
and meet us. He would stay for a few days at a time, sometimes longer." And he and her mother always told her he
couldn't stay long because he needed to travel so often for
business.

God, she'd been such a fool. A brainwashed, idiotic
ostrich that would rather stick its head in the sand than see
the truth that had been right there in front of her for her
entire life.

"Are you certain?"

She glanced up into Taggart's stern face. The rest of
the team was gathered around them, watching her, their
expressions hard. She felt like they blamed her partly for
this. And rightly so. "Yes. Nieto told me it belonged to a
friend, but I'm betting if we dig a little, it will be owned
by one of his companies."

"Do you remember the address?"

"No. But I remember the neighborhood." She glanced around. "I need a map."

Someone shoved a laptop in front of her seconds later, a map on screen. She didn't know the street names or even what the neighboring properties looked like. But she remembered the name of the beach her parents had taken her to play on. It was within easy walking distance of the house. Maybe a few minutes on foot.

She located it on the map, tried to remember which direction they'd walked in to get to and from it. "Somewhere in here," she said, circling a neighborhood of waterfront homes with her finger. "We had an unobstructed ocean view from the back of the house. The lots were big. There was a big garden out back with a tall fountain in the middle. It had trimmed hedges around it. And a sculpture of a dolphin."

Gabe leaned forward and tapped a few buttons to enlarge the satellite map, zooming in on the area she'd indicated. Making it larger. Larger still, until the rooflines and yards became distinct.

Her anxious gaze landed on a familiar landmark in one of them. "There."

Gabe zoomed in closer still and Oceane's heart began to pound. A knot-formation of trimmed hedges came into view in the backyard, a fountain in the center. And the dolphin off in the corner. "This is it."

"Get eyes on this address," Taggart commanded to the room.

People began rushing everywhere.

"How long has it been since you were there?" he asked her.

"I was twelve or so the last time."

"Do you remember the layout?"

"Yes. Though it could be changed now."

Taggart thrust a pen at her and slid a piece of paper in front of her. "Show me what you remember."

She began sketching out the basic floor plan, wanting to do whatever she could to help. Hoping it would be enough to find Brock in time. "How do we even know Brock is really there? The caller could have been lying, just trying to get money."

"It's the only thread we've got, so we're pulling on it," Taggart said, leaning one hand on the table to watch.

Searching her memory, she drew the ground floor. Kitchen, library, dining room. Family room. The upper floor had bedrooms and bathrooms. Her room had its own attached bath, just down the hall from her parents' master suite.

"Is there any place that matches the look of that room?" he asked, jerking his head toward the computer she'd glimpsed on her way in.

Forcing herself to look over at it again, she focused on the horrific image of Brock strung up by those cruel chains. The room was horrible. Cold and sterile. All concrete. Like a bunker.

She sucked in a breath. "The basement. There was a wine cellar down there, and some other rooms I was never allowed in. My fa—" *No.* "Nieto said they were off limits and I was forbidden to go down there without an adult." Because he hadn't wanted her to see what he used that room for. God.

She swallowed, the memories washing over her, conflicting and difficult. He'd been such a kind, attentive father, especially when she was young. Even on the rare occasions when he had spent time with her as an adult. When she was little he had flown kites with her on the beach. Given her piggyback rides up and down the sand and through the lush grounds of the house. He had played hide and seek in its rooms. Read stories to her and tucked her in at night.

Had he been an evil monster even back then? Or had his lust for money and power warped him over time?

"Any tunnels down there or anything like that?" Taggart asked, bringing her back to the present.

She could feel everyone's gazes burning her. Wished she held the power to fix this mess. "It's possible. I heard him mention secret passageways once."

She'd been outside his office while he'd been on the phone that morning. The moment she'd stepped into view his expression had frozen. He'd immediately ended the call and distracted her with an ice cream sundae in the kitchen, and she'd forgotten all about the tunnel until just now.

"Might lead to the beach," Taggart muttered to the others, and signaled to someone out of her line of sight.

She surfaced from her memories, her skin crawling. Was Brock being held and tortured in one of those basement rooms right now, in the place where she had vacationed with her parents all those years? It was too awful to contemplate. "I want to talk to him."

Taggart looked at her sharply. "Who?"

Her heart was racing, her breaths coming faster as the anger hit. "Nieto."

"Not a good idea. And we only have his contact as a go between right now anyway."

"Then I want to talk to him." She raised her chin, looked at Taggart defiantly, anger pulsing hotter with each heartbeat. "Put me on the phone to him. Right now."

"Why?"

Because. Goosebumps broke out on her arms. "Because I'm going to end this." Once and for all.

Taggart shared a loaded look with Gabe for a moment, then waved someone over. The man dialed the contact for her. The room went eerily silent as the phone rang, the sound of it echoing because she was on speaker.

"Yeah?" the male voice answered in Spanish.

She kept her gaze locked with Victoria's as she spoke, drawing strength from her friend. "This is Oceane Nieto.

I want to speak to my father." She only used that term now because she had to.

The man snorted. "I'm supposed to believe you?"

"I don't care if you do or not. Just put me in contact with him. *Now*." The rage was building again. A deep, blinding supernova she couldn't suppress.

"Say I play along and pretend to believe you're his daughter. I'm not gonna give you his damn number, so why don't you tell me what you want to say and I'll think about passing it along to him?"

She hoped someone was tracing the call. They must be. "You tell him from me that I'll come to him—"

Across the table Victoria gasped, shook her head and opened her mouth as if to protest, but Oceane wouldn't stop.

"I'll come to him, but only if he releases Agent Hamilton immediately. You tell him from me that if he hurts Hamilton any more, I'll hate him forever and he'll never get what he wants." She drew a shallow breath. "Tell him right now and tell him he has ten minutes to answer at this number. And you'd better tell him, because if he finds out you didn't pass on the message and he lost his chance to see me, he'll kill you." She hung up, her cheeks on fire, the righteous anger inside her burning out of control.

"Oceane, no," Victoria blurted, but before Oceane could respond Gabe grasped her upper arm and whirled her to face him.

His expression was taut, his pale blue eyes full of rage. And something else.

Apprehension. He was afraid for her.

"What the hell did you just do?" he demanded.

He didn't speak Spanish fluently, so he might not have understood everything. The only one on the team who did was Rodriguez, and he was staring at her in shock, and also maybe a little admiration mixed in. "I…"

Gabe's jaw flexed, his face hard. "What did you say, Oceane?"

"She said she'll meet Nieto if he lets Hamilton go," Rodriguez said.

Murmurs and indrawn breaths filled the air as Oceane stared at Gabe.

"No," Taggart said in an adamant tone, shaking his head. "You're not doing that. It's way too risky. We're not handing you over to him. That's not how we operate."

"I know. That's why I'm going to him voluntarily."

"You can't."

"I can. Unless I'm under arrest and wasn't aware of it?" She raised an eyebrow at him, not caring if she came off as a bitch. She was done with being victimized. With being used. Done with sitting back and watching her life crumble around her, with allowing others to be hurt or killed because of the man who had given her fifty percent of her DNA.

Taggart didn't answer, but a muscle bunched in his jaw.

"Nieto won't hurt me, because he wants me back." For whatever reason. That was the only thing she was certain of anymore. "So if he agrees to free Brock, I'll do a swap for him. You can track me and move in to arrest him once Brock is free." This was the only way, and he had to know it. The best shot they had at arresting Nieto.

The only way to make things right and find justice for her mother, Brock and herself.

Gabe swore and stalked away a few paces, hands on hips as he faced away from her. She winced inside, hating that he'd turned away, but there was nothing she could do. She'd set the wheels in motion and couldn't go back now.

Taggart dragged a hand over his face and sighed. "Shit. I can't legally stop you. But if you go ahead with this, you need to understand that I can't guarantee your protection. And neither can they," he added, looking at the Mexican officials.

"Understood. And I'm going ahead with it." She squelched the ripple of unease that moved under her skin at the thought of undertaking such a dangerous mission. Because dammit, she was the only one who might be able to end this in time.

She glanced at Gabe, flinched at the anger vibrating off him, his ice blue eyes searing her now. She couldn't take his anger right now. She needed to be alone, come to terms with what she'd done and was about to do.

"Now I'd like some time to myself if you don't mind," she said, her voice quieter now, steady even though she was terrified. "Nieto's only got nine minutes left to call me back."

Phone in hand, she turned away from everyone and headed for a private office, scared as hell and sure she'd lost her damn mind.

Chapter Sixteen

Gabe wasn't happy about this. At all. In fact, he was convinced this was a *really* bad fucking idea.

They *might* free Hamilton if they did this. Maybe. Though based on that video, it might already be too late.

They may even get Nieto out of the deal if they were real lucky. But the odds of something happening to Oceane through any part of this plan were way too fucking high. Just thinking about what she might walk into tonight made his blood pressure soar.

"We don't have much time to pull this off," Taggart said to the team in a private office they'd piled into for an emergency meeting. He could see Oceane through the window in another office down the hall, and someone had taken Victoria somewhere. Analysts now thought that the anonymous tip about the target house had been sent by someone working for either Montoya or *El Escorpion*, in the hopes of getting rid of Nieto.

"Nieto's already gotta be suspicious," he continued. "We can't afford to give him a big enough window to move on us, so if we're doing this we're gonna have to go within the next twenty minutes. Our only advantage right now is that he doesn't realize we know where Hamilton is yet."

Shit.

Gabe ran a hand through his hair. He was used to high stress situations, but he'd never had so much at stake personally before on an op.

He struggled to focus, part of his attention on the group of Mexican feds talking to Oceane about the proposed meet up with one of her father's men. What were they talking about? How in hell were they going to protect her if she went through with this?

They can't.

It made him insane. God, he still couldn't believe what she'd done. That she'd volunteered to offer herself up like a sacrificial lamb in the hopes of saving Hamilton.

Already Nieto had changed the damn rules, his contact calling back with an answer just under the ten-minute deadline Oceane had set, rather than calling himself. Not that Gabe or anyone else in this building had expected Nieto to call personally.

The bastard was now insisting she be brought to him first, and saying he would only release Hamilton once Oceane had arrived safely in his care. Gabe had followed on her heels into the office, had tried to talk her out of it. He'd told her flat out that it was too risky, too reckless. He hadn't been gentle about it either.

No, he'd been furious, because it scared the living shit out of him to think of her risking her life this way. She'd been through too much already. He didn't want her facing this too.

Not that his opinion on the matter had done him any good. She'd refused to listen to reason and the Mexican officials were so desperate to get Nieto that they were falling all over themselves trying to help her set everything up.

This was a total shit show. The DEA had no jurisdiction down here beyond protecting themselves and whatever the Mexican government allowed them to do. FAST Bravo would be allowed to perform the rescue attempt to free Hamilton, but only on a joint op with Mexican SF members. They would have zero to do with providing security for Oceane while she walked literally into the lion's den.

Gabe wouldn't be able to protect her. Wouldn't even be able to watch over her because he'd be part of the rescue op for Brock. It made him want to break something. She'd gotten to him over the last few months. Slowly working her way under his skin without seeming to realize it, though he'd been damn careful to hide it. He wished he could wrap her up and hide her somewhere, stop her from doing this. Keep her safe.

"One more problem," Rodriguez pointed out to the group, bringing Gabe back to the conversation at hand. "Without Hamilton we're down to an eight-man team."

"It's all right," Freeman said. "We'll just make certain adjustments in how we do this."

Gabe rubbed the back of his neck, his gut screaming at him in warning. There were so many unknowns to deal with. So many things outside of normal procedure he couldn't begin to count them. Technically they could operate with eight guys, though it would be against protocol. But hell, this entire scenario was against protocol, so it didn't much matter.

"I'll act as your ninth man," Taggart said, making Gabe and the others look at him in surprise.

Taggart was well qualified, that wasn't the issue. He'd served for years in an AFSOC special tactics squadron as a combat controller. He knew the team inside and out, knew their methods and their techniques. Their strengths and weaknesses.

It was still a big goddamn stretch to have him on an op with them.

The reason they trained as hard as they did was so that every man on the team knew each other well enough that they could anticipate what the others were going to do before they did it. They also knew each other's limitations.

That kind of bond could only be forged by countless hours spent training and on deployments together. And now it wasn't just any old hostage they were going to rescue, it was Cap. The stakes and pressure would be beyond anything they'd done before, because as professional as they all were, emotions would be running at an all-time high.

"Any of you object?" Taggart asked, crossing his arms and glancing around at them.

They didn't have time to hash this out any longer and Taggart could hold his own, so Gabe shook his head and got on board with it.

When no one else argued, Taggart nodded once. "All right. Freeman, you'll act as team leader on this one. Lockhart, you're our new point man. I'll go second to last in the stack if we have to do a breach." He gestured to Freeman. "Let's hammer out the details. They're readying a flight for us right now."

Freeman grabbed the drawings of the floor plan Oceane had sketched out earlier. The whole team studied them carefully, cross-referencing with satellite images of the house and grounds.

They picked their entry and exit points. Tried to figure out what kinds of security measures would be in place. How many guards. They would be armed with semi-automatic weapons. Might even have grenades or even RPGs.

This had to be surgical. Insert without detection, use violence of action when they breached the house to take the defenders by surprise. Then get past the armed security, into the basement, find Cap and get him the hell out.

The commander and team leader of the Mexican SF team came in. With Rodriguez acting as chief translator they laid out everything, divvied up assignments. Mexican feds would deliver Oceane to the meeting point and hand her over to one of her father's men. Once she arrived safely, Nieto might release Cap.

But Gabe wasn't holding his breath on that one.

Hopefully the taskforce would at least have eyes or ears on Oceane at all times so they could track her. For all they knew Nieto might not even be at the target house. He might order Oceane to be taken elsewhere.

Fuck. It drove Gabe nuts that he had no say in this, but there was nothing he could do to stop it now. If they were going to save Cap tonight, all of them had to be on their games and focus on the job at hand.

Even if the woman he was falling for was about to place herself in direct and very real danger.

He shoved the thought aside and focused on business. Everything moved fast from there. Before Gabe knew it, they'd been granted a green light for the op from both the Mexican and U.S. governments. The Mexicans would act as perimeter security at Nieto's mansion while FAST Bravo executed the rescue op and moved to the extraction point.

Then Gabe would be forced to wait on the sidelines for word on Oceane…and not be able to do dick all to help her if she got into trouble in the meantime.

"Okay, boys, let's move," Freeman said, pulling on his gloves.

Gabe looked around, but Oceane was already gone.

Heart heavy, he followed his teammates back to their barracks. Everyone grabbed their gear and rushed out to the vehicles waiting to take them to the airstrip. Two private jets were waiting on the tarmac, ready to roll.

They piled on board and buckled in for the flight to Cancún.

No one talked. There was no chatter, no joking around. Even Granger and Maka were quiet. Every last one of them knew the gravity of the situation. If they messed this up, if they breached the house and it turned out Cap wasn't at the target location, he would die.

And Oceane might too.

****

Victoria jerked upright when someone knocked on the door of the hotel room the Mexican officials had put her in near base several hours ago. With everything going on, the taskforce wanted her contained and out of the way, yet available at a moment's notice if she was needed for anything else. Taggart had told her he might send for her at some point. The whole time she'd been in here, she'd thought about Brock, and what she'd seen in that video.

She crossed to the door to see who was there. But instead of finding one of the marshals when she checked the peephole, a Mexican police officer stood there dressed in uniform instead.

"Who is it?" she said in Spanish.

"Miss Gomez, I'm Sergeant Vargas. Commander Taggart wants to meet with you. I'm to take you to him."

She frowned. Everything here was in a state of chaos, but she didn't see why the marshals would allow someone else to come up and get her. Unless the Mexican authorities had overruled them? "Where is my security detail?"

"Downstairs, waiting for you in the vehicle."

Odd. "Did Taggart say what he wanted?"

"No. But his team is heading to the nearby airport, where I am to take you. We must hurry."

Did he want her to fly to Cancún with them maybe? She could ask the marshals once she got to the vehicle.

"One moment." She grabbed her purse from the dresser and unlocked the door.

Vargas stepped back and walked at a rapid clip to the stairs. "Faster than the elevator," he said, holding the door open for her.

Their footsteps echoed in the empty stairwell as they hurried for the ground floor. "This way," Vargas said, pushing open the exit door that opened up into an alley behind the hotel.

A gray van was parked there. Not running. And she couldn't see anyone else inside it.

Suspicion transformed into alarm, a primal warning tingling at the base of her spine.

Not wanting to give herself away, she turned around, hid her unease as she stepped back through the door. This was all wrong. She needed to get the hell away from him. "I forgot a file up in my room. Taggart will need it." She started past the man, intending to race into the lobby and get help.

Vargas shot out a hand and gripped her wrist. "No. We need to leave *now*. The file can wait."

Alarm transformed into fear.

She wrenched her arm free, but just as quickly he snatched her other one and pulled her toward the door.

Heart in her throat, Victoria whirled on him, stared right into his eyes. "Let. Me. Go." She narrowed her eyes at him in warning, hoping her strong stance would be enough to make him release her. "*Now*."

He cursed and grabbed her around the torso, wrenching her off her feet.

"No!" She drove her head back, slamming her skull into his face with a satisfying crack. Vargas bellowed in pain but didn't drop her, kept dragging her determinedly toward the van.

Everything Trinity and Briar had shown her came flooding back.

Victoria twisted around in his grip and drove the heels of her hands into the underside of his jaw, snapping his head back. He tripped, grunted as she landed on top of him.

She scrambled to her feet and took a lunging step away but he managed to snatch her ankle. Down she went, her knees slamming into the pavement with bruising force. With a snarl of rage, she turned on him, used her momentum to break his grip and deliver a solid roundhouse to the side of his head.

He went down, stunned, and she didn't wait to see whether he stayed down.

She ran, her shoes thudding on the pavement, veering around the corner, past a group of startled people and into the lobby. "Help! Help, there's a man after me!"

The two men behind the front desk gaped at her, then hurried toward her. But before she could reach them, a familiar voice shouted from behind.

"Victoria!"

She skidded to a halt, spun around to face two marshals, their faces masks of concern. "A cop," she panted, her knees beginning to quake. "Or a fake one. He came to my room. Tried to get me into a van in the alley out back. He's down."

The one in the lead cursed, glanced at his partner, who took off toward the alley while he came up to her. "Are you all right?" he asked, holstering his weapon, scanning her for injuries.

A wave of queasiness rolled over her. "Y-yes." Oh God, that had been way too close. Who the hell was that guy, and what did he want with her?

She bent over, put her hands on her knees and struggled to breathe. *You're safe. You're okay.* Her nervous system wasn't listening to her, her body still in flight mode.

The marshal put his hand on her back. "It's all right now. Take a minute."

She nodded, but couldn't answer, too overcome by what had just happened. By what *could* have just happened if she hadn't gotten free.

A ringing sound registered a minute later.

The marshal straightened and pulled out his phone. "You got him?" He listened, then nodded at Victoria. "He got him. Guy's not a cop. Apparently someone in the cartel paid him to bring you to them."

She barely suppressed a shudder at the news. "Who?" Terror forked through her at the thought of how close she had come to being their prisoner again. There was no way she could have survived that a second time.

"Don't know. But we're gonna find out." He grasped her upper arm gently, turned her and hustled her through the lobby while people stared at them.

Victoria didn't care about the stares. She just wanted out of here, and back to where someone would know what was going on with the op to rescue Brock. "So Taggart never s-sent for me."

"No. But you're not staying in this shithole a second longer, and we're not abiding by any bullshit protocol down here anymore." He stalked toward the front doors. "I'm taking you back to HQ to wait this out, and I don't care who doesn't like it."

"Good." She was shaken but not hurt. And she was still free. But she was damn lucky on both counts. God, what she wouldn't give to feel Brock's arms around her right now. The thought pushed her precariously close to the tears she was battling.

"I'll call Taggart."

"No." She grabbed his hand when he raised his phone to his ear. When he looked at her sharply, she shook her head. "Don't. I don't want anything to distract from the rescue op. I'm fine. This can wait until after."

He stared at her a second, then nodded and ushered her toward a car parked at the curb. "How did you get away?" he asked as he slid into the driver's seat beside her.

Victoria wrapped her arms around herself and took a deep breath. "I head-butted him, then gave him a round-house to the side of the head." And damn, it was empowering to realize she had fought back and saved herself this time. She owed Trinity and Briar a big thank you when this was finally all over.

One side of the marshal's mouth kicked up. "Well, good for you." He chuckled as he pulled out into traffic. "Good for you."

She didn't care about that now. "Have you heard anything more about Brock? Or Oceane?"

His expression sobered. "No. But the team's on their way down there with her now. Won't be long until we know something more. And if you're at headquarters, you'll know as soon as it happens."

Closing her eyes, she fought the sting of tears and the sense of hopelessness invading her. Oceane was putting herself in grave danger to do this. Brock's life depended on her convincing Nieto to let him go, or his teammates finding and freeing him in time.

But with every second that passed, the odds of him surviving dwindled more.

****

Oceane's heart pounded against her ribs as the *Federale* drove her to the meeting point. A park a few miles from the Cancún vacation house, where her father had pushed her on the swings when she was little.

They had been given the location only a few minutes after she'd texted the contact upon her arrival at a local airstrip. A precaution, to ensure the police wouldn't have time to set up a sting to arrest the man coming to get her.

She knew the park well. Once, she and her mother had set up a picnic on a blanket beneath the shade of a grove of palms and together they'd eaten lunch, finishing off the meal with the special chocolate cake they'd made, spiced with cinnamon and cayenne.

One of so many treasured, happy memories she had of her little family. She'd felt so secure. So safe. But it turned out it had all been a lie.

She pulled herself from her reverie as familiar landmarks caught her attention and ordered her nerves to calm. They had planted a tiny tracking chip in the underwire of her bra. Even with a scanning device, no one was likely to find it. The Mexican federal agents were using it to track her to wherever she was taken. From there they would move in to arrest Nieto, while Gabe and his team would try to rescue Brock. Then…

Then she would finally be free.

She focused on the scenery outside her window. The city was so beautiful at night with all the lights gleaming. Since it was almost one in the morning all the shops and restaurants were closed, only the occasional bar open. The streets were quiet, the sidewalks all but deserted as they approached the park.

"Are you ready?" the fed up front asked her.

"Yes." *As ready as I'll ever be.*

He parked under a streetlight, making it easier for the men coming to get her to see it was only her and the driver in the car. He stepped out and opened her door for her.

She took a steadying breath. This was it. No turning back now.

She stepped out of the vehicle, locked her shaking knees and looked around. The fed stayed beside her, his body partially blocking hers as another vehicle drew up. A sleek Jaguar. It parked across the street, the engine still purring.

The driver's door opened.

A bittersweet pang hit her when she saw the familiar man climbing out. "David," she said, a wave of anguish threatening to crash over her. She had known Nieto's head of security since she was a child. What atrocities had he committed or covered up on Nieto's behalf?

The handsome, middle-aged man smiled at her, his expression so kind it made something sharp twist in her chest. "Hello, *mija*."

She swallowed back the tears burning the back of her throat, her mind at war with itself. He'd always been so kind to her. How was it possible he was involved in all the atrocities her father was responsible for? "Is it just you?" She had expected more of an armed escort.

"Yes. We thought you'd be most comfortable that way." He held out a hand toward her. "Shall we go?"

She forced herself to nod, step away from the agent and cross the road to where David waited, strangely comforted by his presence.

The park behind him was enclosed by trees and other vegetation. It looked deserted, but she knew David would have set up at least one of his men there with a rifle, just in case. She shivered, the sense of security she had always felt around him ripped from her.

She climbed into the Jag. The interior smelled brand new, the sweet scent of high-grain leather rich in the air. "Is he waiting for me?" she asked as David pulled away from the curb.

"Yes. He'll be so happy to see you. He's been waiting for this a long time."

She rubbed her damp palms over her jean-clad thighs. "So have I." She pushed back the anger and sadness building inside her, the questions crowding the back of her throat. Losing her cool with David wouldn't do anyone any good. She would wait until she confronted her father to let it all out.

At least she was safe now, strange as that thought was. Her father had gone to extraordinary lengths to try and bring her back to him alive, and he had sent David to get her personally. She was precious cargo to him, after all. Though she still didn't understand why in light of everything he'd done.

"Has Agent Hamilton been set free?" she asked.

"I'm not sure."

Bullshit. David knew everything that went on with her father's activities.

"That was the deal. My father needs to let him go. Now."

"You can talk to him about it when you see him."

She sat there fuming, trying to think of a way to sway him. Or at least have him convince Nieto to let Brock go.

David made several sharp turns when he reached the city center. She glanced in the side mirror, wondering if any of the headlights behind them were from someone on the taskforce following her. Perhaps the federal agents were watching them via satellite, or maybe CCTVs or drones, she wasn't sure.

Instead of continuing on toward the water as she expected, David wound his way into a cramped back alley and parked behind a building.

Her stomach muscles tightened. "What are you doing?"

"Taking precautions," he said calmly, and handed her a bag. "Take off everything you're wearing and change into these. Everything. Bra and underwear too."

She blinked at him, opened her mouth to argue but realized that would make it look even more suspicious. Except without the tracking chip in her bra, the feds wouldn't know where she was if they lost visual contact at any point.

"I'll wait outside," David said, and stepped out.

Not having a choice, she changed clothes, the task twice as awkward because of the cramped space in the front seat.

She put on the new clothes from the bag and stuffed her own back into it. When she was finished she glanced up to make sure David still had his back to her and fumbled with the underwire of her old bra. He would check to make sure the new bra and underwear weren't in the bag, so she had to transfer the chip somehow.

Her fingers were clumsy, the stress starting to get to her. She cursed as her grip slipped.

Hurry. Hurry.

The chip was soldered to the wire. She used her nails to try and pry it free. It didn't budge.

Frantic to do this before David turned back around, she used her teeth, biting down with all her might. The chip cracked free.

Sending up a silent thank you, she quickly shoved it into the bottom of the new bra cups, stuffed the old bra into the bag and smoothed a hand over her shirt.

David opened the door a crack. "Done?"

"Yes." God, her heart was hammering. She schooled her features into a calm mask, determined to hide her anxiety as he took the bag from her, checked that everything was in it and then walked over to toss it into a garbage can nearby.

"Step out. We're switching vehicles."

She got out, stiffened when he pulled something out of his coat pocket.

His dark eyes met hers in the dim light filtering into the alley, a flare of sympathy flashing in them. "It's a detector wand, not a gun," he said softly, and stepped toward her.

She stood absolutely still as he ran the device over the length of her body, pausing at the bottom of her breasts. He glanced up into her face for a moment.

Her heart rocketed into her throat. Had he figured out what she'd done? But he merely finished the sweep down to her feet and back up, stopping once more at bra level.

"Underwire," she explained tightly, hoping the annoyance covered the stress in her voice. "But maybe you'd like to check my fillings too, just to be safe?" She raised an eyebrow, letting some of her resentment bleed through. It was realistic enough to be believable.

David lowered his gaze and shook his head, giving a slight wince. "I had nothing to do with that, by the way." Before she could say anything, he pulled out his phone and called someone. "We're ready. All clear? Good."

He was tucking his phone away when a car pulled into the far end of the alley. A minivan. "This is us. Come on." He grasped her upper arm and walked her to the waiting vehicle, his grip gentle but firm.

"Where are we going?" she asked, hoping she hadn't damaged the chip during the transfer. If she had, she was screwed.

"Home," was all he said.

Oceane climbed into the back with him behind the two men up front, and they drove away.

A sense of unreality hit her. After all this time she was about to face the monster who had haunted her dreams since the terrible night when those armed men had stormed her home. Marking the beginning of the destruction of her entire world.

I'm going to face him for you, Mami, she vowed as she stared out the window as the darkened city passed by. *I'm going to get answers.*

And then I'm getting us both the justice we deserve.

Chapter Seventeen

Until this moment, Manny had never known time could pass so slowly. It felt like he'd been waiting days instead of minutes for the call to come in.

His heart jumped when his cell phone rang. David. "Yes?" He held his breath, awaiting the reply. *Please let her be there. Let her be okay.*

"We're five minutes away."

A huge smile broke over his face, relief rushing through him. They'd done it. It had worked. "She's there?"

"Right next to me."

He closed his eyes, sagged forward to plant a hand on the tabletop. *Thank you, God. Thank you.* He'd waited so damn long for this. "Is she all right?"

"Of course. Do you want to talk to her?"

"No. Not yet." He needed a few more minutes to compose himself, and he didn't want their first words to each other after all this time to be over the phone.

The reunion he'd dreamed of was tempered by the knowledge that she had been working with the Americans and his own government. This might well be a trap, but his men were careful and he was willing to risk it. They had emergency evacuation procedures in place just in case something went wrong.

His first priority, however, was his daughter's safety. Even if there was an attack, he would not leave without her.

He rubbed a hand over his mouth, his mind working fast. He'd thought many times of what he would say to her if he ever had the chance. Oceane would be angry and scared and confused and he didn't blame her for any of it. He had a lot of work to do if he wanted a chance at repairing the damage he'd done to their relationship.

Manny didn't deserve another chance with her, not after the things he'd done, but he would take it. More than that, he would guard it, nurture it with all of his energy for the rest of his life, however long that might be. As of tonight he was a new man, with a new life waiting for him.

The mansion's security system beeped a few minutes later, alerting him that a door had been opened. His pulse thundered in his ears as he stood in the entryway to the kitchen and waited.

David appeared first, his face lit with a secret smile. Then he stepped aside, revealing the beautiful young woman standing behind him.

Manny exhaled in a painful rush as Oceane stepped forward, barely stemming the impulse to rush over and wrap her up in his arms. Looking at her was like a punch to the gut. It had been almost a year since he had last seen her. How could he have forgotten how the sight of her made it feel as though his heart would burst open?

Her skin was a pale, creamy brown, shades lighter than her mother's had been, her hair a deep chocolate and less tightly curled, but the eyes and everything else about her were pure Anya.

A wall of emotion hit him, the force of it taking him off guard. His throat closed up, guilt and grief and regret all but choking him.

She stopped where she was, her body stiff, her blue-gray eyes cold as winter as she stared back at him. Full of hatred and a loathing that shredded him inside.

His fault. All his fault. God, if he could go back and change the past he would do things so differently. He would have told her the truth long ago and taken more steps to ensure she and her mother were protected. If he had done those things, Oceane would be rushing into his arms right now and Anya would still be alive.

He cleared his throat, unable to help the smile tugging at his mouth. He was so damn glad to see her again. "Hello, Oceane. I'm glad you're here."

She didn't answer, just stared back at him with those icy eyes, the pain embedded there slicing him up.

Patience.

It wasn't something that came easily to him. He was now accustomed to getting whatever he wanted when he wanted it, but for her he could exercise some patience.

He sighed. "Why don't we sit down and talk," he suggested, gesturing behind him to his office. The most secure room in the house, where even a bug David might have missed on her wouldn't transmit anything.

She studied him a long moment, then relented and took a step forward, gazing around at the lavish décor and furnishings of the main floor. "This isn't the same house we used to stay in."

"No. I thought a change of venue was best. Make a fresh start." The property wasn't far away from that house, though, only four lots north up the beach.

He took a breath, forced his tight stomach muscles to relax. They would be leaving here in another hour or two, once everything was in place. Then he would have all the time he needed to repair their relationship. Until then, he had to make her comfortable enough to relax a little.

"Just in here." He stepped aside to let her pass him, aching to hug her the way he used to. There was a time when her face would light up at the sight of him. When she had looked at him like he had hung the moon.

Those days were gone forever. But perhaps they could have something almost as good, in time.

She took the tufted leather chair he indicated as David shut the door for them. She seemed calm enough on the surface, but her nerves showed in the way she rubbed her hands on her thighs and the way her gaze darted around the room.

"Would you like something to drink? Or eat?" he asked.

"No." She met his eyes, her inner strength shining through. "I'm here, as promised. Where is Agent Hamilton?"

"Nearby."

"You agreed to release him immediately if I came to you." She raised her chin, her whole being radiating a defiance that had him hiding a smile. She had more of him in her than she probably wanted to admit. "I honored the terms of our agreement. Now let him go. You promised. I need to see you do it."

He nodded. "I will within the next hour or so."

Anger flashed in her eyes. "No. *Now*."

Suspicion took root. "What is he to you?"

She faltered for an instant, caught off guard by his question. "An acquaintance."

She was lying. "He must mean more to you than that, given your reaction."

Her eyes narrowed. "Your men tortured him," she said in disgust.

Manny didn't react, though his conscience squirmed a little under the censure in his daughter's gaze. "I'm not involved with any of that."

She stared at him in disbelief. "They're your men. And no matter how *involved* you are or aren't, you didn't stop it, either."

Sighing, he leaned back in his chair. He'd been hoping to delay this conversation until later, but it was clear they had to have at least part of this out here and now. "Whatever they told you, there are many things going on here that you don't know about. Things you don't understand."

Her mouth twisted into a bitter smile. "I wonder why that is?"

"I was trying to protect you. You were just a little girl."

She shot from her chair, hands knotted into fists at her sides. "No. I haven't been a little girl in a long time. You were trying to *control* me. Keep me ignorant of everything that was going on. Hiding the truth from me as much as possible, and, stupid me, I believed it all. My entire *life* has been a lie."

SHE WAS SHAKING inside, slowly coming apart at the seams, stitch by stitch.

None of this was going according to plan. Oceane had expected some deviation, but not this. Not arriving at the wrong house and Brock still being held prisoner.

Was the tracking device still working? She wasn't even sure this place was in the same neighborhood as the house she had shown Taggart and the others, and without the tracker the taskforce would never find her.

Nieto's expression was so damn calm she wanted to scream at him. "I know you're upset. And I understand it's my fault."

"You're damn right it's your fault. It's *all* your fault." Now that she was here before him, she couldn't keep the acidic words inside her any longer. If she didn't let them out, they would eat her alive.

Nieto drew in a deep breath, held up a hand. "Look. I realize there are a lot of things we need to talk about. But I need you to know that everything I did, everything I hid from you, was for your protection. I did everything in my power to keep you safe, and even that wasn't enough in the end. When I heard that you and your mother had been attacked at home, I thought…"

He stopped, seemed to struggle to hold onto his composure before continuing. "I feared the worst. And ever since I found out you had fled to the States, I've been working to bring you back here the whole time, so I could explain everything where I know you would be safe."

She shook her head, emotions ripping through her in a chaotic torrent. Betrayal. Rage. Grief. A deep, aching sadness that would never go away. "You had a tracking device implanted in my mouth without me knowing. You hunted us down in D.C. because you were afraid we had betrayed you, and then you killed my *mother*."

He blanched and shook his head, emphatic. "*No*. No, I swear it. I sent Arturo to get you, bring you back to me. Juan was supposed to locate you with the tracking device and have his men provide security during the extraction, that was all."

All? Oceane stared at him, her heart imploding.

The tears she had been battling were too much to hold back any longer. They dripped down her cheeks and she angrily swiped them away. Her voice shook as much as her body as she responded. "Those men *raped* her, do you understand? They violated her. Then they butchered her with knives. I was there. I saw her stumble out of the house, naked, bleeding from all the wounds."

She sucked in a breath and jabbed an accusing finger at him, wished it was a gun instead so she could shoot him in his black, evil heart. "I had to sit there by her side, hold her hand and watch her bleed to death. There was nothing I could do to save her or ease her pain. My mother, the person I loved more than anyone else in the entire world. Do you *understand* that?" She screamed it, all the pain pouring free after being bottled up for so long.

A terrible silence engulfed the room as he stared back at her.

"Yes," he finally said, looking ill, his jaw flexing and his hands balling into fists on his desktop. "Believe me, Juan will pay for what his men did. I will see to it."

Did he really believe that would make anything better? He was insane. "She's dead because of you. And now you're dead to me too."

His expression turned stricken. "No. Don't say that."

She shook her head, held up a hand to stop any other arguments. She didn't want to hear his lies. "I've said everything I had to say to you. I came here to see you, did everything I said I would. Now free Agent Hamilton and let me go. You and I are done."

"We're *not* done," he shouted, slamming his hand on the desk.

She jumped and sucked in a breath, ready to bolt for the door. His face was red, his eyes bulging in a way that terrified her. She'd never seen him like this, the monster beneath the handsome veneer slipping above the surface. While she hadn't expected him to just let her walk out of here, until this moment she hadn't been afraid that he would hurt her.

Now she wasn't so sure. But even if she got out of this office, she would have to get past David, and David would do whatever her father told him to.

Her father struggled with himself for a long moment, then exhaled and leaned back to regard her more calmly. "All right. You've said your piece. Now you're going to listen to mine." He thrust a finger at her chair. "Sit down."

"N-no."

"Sit. *Down*."

"Or what? You'll hurt me too?"

Something flashed in his eyes. Surprise? "Don't push me."

The menace in those quiet words sent a shiver through her. Reaching behind her, she gripped the arms of the chair and dropped onto the seat, her pulse hammering in her throat.

Someone knocked on the door. David opened it. He glanced between them, his gaze pausing on her almost in concern for a moment before he addressed her father. "He's on the way. Should be here in about ninety minutes."

"Thank you," her father muttered, his eyes still spearing her. "We'll be out shortly."

David shut the door and a chill rippled up her spine as his words registered.

"You are my only child," her father continued as though there had never been an interruption. "My sole heir. While I've been searching all over for you, I've also been reorganizing my estate. It's true that a sizeable amount of what I have came from less than legal means. But everything else came from legitimate sources."

"Some of which I unknowingly helped you launder," she snapped, sick with rage and despair. And alarm. She wanted out of here. Had stupidly thought Nieto would let Brock go if she came.

His jaw flexed again, but this time he let the verbal slap go. "I pushed you into becoming a financial adviser for a reason. I knew that someday you would have a huge amount of money to manage, and I wanted to be sure you could handle it. Now the time has come. I've been restructuring everything so I can begin to show you what I've created, let you take over more and more of the business side until I pass it all to you when I die."

"I don't want your filthy blood money."

"It's yours, whether you want it or not. It's your birth-right. And I'm going legitimate. I wouldn't expect you to work with or keep money that came from my other sources."

Like that made it okay? Did he honestly think she would want this? Even consider it, or...she didn't know, be *happy* about it? He was insane.

He waved a hand impatiently. "I realize that you and I have a lot of things to work through. I can only hope that in time we can rebuild at least part of what we had. It will take effort on both our parts, but you have to know that even with all that's happened, no matter what happens, I have always loved you and always will."

It hurt. Hurt so bad it felt like her chest was being split open. Because she'd loved him too once. Loved him to pieces. To the point where had she and her mother not been driven from their home that awful night, she might have been able to forgive him for lying to her about everything else once she'd learned the truth.

Maybe. Though she would never know now. Too much had happened. She would never give him another chance.

"Who's on the way?" she demanded now, desperate to change the subject because it was all she could do not to launch herself across the desk and attack him. "What did David mean?"

He hesitated a moment before answering. "My pilot."

No. "What?" she gasped.

"We're leaving."

Like hell.

She shoved to her feet and took a stumbling backward step toward the door, afraid to take her eyes off him, her heart thundering in her chest. "I'm not going anywhere with you."

His jaw tensed, a sign his patience was growing thin. "Yes, you are."

She whirled and lunged for the doorknob. Managed to twist it and yank the door open, only to run smack into David. He caught her by the upper arms to steady her.

But then his fingers locked around her arms like manacles, and the taut expression on her face made her insides shrivel.

His black gaze cut to her father, still behind his desk. "They're attacking the other house."

Oceane gasped, cringed when her father shot to his feet, his livid gaze snapping to her. Scalding her with its fury. "What did you do?" he demanded. "How did you know?"

"There's no time for this," David interrupted, tugging her firmly into his side. Protecting her from Nieto, yet unwilling to let her go.

She pulled and struggled, frantically tried to get free, her mind racing. Nothing in her world made sense anymore. She needed to get the hell out of here. Find a way to escape.

Nieto's lethal gaze swung from her to David. "You know what to do. Go."

Go where? Oceane dug in her heels and tugged against David's grip, shaking her head. "No."

"I don't have time to explain," David said curtly, dragging her toward the staircase that led to the lower floor.

Panic hit her. "Stop!"

His grip remained solid on her arms. "Don't fight me," he warned, but there was also the edge of a plea in his voice. "I don't want to hurt you. Please don't make me hurt you, Oceane. I couldn't take that." Ignoring her struggles, he continued forcing her toward the stairs.

Chapter Eighteen

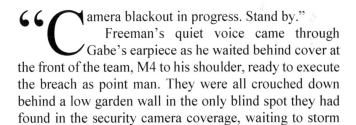

"**C**amera blackout in progress. Stand by."

Freeman's quiet voice came through Gabe's earpiece as he waited behind cover at the front of the team, M4 to his shoulder, ready to execute the breach as point man. They were all crouched down behind a low garden wall in the only blind spot they had found in the security camera coverage, waiting to storm the place and rescue Cap.

On the opposite side of the property, the Mexican team waited for the same. Someone on the taskforce was busy trying to disable the system, hopefully buying them a window of surprise.

Rodriguez crouched beside him, breaching tool in his hands. As soon as he blew the door to the main floor open, Gabe would be the first one through it.

A loud thud reverberated through the sultry night air, coming from the other side of the house. Gabe's head snapped up, looking at the others. They all looked as tense as him. What the hell? Had someone spotted them?

Another thud, and then yelling in Spanish.

Christ, the other team had breached too soon.

He popped up to check the side door of the house. With the element of surprise gone, they had to get in there immediately. "Freeman—"

"Execute."

Gabe broke from behind the brick wall and charged the short distance across the lawn toward the door they were using for an entry point. More shouts rang out from the other side of the house, followed by the sporadic crack of gunfire.

Gabe bit back a snarl of fury. Fuck, if this cost Cap his life, if Oceane was in there and in harm's way because the other team had just fucked up, Gabe would tear someone apart.

Oceane had insisted her father wouldn't hurt her, but Gabe wasn't so sure. Men like Nieto were never predicable. And when cornered, they were the most dangerous.

Rodriguez reached the door first, rammed the reinforced door with the breaching tool twice, three times until it opened slightly. Then he reared back and smashed his boot against it, and it finally gave way.

No need for night optics now. Gabe pushed his NVGs up onto his helmet mount and scanned for targets as he swept into the lit house, using his knowledge of the layout to navigate. If Cap was here, he would be down in the basement. The team had to get to him before his captors did.

Plaster sprayed a foot to Gabe's right, the shot echoing in the air. He glanced to his right, glimpsed the shooter trying to duck back around the corner of the wall. Swinging his weapon around, he fired, tagging the guy in the shoulder.

The man's weapon clattered to the floor as he fell out of sight. Gabe swiveled to clear the other side of the room, waited as Maka and Prentiss rushed past him to clear the next.

"Main floor clear. Heading upstairs," one of the Mexican team leaders called out. Moments later the other team raced up the stairs toward the second floor. Somebody shot at them but it quickly stopped.

Gabe didn't even glance up, busy with his own team as they did a sweep of the main floor themselves, to ensure it really was clear. "Clear," he reported and headed for the top of the stairs that would lead to the basement. It was dark down there. He flipped his NVGs down.

"Clear," Freeman echoed a moment later. As team leader, he would be near the back of the line. "Let's move."

As soon as Gabe felt his teammate's hand squeeze his shoulder, he switched on his NVGs and started down the stairs. A hand popped out from around the corner below, holding a weapon. The instant the shooter came into view Gabe stepped to the side and fired, hitting him in the chest. The man dropped, his rifle still clutched in his hands.

"Tango down." Gabe raced for him, ready to put another round in him, but he didn't twitch. Gabe kicked the weapon away as his teammates rushed past him down the stairs.

More shots rang out from up ahead. The distinctive sound of an M4 firing answered.

"Tango two down," Granger said.

Gabe spun around to check the stairs above them. Still clear.

He turned and ran after his teammates, his heart rate picking up now that they were getting close. If Cap was down here they would find him and get him the hell out.

Gabe just prayed they wouldn't be carrying his dead body with them on the return trip.

****

Seated in an empty office at the far end of the head-quarters building, Victoria pressed her clasped hands to her lips as she sat on a bench, elbows propped on her thighs. Her eyes remained glued to what was happening on the other side of the window.

In the center of the long building, various Mexican and American officials were all gathered around their stations, monitoring whatever was happening on the other end of their comms.

Tracking intel. Satellite data. Working informants. Analyzing security and CCTV footage.

Anything and everything they could get their hands on.

While she sat stuck alone in here, slowly losing her mind with worry.

Officials had interrogated the man who had tried to capture her. He had apparently been hired by someone linked to Nieto, who worked in Mexican customs and im-migration. The man didn't know what Nieto wanted with her, he'd simply wanted the money for delivering her to Nieto.

The cartel had informants everywhere. Someone, maybe her would-be-kidnapper's contact, had alerted the network the moment she and Oceane had touched down on Mexican soil. And likely the moment FAST Bravo had too.

That's how they had gotten Brock.

She blew out a shaky breath, bounced her knee up and down, unable to tear her gaze away from what was going on in the main room. They wouldn't allow her to watch what was going on. But she knew the gist of what was happening.

Oceane had disappeared shortly after the drop off. Whether or not they had been able to start tracking her again was unclear.

As for Brock...

FAST Bravo was on site and in position at the target house Oceane had identified for them. That was all Victoria knew.

The strain was slowly killing her. Her emotions were all over the place. Fear for Brock and Oceane kept swamping everything else.

A screen off to one side at the far end suddenly came to life. She raised her head.

It showed a darkened landscape, painted in shadows and a weird, neon green. The camera swiveled to the left, and a man's face appeared.

Agent Rodriguez.

Victoria sucked in a sharp breath and surged to her feet. The team. It was a live feed from someone's helmet cam.

She was up and heading through the door before she even realized she had moved. Her eyes remained glued to the video feed at the far end of the room. People stopped what they were doing to gather around it, blocking her view. She hurried toward them, her shoes silent on the carpet, straining to see what was happening.

Blurs of motion. Shadow and light. The distinctive crack of gunfire.

Her heart shot into her throat. Stuck there and wouldn't go back down. Choking her. She struggled to suck in air, pushed her way through the knot of bodies blocking her view.

Brock. Had they found him? Was he alive?

More gunfire.

She stood on tiptoe, managed to catch a glimpse of the screen between the moving bodies in front of her. The inside of a house. Bright. Men in tactical uniforms rushing around, weapons up. Then whoever wore the camera turned and headed away from the others. Into darkness.

"You can't be here," a man said next to her.

Victoria glanced over to see one of the Mexican officials who had taken her to the hotel earlier. The one that insisted she be kept out of headquarters during sensitive operations.

She pulled her arm away when he reached for her. "No. I'm staying."

His expression hardened. "No, you're not." Without pause he gripped both her upper arms, spun her around and began marching her away, back to the office they'd put her in.

"I need to see," she cried, twisting away. She needed to see if they found Brock. Whether he was still alive or not.

"*Stop*," he commanded, giving her a shake that shocked her into going still. "You can't help anyone now. You have to stay out of the way." He towed her away from the others.

Victoria relented and went with him, casting a desperate glance over her shoulder at the screen. She could barely see it now.

The team was moving through the darkness now. She couldn't make anything else out.

Her last glimpse of the screen showed more of the same. And no sign whatsoever of Brock.

****

Brock struggled toward consciousness as another shudder wracked him. It didn't seem as cold anymore. He kept fading in and out. Not a good sign.

He was hypothermic, his thoughts sluggish, even the pain signals slow to reach his brain. He was alone. The bastard beating him was gone, maybe because he'd decided it wasn't much fun to beat on an unconscious man.

He was still hanging by his wrists, locked in complete darkness. The shudders and shivers were getting fewer and farther between, his muscles too exhausted to expend the energy to try and warm him.

His breathing rate increased, a surge of adrenaline flooding him. Survival instinct kicking in.

Instinctively he knew his body was shutting down from the prolonged exposure to the cold. And that if he went under again, he would die.

He fought the pull of it, the lure of painlessness and oblivion, tried to use the pain to center him. Keep him awake. But it was getting harder and harder to think. His eyelids were weighted down with concrete. Or maybe they were swollen shut. It was peaceful when he went under. No more fear. No more suffering.

Stay awake.

He shook his head, gritted his teeth that were hardly even chattering now. Now he was completely numb except for the pain in his wrists and shoulders, though they weren't as sharp as they had been. It was so much easier to close his eyes and let go. All he wanted to do was sleep.

Tori's face appeared in his mind. Her dark eyes were worried, her expression full of desperation as she knelt in front of him and took his face in her hands. "Brock. Brock, don't close your eyes."

He forced his eyes open to look at her. But she wasn't real. She was only in his mind. He closed his eyes again, struggled to hold onto her image. *You have to stay awake.*

She gave him an encouraging smile, her eyes begging him to keep trying. "That's right. Hold on."

Can't.

"Please. Fight it."

He squeezed his eyes shut, choked back a sob. It hurt so bad. He couldn't take anymore. *Need you. Need you to help me through this. Please.*

"I'm right here, and I will. Now fight it. For me."

Trying. Help me...

221

A muted thud broke through his trance. His head jerked up. He struggled to open his eyes to the black ceiling above him, ears straining to hear something else.

Another thud. Louder this time.

Muffled yelling. Running footsteps outside in the hallway past the room Brock was in.

Then gunshots. A pistol. Followed by semiauto rifle fire.

He sucked in a breath, hope pouring a blast of warmth through his cold body. Someone was attacking the compound.

His heart beat faster as he listened, trying to piece it together. Was this about him? His team coming to rescue him?

The door flew open. Brock slitted his one functioning eye to squint at the silhouette of the man rushing toward him. There was no mistaking the outline of the extendable rod in his hand. "Wake up, asshole," he snarled at Brock.

Brock didn't think. He reacted.

Using his remaining strength, he waited until the man came close enough, then swung his legs out, biting back a scream as the manacles sliced into his wrists and tore the muscles in his shoulders. Something popped.

Sucking in air, roaring in agony, he parted his knees enough to clamp his thighs around the man's neck. His victim swore and tried to wrench away. Swung the rod at him. But this time he had no leverage and Brock wasn't going to endure any more.

Brock gritted his teeth, his entire body shaking as he clamped down with everything he had. A feral cry of rage and agony tore from his chest as he squeezed the man's neck, taking blow after blow as his tormentor tried to fight his way free.

He couldn't let go. Wouldn't, until the last of his strength gave out.

Gunshots rang out from somewhere outside the room. Brock didn't let go, struggling with all his strength to keep his knees locked in place.

The man's struggles slowed. Grew weaker.

Brock wrenched his lower body to one side, hard as he could. A crunch sounded. The bastard's dead weight dropped all of a sudden. It was too much.

Brock howled in agony as his wrists shredded from the additional weight. The man fell from his grip and slid through Brock's legs, hitting the floor hard.

Brock was sucking in air, a blinding haze of pain clouding his mind when he finally realized more men were coming through the door.

"Cap. Cap, you good?"

Brock couldn't answer, so grateful to hear Rodriguez's voice that he sagged, his body convulsing with a sob.

"Fuck." Granger. "Hang on, Cap. I got you." He wrapped solid arms around Brock's hips, hoisting him slightly to relieve the strain on his wrists and shoulders.

Brock groaned in pitiful relief and dropped his head to his chest, unable to speak.

"Help me get him the fuck down," Granger snapped.

"On it." Lockhart.

The familiar, dreaded cranking sound started up, came faster and faster, and Brock was slowly lowered toward the floor. Granger held him up, his grip solid around Brock's hips. Somebody else rushed forward to grab him around the waist. He yelled as pain sliced through his ribs, tried to wrench away and got nowhere.

"We got you, Cap. We're getting you out of here." Freeman.

The pressure on his sore ribs eased. His arms slowly lowered to his sides. No longer suspended by the chains, his entire body sagged like a ragdoll as his teammates lowered him gently to the floor on his back. He dimly heard them dragging the dead man's body aside.

"It's like a fucking meat locker in here," Granger muttered, already fumbling with one of the manacles. Someone was cutting the ties on Brock's ankles free. His legs flopped apart when it snapped, lay limply on the icy concrete. "Get a blanket."

Brock faded out, came back when someone tucked a blanket around him. The overhead light was on now. He blinked his one eye, staring up into Khan's worried face.

"Hey, man," Khan said. "You're gonna be okay. We'll have you out of here in a minute. Just hang on, all right?"

Brock sucked in a breath as Granger finally got the first manacle off. He struggled to turn his head to see who was working on the other one.

Blood coated his wrists and hands, the torn flesh there like raw hamburger. Maka was there, his face set as he strained to force the metal halves apart. Brock yelled when the second one snapped open, tearing into his shredded skin.

"Sorry, Cap. I'll let you punch me in the face later. Now take a breath and brace yourself, because this is gonna fucking hurt."

It hurt to breathe, much less take a deep breath. The little air he managed to suck in left his lungs on a scream when Maka grabbed his arms, pulled him upright and then bent to lever Brock across his wide shoulders.

Fire burned through his ribs, through his arms and down his spine. When he could finally get a gasp in Maka was already on his feet and heading for the door. Glad as he was to be rescued, Brock wasn't sure he could handle being carried right now.

"I c-can walk," he gritted out.

"Not today," Maka replied, and rushed out of the hellish room.

The difference in temperature was immediate and startling. Brock groaned in sheer relief as the air seemed to warm with every step Maka took.

Time blurred. His head spun. He faded in and out during the trip up the stairs. Might have puked once.

He came to sometime later with the sound of rapid Spanish floating around him. Maka was carrying him through what looked like the main floor of the house, and there were Mexican forces all around them.

"Tori," he rasped out when Maka carried him outside into the warm night air.

The big guy went to his knees on the lawn, eased Brock off him onto his back on the grass and peered down at him in concern. "What's that, Cap?"

No, not Tori. They didn't know her as Tori. "Vict-to-ria."

Maka shook his head, wrapped the thermal blanket more tightly around him. "You'll see her soon enough." Brock wanted to ask what he meant but Maka was already looking back at the house. "Khan! Get your ass over here."

"Nieto," Brock managed. "Was here earlier."

"I'll inform Taggart."

The team medic came running over, knelt beside Brock. "Hey, Cap. Let's take a look at you." Khan unwrapped the thin thermal blanket and started checking him over.

Fire. Fire burning in his shoulders, wrists and ribs. Everything else was icy cold. His teammates gathered around him, all trying to help.

"Gimme some room, dammit," Khan snapped, and everyone else backed off.

Brock closed his eyes, let himself drift until Khan tried to move his right arm. Brock let out a snarl and tried to curl in on himself but his muscles wouldn't cooperate.

"Damn, Khan, stop moving him," Lockhart said.

"Will in a sec." The medic continued to check him over. "They've got an ambulance coming for you, Cap.

I'm gonna get an IV started, get some fluids into you and then—"

A sharp whistle cut through the air.

Brock rolled his head to the side, managed to focus on Taggart as their commander rushed out of the house. He was dressed in tac gear and carrying a rifle.

"We got a situation going down a few houses north up the beach," he said, pointing behind him. "Nieto's trying to make a run for it with Oceane. Mexican SF wants us to help stop him, so we've gotta haul ass."

Chapter Nineteen

Oceane's heart was in her throat as she fought to break free of David's grip. His fingers were like steel as he dragged her down a staircase hidden beneath the butler pantry floor.

"You can't do this," she cried, twisting and pulling. "David, *stop*."

"Can't," he replied, his stride never slowing. As though her attempts to break free were no more bothersome to him than a mosquito buzzing around his head.

Panic knifed through her. Nieto had her now. Everything was in chaos. He may not hurt her, but neither would he let her go. And she had no idea where her rescue was, or if the team even knew her location now.

A light appeared from somewhere up ahead along the corridor. The radio on David's hip squawked.

"I'm bringing the boat up now," a man said.

Boat? "Where are you taking me?" she demanded. God, she needed to stall. Find a way to delay their departure long enough to give the team coming for her time to get here.

What if there is no team coming for you?

Terror slithered in her belly, cold and oily. "David. Tell me, dammit!"

"To somewhere safe," he said, hurrying along the tunnel.

They seemed to be moving downward, the angle increasing as they went. There was no breaking his grip. Even when she stumbled and went limp, becoming a dead weight in a desperate attempt to get him to drop her, his fingers remained locked around her arms.

Finally, they reached the source of the light. A small safe room stood off to one side, its thick steel door open. Nieto appeared in the doorway and her stomach lurched.

His expression was icy cold as he stared at her, a pistol in hand. For one fleeting instant, she was afraid he would shoot her. "How long do we have until they come for you?" he demanded.

She swallowed, debated her answer for a moment before responding. He knew she had been with the authorities. No point denying it now. "I don't know." She didn't dare add that they might not know where she was. If he was worried about cops arriving, maybe he would just leave on his own, without her.

He shook his head, his jaw tight. "You don't know what you've done."

"What *I've* done?"

He glanced toward the end of the tunnel where another steel door stood between them and whatever was on the other side. "It doesn't matter now. It won't change anything." He checked his watch, looked at David. "Let's go."

David began to pull her forward once more, and a fresh shot of alarm sliced through her. "You can't just kidnap me!"

"You're my daughter," Nieto called back to her, marching ahead of them toward the steel door. "I'll do whatever it takes to keep you safe."

"Then let me go," she begged, too afraid to keep the fear at bay any longer. "That's the only way you can keep me safe now."

He whirled on her, his eyes blazing in the eerie overhead lighting. "Never."

Her heart sank along with her stomach. She didn't know this man. Had never known him at all.

He paused at the door, checked his phone. After a moment he looked back at David. "They're here. You ready?"

"Ready."

Her father hit a switch, plunging them all into darkness. Then he opened the steel door.

Oceane stopped struggling for a moment, peering out into the night. The rush of the surf against the beach reached her ears, the salty smell of it filling her nose. And above the sound of the waves, the distinct roar of a powerful boat engine racing toward them.

A speed boat. Probably like the one she'd been on before with Nieto. Small and fast enough to get them offshore without being detected. Able to slip past the Coast Guard and out to sea before anyone could catch them.

Distress pulsed through her, along with a renewed resolve to fight. She twisted in David's grip, kicked at his shins as he held her prisoner. "No, you can't do this." She was beyond the ability to try and argue her way out of this, the words bursting from her, flinging them at Nieto like bullets. "I don't want this. I don't want any of this. This is *your* life, not mine. You've already taken everything from me—*everything*. I won't let you take my future too."

It might have been her imagination, but she thought David's body went rigid, his grip easing slightly. She twisted her face up to peer up at him, faint moonlight illuminating his features. She wasn't too proud to beg. Not if it freed her.

"David. Please, I'm begging you. I've known you forever and you always looked out for me. You know about what happened to me when Ruiz's men attacked our house. How my mother died because of Montoya. I watched her die. I don't want to be part of that life anymore. Please, don't do this."

His grip eased even more. She could feel him hesitating. Battling with himself. Knew instinctively that appealing to him was her only shot at freedom.

"David," Nieto warned, taking a menacing step toward them. "Get moving. *Now.*"

But David didn't move. "At least listen to her."

"I don't have fucking time to listen. *Move.*"

"She's right. If you really want her safe, if you really love her like you say, you'll do as she says and leave her here. You know it's the only way to ensure she makes it out of here alive."

Oceane gasped and stood frozen, heart knocking in her throat, hardly able to believe what she had just heard. Her eyes pinged back and forth between Nieto and David, waiting to see what would happen next.

Nieto stared at him for a moment in stunned silence. She saw the exact moment he snapped, his face contorting with rage. "God dammit," he snarled, and lunged toward her.

She shrank away, a cry locked in her throat but David shoved her to one side. Out of the way.

She stumbled and hit the corrugated metal wall with a thud, fell to her knees. When she scrambled up, pushing the hair from her face, her heart stuttered at the sight before her.

David and Nieto were facing off, fifty feet apart, each of them holding a pistol on the other.

Nieto's hand never wavered. "David, put it down."

"Let her go. We leave her right here in the tunnel and run for the boat. We'll make it out. But we leave her *here*."

"Fuck you." Nieto raised the weapon.

They fired simultaneously.

Gunshots exploded, the sound amplified by the tunnel. Oceane screamed, her hands flying to her ears as she stared in horror. They were both down. She took an automatic step toward David. He had saved her. She had to try to help him.

But when she got up close, she saw it was too late. The bullet had pierced his heart. His chest wasn't moving. His eyes were already vacant, staring up at nothing.

Nieto groaned from up the beach, cursing as he rolled to his side on the sand. "Oceane," he gasped. "Come. Now." He struggled to his feet, began lurching down the beach.

David was dead. She had to run.

She stood and whirled away, ready to race back up the tunnel. Escape Nieto and this whole nightmarish situation. But she hesitated, looking back the way she had come. What if there were more armed men at the other end of the tunnel?

"Oceane," Nieto called back, his voice desperate. Rough. "Please. Don't go."

The plea turned the sand into glue beneath her feet, immobilizing her.

"Don't leave me…" This time it was weaker, the words edged with a pain that sliced through her like a blade.

She made the mistake of turning around.

The sight of him sliced through her heart like a razor blade, blindsiding her. Blood covered his shirt. Spilled out from beneath his hand. The pain on his face was horrifying.

Something inside her refused to turn and run. Something too deep for her to understand that kept her there, staring at him.

He made it another four strides before falling to the sand. His head turned, his gaze seeking and locking onto her. "Oceane…"

Her heart broke at the despair on his face. She couldn't leave him to die. Not like this.

Cursing, she broke from the tunnel, running toward him without conscious thought, dimly aware of distant shouts coming from behind her down the length of the tunnel. Her feet flew over the sand as she raced to the figure lying on the beach.

Sand sprayed up around them as she slid to her knees beside him, reached for his shoulder. "Father." She didn't know where the word came from, or the tears thickening her throat, making it hard to breathe. She just knew she wouldn't be able to live with herself if she left him like this.

He groaned, reached up a shaking hand to grip hers. "Oceane, listen…"

She helped him roll to his back, gasped. In the pale moonlight his whole chest glistened black, the scent of blood cloying and metallic on the warm breeze.

"I'm sorry," he wheezed, one trembling hand reaching for hers. Clutching tight.

"Shh," she said, shock washing over her at the amount of blood pouring from his chest, her emotions conflicted. Confusing. Even after everything he'd done, he was still the man who had once read her bedtime stories and treated her like his cherished princess. And right now, he was slowly bleeding to death in front of her.

Not knowing what else to do, she dragged his head and shoulders into her lap, put her hands on his chest and pressed down. She couldn't leave him to bleed to death all alone. The part of her that remembered him as a warm, loving father when she was young kept her there trying to help him, while the other part that knew he was a monster told her to run.

If he lived, he would go to prison. She wanted both of those things.

"I never meant to…" He choked, convulsed in her arms.

"Don't talk. Just be still. Help is coming." She swiveled around, searching desperately along the beach for someone to help them. Had someone been running down the tunnel toward her or not?

"Only wanted to protect you," he moaned, his grip on her hand frantic, bringing her focus back to him. "When I couldn't anymore… Had to get you back… Any way I could."

"I know. I know," she soothed, not knowing what else to say. Much as she hated him, he was still her father. She would not leave him here to die on the beach. It wasn't how she was wired. Not even with everything he'd done. "Be still, now. We have to get this bleeding stopped."

"No. Too…late," he rasped out.

She squeezed his hand. "It's not." She thought she saw shadows moving along the bluff. Could anyone see them? "Help!" she called out. "Someone help us!"

He tugged on her hand. She glanced down into his face. "*El Escorpion*," he managed, and turned his head to spit out a mouthful of blood. "Know…who."

She stilled, her heart thudding as his words penetrated the fog of panic swirling in her brain. "You know who he is?"

His lips moved, his eyes glazed with pain and a despair that sent a shiver ripping down her spine. "Ins…surance. F-for you."

He was going to tell her the name so she had leverage to use to protect herself with if need be. Because he knew he was dying.

Tears clogged her throat. He was such a complex, confusing man. Making her hate him one moment, and acting like the protective father she remembered the next. Damn him.

Shoving all that aside, she leaned her head closer to his mouth. The name was critical in helping bring down the *Veneno* cartel. "Who is *el Escorpion*?"

"D-Diaz," he gasped, his body writhing in the sand. Trying to escape the pain while his blood coated his torso, coating her hands, her lap as it seeped into the sand beneath them.

"Diaz," she repeated.

"F-Fernando…Pa…Pascal…"

Fernando Pascal Diaz. The head. The man behind this whole evil empire. The man ultimately responsible for all the terror and devastation she and her family had suffered.

Her father groaned and went slack in her arms.

No. She shook him once. "No. No, you stay with me," she ordered sharply, her voice cracking as a tear landed on his face. *You can't leave me too.*

"I…love you," he whispered, his body growing heavier on her lap. "Always h-have." He took a horrible, rasping breath, choked. "Please… For…give me…"

She couldn't answer for a moment, her throat was too tight, too many conflicting emotions tearing her apart inside. "Shush," she ordered at last. "Don't talk anymore."

His eyes slid shut. His body went slack.

"Dammit, *no*!" She bent over him, cradling his upper body, commanding him to hang on.

Then a sound registered through the torrent of emotion crashing over her. Someone was yelling her name from behind her down the beach.

GABE'S HEART LURCHED to a halt when his gaze landed on the bodies crumpled up on the beach.

Oceane.

All he could see was her bent over someone. A man. The front of her light-colored shirt was covered in black.

Blood.

"Oceane!" His boots thudded on the sand as he raced for her. God, if she'd been shot—

She looked up, locked devastated eyes on him. "Gabe," she cried out, the pain in her face crushing his chest. Nieto. She was cradling her father.

He skidded to his knees beside her, took her face in his hands, scanning her for injury. She was his number one priority. "Are you hurt?" he asked, his voice urgent.

"David. Nieto shot him," she whispered brokenly, and turned back to bend over her father. "He's unconscious."

Gabe pulled her upright by the shoulders, forced her to look at him. "Oceane. Are you *hurt*?"

Tears flooded her eyes as she looked up at him. Then she shook her head.

His heart eased a few inches down his esophagus and he relaxed his grip. "Okay. Let me see him."

She shifted out from underneath her father, still cradling his head and shoulders in her lap. Gabe set two fingers beneath the edge of Nieto's jaw. He waited, detected a faint pulse.

"I need more room," he told Oceane. She scrambled out of the way, gently laying her father's head on the sand and hovering next to him.

Gabe leaned over and ripped the halves of Nieto's blood-saturated dress shirt off him. Two bullets had penetrated the center of his chest. Given the position of the wounds and the amount of blood he'd lost, Nieto's wasn't going to live longer than another few minutes, if that long.

"Please. Do something," Oceane begged. "I know who he is and what he's done. But I don't want him to die like this."

He would have left the bastard to die, but there was no way he could ignore that plea. Gabe placed his hands over

Nieto's chest and pressed down hard in an effort to stem the bleeding, at the same time looking over his shoulder. Men were rushing toward them. Including Khan.

"Need you over here," Gabe shouted to him.

Khan ran up, tossed his med kit on the sand at Gabe's feet and knelt down to do a quick assessment. Two seconds later he glanced up and gave Gabe a telling look.

"I know," Gabe murmured. "Just do what you can." Maybe Nieto would pull off a miracle and survive long enough to make it into surgery. Then he could live through a trial in the U.S. and die at the end of his life sentence instead of here on this beach.

Khan started working, talking on the radio as he did, calling for emergency medical transport.

Gabe moved back, edged around to hunker down next to Oceane. He wanted to haul her into his arms so badly but she was totally focused on her father so he wrapped an arm tight around her shoulders in a silent show of support and tucked her close into his body.

She stared at Khan's hands as the medic worked, her face pale, seemed to be holding her breath.

He hated that he couldn't shield her from this and the coming pain. Christ. Wasn't it bad enough that she'd watched her mother bleed out in front of her months ago? It was too fucking cruel that she had to watch her father do the same, even with their bad history. She was clearly distraught and desperate for him to make it.

Less than a minute later Khan stopped trying to get an IV into Nieto's arm, pulled his fingers from the man's pulse and immediately started chest compressions.

Oceane made a choked sound. She seemed to steel herself, then reached for Nieto's hand. "I'm here," she told him in Spanish. "You're not alone."

It was heart-wrenching to watch. Gabe slid an arm around her waist and drew her back, making room for the paramedics who had just arrived.

She resisted for a moment then stopped, her body rigid as he eased her to her feet and drew her a short distance away. He coiled one arm around her and reached his free hand up to cradle the back of her head, pulling her cheek to his chest. Her hands clutched at the front of his tactical shirt, fine, rapid tremors wracking her. "Did he hurt you?"

"N-no."

The medics paddled Nieto three times before calling it.

Oceane made a low, devastated sound and buried her face in Gabe's chest. He closed his eyes, tightened his hold on her. "I'm sorry," he whispered against her temple. It was such a pathetic thing to say at a time like this, but it was all he had.

She started to shake harder. "I can't," she quavered. "I c-can't take this. Please."

Fuck. Making a snap decision he bent his knees, scooped her up and started carrying her down the beach as fast as he could.

By the time he reached the staircase that led up the slope, she was crying on his shoulder. Part of him was glad that she was able to release at least a little of her grief. She felt so damn good in his arms, he just wished he was carrying her under totally different circumstances.

Up on the lawn he stopped in a secluded spot of the garden where a screen of shrubs and trees shielded them from view of all the people crowding the yard. He would take her to the Mexican feds who were leading the task-force in a minute, but not until she was calmer.

Sinking to his knees on the grass, he shifted her onto his lap and tucked her in close, resting his chin on the top of her curls. And just held her. Giving her a safe place to hide while the shock and adrenaline tore through her body. Giving her the only comfort he could.

Finally, she calmed a little, her shoulders hitching with her jagged breaths. He eased his grip but kept her close, rubbed a hand up and down her spine.

With a heartbroken little sigh that twisted his insides, she went limp against him. The scent of blood swirled strong in the air. He wanted to take care of her, clean her up and stay with her.

"Sweetheart, look at me," he murmured.

Her hands stayed locked in his shirt. She drew an unsteady breath and lifted her head from his shoulder to look up at him with puffy eyes.

Gabe slid the hand in her hair down to cup her cheek. Her skin was warm, like velvet as he swept his thumb across it, wiping the tear track away.

"I didn't want him to die," she whispered. "I thought I hated him, but… I wanted him to go to prison, not die that way."

Ah, sweetheart.

"They're all gone." Her tone was wooden, empty. "My family's all gone."

You've got me.

He wanted to say it so bad he had to choke the words back. Because he couldn't say them. It would cruel to give her false hope that anything between them could last when she was in WITSEC.

But staring down into those pain-filled, red-rimmed eyes, Gabe couldn't take it.

He tipped her face upward, caught the slight flare of surprise in her eyes and the hitch in her breathing as he brushed his lips over hers. Once. Twice.

Her hands released his shirt to curl over his shoulders and she leaned up to press her mouth to his. Gabe swallowed a groan and slid his fingers into her curls, squeezing gently instead of gripping tight and crushing his mouth to hers as he wanted. He couldn't help but skim his tongue along the seam of her lips, steal inside to touch hers, caress lightly when she parted for him.

Before things got out of hand, he lifted his head, flexed his fingers in her hair. The curls wrapped around his fingers, clinging as though they didn't want to let go. He felt exactly the same way.

Oceane stared up at him, the shock and pain momentarily gone from her face, a slight flush on her pale cheeks visible in the moonlight. "Oh…"

Yeah, oh.

What the hell he was going to do about this, he didn't know. But that was something for him to worry about later. "I've got to take you to talk with the head of the taskforce," he told her, wishing they had more time. He would love to be able to take her away from here.

To some fancy hotel where he could strip those bloody clothes off her, carry her into the shower and clean her. Dry her off, then carry her to bed and hold her in the darkness. Be there when the pain came back to attack her in the middle of the night.

Because it would. And it would keep attacking her for weeks and months yet.

She sagged, closed her eyes. "I can't."

It sucked that they wouldn't give her time to decompress, but with a case this important there was no time to lose. "I'll stay with you."

Her eyes opened and she stared up into his face. "Thank you."

She didn't have to thank him for that. "Come on." He slid her off his lap, wrapped a steadying arm around her waist and stood, pulling her with him.

"Did you get Brock out?"

His heart squeezed that she would think of Cap at a time like this. "Yeah. We got him out."

"And he's alive?"

"Yeah."

She exhaled, sagged against him. "Thank God." She looked into his eyes. "Will he be all right?"

"Not sure. Khan was checking him over when we found out what was going on with you. I dropped everything and ran."

She stayed pressed to his side as they emerged from their hiding spot. "Where is Victoria? Does she know Brock's been rescued?"

"Not sure. I'll make sure she knows."

A group of agents spotted them. One of them waved at someone behind him and rushed toward them.

"Two good things came out of this mess," she said as they kept walking.

He glanced down at her in surprise.

Her face was set. "You rescued Brock. And I know who *el Escorpion* is."

Chapter Twenty

Brock surfaced from the blackness when a nurse came into his room to hook up another bag of fluid to his IV drip. He pried his left eye open, could barely see through the slit between his lids, the right one swollen shut.

He felt like he'd been hit by a fucking truck.

The last thing he remembered was Khan working on him, then Taggart saying Oceane was in trouble. Everything after that was a blur. His entire team had raced off to help her, leaving him with paramedics. He'd faded in and out on the way to the hospital.

The nurse smiled at him, the first rays of dawn coming through the window behind her. "How is your pain?" she asked him in accented English.

"Okay." It sucked, actually.

On a scale of one to ten, he was at a nine-point-eight. All the jostling around and examinations by the medical staff seemed to have aggravated everything. He'd still been hypothermic when they'd put him in the ambulance. Bringing up his core temp had been their first priority.

They'd given him warmed IV fluids, wrapped him in layers of blankets until he'd probably resembled a mummy.

It had been hours since his team had rescued him. He hadn't heard anything since. Had no idea whether Oceane was okay or whether the Mexicans had managed to take Nieto into custody. And of course, he'd been thinking a lot about Tori. About what she meant to him, and what he was prepared to do to be with her.

He had a lot of thinking to do about what he truly wanted going forward. Almost dying had a way of making things so clear. All he knew was, he had to find her. Had to figure out a way to make it work between them. He needed her.

He bit back a growl as he shifted on the bed. His body was a mass of bruises. His wrists were bandaged up and they'd immobilized his right shoulder after reducing the dislocation. They'd taken x-rays of his face, arms and ribs. Nothing was actually broken except his nose, but he had a lot of soft tissue damage and there were two hairline fractures on the right side of his ribcage.

But at least he was still breathing. For a while there he hadn't been sure he would make it.

"The doctor said a plastic surgeon will be in soon to stitch your face," the nurse told him, gently tucking the blanket around his shoulders, careful not to jostle him.

"Okay." The Emerg doc had closed the gash with adhesive strips in the meantime.

"Do you need anything? Something to eat?"

"No. Thanks." He just wanted to know what the hell was going on with his team and the op.

The plastic surgeon arrived a few minutes later. He injected freezing into Brock's face and began the task of stitching up the skin that had split over his nose and beneath his eye. Brock couldn't feel the curved needle going in and out, but he could feel the tug of the sutures as they pulled through his skin.

He closed his eye, focused on taking slow, shallow breaths to spare his ribs, and thought about what he'd just survived. That had definitely sucked way harder than SERE school, and he'd fucking hated SERE school.

A knock sounded on the door. Brock cracked his left eye open as Taggart walked in.

"Making you all pretty again, I see," his commander said with a slight smile as he approached the bed.

"What happened?" Brock demanded. "Did you get Nieto? Is Oceane safe?"

"Can you not talk?" the surgeon asked, intent on his work. "I need you to keep your face perfectly still."

Taggart walked around to the side of the bed opposite from the surgeon and gripped the side rails. "Nieto's dead. And yes, she's safe."

Good. Bastard. "Who got him?" He barely moved his lips as he spoke, keeping his face as still as possible for the surgeon.

"His bodyguard."

"Seriously?"

Taggart nodded. "He and the bodyguard apparently got into an argument about Oceane. Nieto wanted to take her and the bodyguard wouldn't let him. They shot each other."

"In front of her?"

"Yes."

Ah, shit, the poor thing had been through hell. "She all right?"

"She's holding up as well as can be expected." Taggart's pale turquoise eyes swept over him, coming back to his face to watch the surgeon put the last few stitches in.

The doctor cut the last suture and sat back to study his work. "You won't look like new when it's healed, but the scars shouldn't be too noticeable."

"Thank you," Brock said.

"You're welcome. Rest if you can."

Taggart straightened and crossed his arms as the doctor left. "How you feeling?"

"Fantastic."

One side of that hard mouth lifted. "You gave us all one hell of a scare, Cap. Pull a stunt like that again, I'll kick your ass."

Brock snorted out a laugh, winced as it pulled his ribs. "Don't make me laugh."

"Roger that. I'll make sure no one lets Maka or Granger in here."

"Good idea."

"What's the prognosis, any idea yet?"

"Mostly just soft tissue damage. They put my shoulder back into joint. Not sure yet if I'll need surgery. I haven't talked to an orthopedic surgeon yet, so I don't know what kind of recovery I'm looking at." He just prayed this wasn't a potentially career-ending injury.

"Don't worry about all that right now. We're all just glad you're still with us."

"Me too."

"I know you're supposed to be getting some sleep, but I brought someone I thought you might want to see. You up for another visitor?"

Brock focused on him, wondering if maybe Taggart had called his parents. He could just picture his mom out there, wearing a hole in the hallway floor outside his room right now. "Who?"

"Hang on a sec." Smiling to himself, Taggart got up and headed for the door. "I'll be right outside if you need me."

The door slid shut behind him, then opened a moment later, and his heart did a crazy cartwheel at the sight of Tori stepping into his room. "Hey," she said softly, a wobbly smile on her face as she rushed over to him.

For a moment it felt like his chest might explode. Emotion closed off his windpipe, making it impossible to breathe, let alone speak. "What are you doing here?" he finally asked, overwhelmed as she bent and kissed his forehead, then brushed her lips over his.

She scanned his face with worried brown eyes. "I threw a tantrum, basically. Yelled and swore at people in both English and Spanish. Refused to cooperate or be reasonable until someone brought me here to see you. Taggart finally took pity on me."

His throat thickened. God, he loved her. But he still wouldn't say it. It would only hurt her more when she had to leave this time. That was the only thing holding him back. "I want to hug you so bad but I can't move my arms."

She sank into the chair the plastic surgeon had used and cupped the side of his face gently, running her tear-drenched gaze over him. "God, look what they did to you."

Yeah, it wasn't pretty. "There goes my modeling career," he said dryly.

She gave a watery laugh. "No. You'll still be as heart-stoppingly gorgeous as ever when you heal up."

Not even close, but he didn't care because he was alive and she was here. "You're biased."

"Maybe." She stroked his hair. "I saw the video they sent. I think I died a little." Her voice wobbled and his heart squeezed.

"I'm sorry you had to see that."

She nodded. "You heard about Nieto?"

"And Oceane."

"Did you also hear he told her who *el Escorpion* was?"

No way. "Really?"

"Yes. They're planning a sting to catch him right now." She gave him a little smile. "So it's almost over. And I've bought myself a couple of days to stay with you until they transfer you back home."

"Yeah?"

"Yeah. And the best part—I get to be your personal nurse as long as you're in here."

"Hope I'm here a long time then." He grinned, feeling no pain in his face as his numb skin pulled with the movement. "Do you give sponge baths?"

Her eyes twinkled. "For you, yes."

"I can't wait." He wouldn't think about her leaving yet. It hurt way worse than the damage done to his body. He couldn't stop looking at her. What would she say if he broached the idea of him going with her when she left D.C.? Would she even consider it?

"Good." She sighed, ran her fingertips down the unfrozen side of his face. "Get some sleep. It's over and you're safe now. I'll stay right here beside you, like you did for me the night we met."

He appreciated that, but this wasn't even close to over. Not with Montoya and *el Escorpion* still on the loose.

****

Fernando's hand froze when he heard the noise, the forkful of beans inches from his mouth. He swung his head around to stare at the back door, listened intently.

Rapid footsteps. Someone running toward them.

He shot to his feet, grabbed the pistol lying on the table and aimed it at the door. It flew open, revealing the young boy he had paid yesterday to act as a lookout. "*Señor*, they are coming," he blurted, his eyes wide and frightened.

Cold ripped down his spine. *They're here.* But how?

"Run," his bodyguard said, shoving from his chair, their breakfast barely touched on the table as he reached for his rifle. "I'll meet you at the car."

A spurt of panic flashed through Fernando as he raced out the back door of the small house they had stayed the night in. The sidewalk out back was all but deserted, the first rays of daylight spilling around the buildings and onto the street of the quiet village.

"Diaz! Stop and put your hands up!" someone shouted behind him. Pounding feet thudded on the concrete.

He threw a glance over his shoulder, a wave of terror flooding him when he saw the uniformed men moving along the alleyway. They wore military fatigues and black balaclavas to hide their faces, carried assault rifles.

Mexican Special Forces. How the *hell* had they found him?

He put his head down and ran, focused on executing the escape plan he and his bodyguard had gone over last night, just in case. Part of him had known this day was coming. It was why he had left his family and set out on his own a few days ago. He just hadn't expected it to happen so soon.

His feet flew across the pavement. He couldn't surrender. They would just use him to get to his family.

Saying goodbye to them the other night when he'd tucked them into bed was the hardest thing he had ever done. The children were too young to realize what was happening. What his words had meant. But he had known. And so had his wife and mother.

Gunfire erupted behind him. Fernando risked a glance back to see his bodyguard standing at the corner of a building, firing at the approaching men. Buying him a precious window of time to escape with.

Fernando jumped into the waiting vehicle, fired it up and screeched away from the curb. A military vehicle veered out onto the street ahead of him and stopped, blocking his way.

He slammed on the brakes, threw it into reverse, turned to brace one arm across the back of his seat as he sped backward, wrenching the wheel to one side to make the turn. The vehicle skidded around, jerked as he put it in drive and hit the gas. Gravel sprayed from beneath the tires as he sped back the other way.

His bodyguard lay dead on the sidewalk, sprawled on his back.

Fernando whipped past him, desperation pushing him to go faster. Figure out how to escape.

More vehicles shot out ahead of him. He hit the brake again, his body jerking against the seatbelt. His gaze darted up to the rearview mirror. The vehicles behind him were closing in now.

He was trapped, the alleyways between the houses too narrow for his car. And he would never make it out of here on foot.

He pursed his lips. He would have to ram through them. It was the only option he had left.

Gripping the wheel tight he stomped down on the accelerator. The car shot forward, picking up speed as it hurtled toward the stopped vehicles ahead. It was going to be one hell of a crash, but he had to try. If he could just get through he could escape to a neighboring village, pay someone to get him to safety.

Men jumped out of the vehicles, raised their weapons.

Fernando sucked in a breath and braced himself, ducking down low in the seat.

Shots rang out, slamming into the hood like hail in a storm. They smashed the bullet-resistant windshield, blinding him. They kept coming, like angry bees, too fast for him to count.

The engine screamed as he raced toward the vehicles.

But the windshield finally gave way.

Bullets pierced the glass. He gasped as fire burned in his chest, the pain staggering. His hands dropped from the wheel. The vehicle skidded sideways. Crashed into something.

Stunned, blinded by pain and the blood on his face, he fumbled with the door handle, managed to shove it open.

He fell out of the vehicle, tried to drag himself along the sidewalk.

To his right he caught a flash of movement. An elderly woman stood frozen in her doorway, her eyes wide with horror.

"Help me," he begged, trying to drag himself toward her. They were coming for him. He needed to get inside. Hide.

She whirled away and slammed the door in his face.

Fernando groaned and pulled himself up onto the curb, his energy already fading. The burn from the bullet wounds was agonizing, far worse than he had imagined. It stole his breath, made his vision blur. The scent of his own blood filled his nostrils, making his stomach lurch.

Running footsteps echoed in his ears.

He was half-sprawled on the pavement, his arms struggling to bear his weight. Unable to summon the strength to go an inch farther. It was getting harder and harder to breathe now, his heart racing. Too fast.

Everything was happening too fast.

Rough hands grabbed him from behind. Shoved him flat on his stomach and wrenched his arms behind him. Someone flipped him over onto his back. He fought to breathe, stared up at the shadowy shapes converging around him. Blocking out the light.

One man crouched next to him, triumph in his dark eyes. He said something that Fernando didn't catch.

Everything was fading now. His vision blurred, grew dark. The pain began to fade. He barely felt them poking and prodding as they tried to keep him alive.

It was better this way. Better for his family if he died.

A searing bolt of grief speared through him as he thought of his children. Of the empire they would inherit one day.

His body went limp. His eyes bulging as his lungs stopped working. But his mind kept going for a few seconds.

Enough time for him to be grateful that at least the cartel wouldn't die with him. Because contrary to what people thought, he wasn't the head.

No. So even as he lay dying on the sidewalk in this tiny, remote village, *el Escorpion* was still very much alive.

Chapter Twenty-One

S eated next to Brock's hospital bed, Victoria curled her fingers around his, her heart aching at what he'd been through. She wished she could make all of this go away, heal him with her touch, but of course that was impossible.

Right now, he was out cold from whatever medication they'd put into his IV an hour ago and she was glad he was getting some sleep and no longer in pain. His body needed the reprieve. He was a mess.

Both his eyes were completely swollen shut now, the lids shiny and deep purple. The jagged scar across his nose and upper cheek looked sore as hell with all the stitches holding his skin together.

His whole chest and ribs were a mass of welts and bruises. She hadn't seen his wrists without the bandages, but she already knew what they would look like because hers had been the same. It would take weeks for him to heal, even if it turned out he didn't need surgery for his shoulder.

At least the evil son of a bitch responsible for the

damage was dead. Well, him and Nieto. It wouldn't make Brock heal any faster, but it would help him mentally moving forward. He was strong. She wasn't worried about him recovering from this, she just wished she could be there for him while he did.

He still had some dried blood on his face and chest. She hated seeing it on his skin.

She got a warm washcloth and a towel from the washroom and came back to him. This was stolen time they shouldn't have had together. She wanted to milk every second of it for all it was worth.

Careful not to wake him, she started on his face, gently washing the blood from his cheeks and chin. Down his throat where his pulse beat slow and steady.

When she reached his chest, he stirred. She froze, the washcloth poised an inch above his skin. He turned his head toward her slightly, his left eye opening a millimeter or two. "Sponge bath time?" he rasped out, his voice hopeful.

She laughed softly. "Only if you behave. Sorry I woke you."

"No. I wouldn't want to sleep through this."

With a wry grin she resumed cleaning him, using light pressure over his bruises. "I wish I could kiss each of these better."

"I'm down with that. Couldn't hurt to try."

She bent and touched her lips to the welt at the top of his left pec, then raised her head to look at him. "How's that. Any better?"

He pursed his lips, his brow furrowing. "Not sure. Do it again."

She did. Twice. And added a few kisses to a neighboring welt for good measure. She looked up. "Well?"

"Think it's working. Keep going."

Smiling now, she did, working her way across his chest with light kisses as she washed the rest of the blood away. "There." Easing up, she pressed her lips to his and sat back. "How do you feel?" she asked, serious this time.

"I'm okay."

It broke her heart how strong he was. "Are the pain meds still working?"

"Not really."

"Your ribs bothering you the most?"

"And my right shoulder. Freezing's starting to wear off on my face, too." He wiggled his nose around.

"Stop that."

"It's itchy."

"Where?"

"The tip."

She carefully scratched it.

"Oh, yeah, that's good," he groaned. "And the left side of my neck, too."

She scratched that one too. "You're high maintenance."

He laughed, then winced. "Nope. No laughing."

"Sorry." She smoothed his hair back from his forehead, used the cloth on a streak of dried blood there. "I'll wash your hair later. You hungry now? Thirsty?"

"Yeah, both."

He couldn't use his right arm and shouldn't be moving the left one either until the orthopedic surgeon had checked everything over. "Hang on." She grabbed the cup of water from the little stand beside the bed, angled the straw into his mouth. "Your options for breakfast are some cut up fruit, scrambled eggs, and a piece of toast. What do you feel like?"

"All of it."

She forked up some fruit. "Here's some pineapple."

His mouth stretched into a grin as he chewed. "I could get used to this. You hand feeding me while I lie in bed."

"I'll bet you could." And so could she. She loved being able to take care of him when he needed her.

But it wasn't going to last. They weren't meant to be.

Her heart lurched. Threatened to turn to ash in her chest.

She fed him his breakfast until it was gone, then gave him more water to finish. When she turned back he was wiggling the outstretched fingers of his left hand toward her. She took his hand, lowered it to the bed so he wouldn't move his wrist. She remembered how much hers had hurt.

"How long do we have left?" he asked.

The ache in her heart intensified. "Not sure. I'm kind of on borrowed time here. They want to get me back to D.C."

"Yeah." He squeezed her hand. "I'm real glad you were here, though."

Everything they hadn't said to each other swirled in the air between them. Making her pulse pound in desperation. "Me too."

Before she could say anything else, a light tap on the door made her twist around. Commander Taggart stepped inside. "How's our boy doing?"

"He ate some breakfast."

"That's good." He strode over to the other side of the bed, gripped the railing as he peered down at Brock. "Rest of the boys are all down in the waiting room. I told them no visitors until after you got some sleep. And I told Maka and Granger they're banned until further notice."

One side of Brock's mouth kicked up. "Bet they didn't like that."

"Nope. Now they're both pouting." He put his hands in his pockets. "So. Something big just happened."

Victoria turned her full attention to him. "What?"

"Mexican SF got *el Escorpion*. He's dead."

The news was such a shock Victoria could only stare

at him. Was it possible? "Who was it?"

"Guy named Fernando Diaz."

Her brow furrowed as she tried to place the name. She'd come across someone named Diaz rumored to be part of the cartel back when she had done her research for her second book. He hadn't seemed to be all that important in the chain of command she had uncovered, though. Was it the same man?

"That's good news," Brock said.

Taggart nodded. "And there's more. Sanchez was arrested too. He's already admitted to being one of Ruiz's, and now he's working for Montoya. He gave them a possible location on Montoya. Some codenamed location Ruiz used to use. If they can figure out the location, they're going after him tonight."

At his words, Victoria's pulse thudded. "What's the code name?"

Maybe it was the tension in her voice, but Taggart looked at her sharply. He considered her a moment, then answered. "Can't remember. Something about a rattlesnake in Spanish."

Rattlesnake? She stared at him, the word tweaking something in her memory. It was familiar. She remembered learning something important about it during her research for her second book. Something that related to a place. Dammit, why couldn't she remember?

"What is it?" Brock asked.

"My files. I need to access my files online." She turned to Taggart. "I need a laptop."

"I'll get one. Wait here."

She got up and paced as he left. She thought best on her feet.

"What's going on?" Brock asked.

"I recognize the rattlesnake bit." *Wait.* She stopped. "You read my second book. Do you remember it being in there?"

His expression brightened. "Yeah. Shit, it was only mentioned once, and kind of in passing." He frowned, thinking. "What did it say?"

She nodded and waved her hand in a circle in encouragement for him to keep pulling on that thread. "It's a place. The name of a place. Something in Spanish, right?"

"Yeah, I think so." He frowned. "Damn, what the hell was it again?"

She wracked her brain along with him. Snake head? Fangs? Venom? That was the literal translation for the *Veneno* cartel. Venom.

She made a sound of frustration, grabbed handfuls of her hair. "God, why can't I remember it?" Montoya might be headed there now. If she could remember what the hell it was called, maybe she could remember where it was and find it on the map. Give the team a location so they could get a jump on him.

She paced for another few minutes, then dropped into the chair beside Brock's bed. She took his hand, kept thinking, but the exact wording eluded her.

At last Taggart came back in, carrying a laptop. "This thing's pretty ancient," he told her, setting it up on the rolling table next to Brock's bed and plugging it in for her, "but they said it works and the connection's decent."

Victoria went right to work, going to the website where her files were stored. The network wasn't secure by any means, but she didn't care if anyone knew she was accessing her old files. All that mattered right now was finding Montoya before he melted away someplace.

It took her three tries to get the password right. Finally, she was in.

She clicked on the third file marked *Notes*, urgency thrumming through her. Taggart and Brock watched her every move as she scrolled through the documents stored in the file. Then she came to the one named *Locations*.

"Bingo," she murmured, and opened it. Her heart

beat faster and faster as she skimmed the contents, then skipped once.

There. There it was.

"*Cola de serpiente de cascabel*?" she said, looking up at Taggart for confirmation.

Surprise flashed in his aqua eyes. "Yeah, that sounds about right."

Holy shit. Her heart was pounding. This might mean the end of Montoya. "It means tail of the rattlesnake. It's named for a rock formation that looks like the rattles on a snake's tail."

His posture tensed, his expression intensifying. "Do you know where it is?"

"Yes. In the middle of Chihuahua. Here." She clicked on the link to a map she had included, pointed to the spot with her finger.

Taggart held up a finger and whipped out his phone. "Get us the best satellite images of Chihuahua you've got," he said to whomever he'd called. "I'm bringing Victoria Gomez into HQ right now. I think we might have a target location for Montoya."

****

So Nieto and *el Escorpion* were both dead.

Juan couldn't help but smile to himself as he drove the Jeep behind the rock formation and killed the engine. Shaped like the end of a rattlesnake's tail, it would hide him until he left in the morning. Ruiz had used this place in the past, bringing only his most trusted men here. Now that he was in prison, Juan was the only one to use it.

With all of his rivals either dead or behind bars, there was no one left to stand in his way. The remnants of the cartel would be in chaos. Using Ruiz's former network, he would step in and take control. Everyone would answer to him. He would kill anyone who challenged or posed a threat to him.

He was going to be fucking rich beyond his wildest dreams.

The sun was just about to set over the ridge to the west. He gazed around the vast emptiness surrounding him, taking a deep breath of the dry, hot air. The chirp of *chapulines* was the only sound in the quiet. Nobody around for miles.

He shifted the backpack on his shoulder as he walked toward the small wooden cabin. Inside he would have a hot meal, enjoy the bottle of whiskey he'd brought and the cigars Ruiz always stocked in all of his places, even out here. He dropped his bag inside, grabbed the shovel from beside the door and walked back out into the sunset.

Through a contact at the prison, Ruiz had worked his network to give Juan a map showing the location where he'd buried emergency cash reserves on the property. Enough money to buy whatever and whoever he needed to stay off grid while he planned his next move.

Reaching the approximate spot marked on the map he pulled from his pocket, he stabbed the blade of his shovel into the dry earth and jammed a foot down on it. In all, there was over twenty million U.S. dollars buried out here. It would go a long way in aiding him on the coming takeover.

Juan whistled to himself as he dug, not minding the physical work, more at ease than he had been in years. For the first time in forever, he had a whole night to himself in a place he could let his guard down and truly relax.

Tonight, he would celebrate all his victories. Tomorrow, he would begin taking what was his.

****

Montoya had no idea he wasn't alone out here. Or that he had just walked through the crosshairs of a sniper rifle.

Stretched out in supported prone position, high up on the ridge overlooking the small valley and the rock formation that marked the location of Ruiz's old hideout, Gabe tightened the focus on the sight of his weapon.

He and Colebrook were hidden behind a cluster of boulders camouflaged by clumps of sagebrush. Taggart was waiting a hundred yards down the slope behind them with the rest of the command staff, while the Mexican SF team moved into the valley on foot to take Montoya.

The goddamn evil and twisted excuse for a man who had betrayed Oceane, killed her mother, and almost killed Freeman's fiancée, Rowan. Gabe's orders were to provide recon and shoot Montoya if he tried to escape before the Mexican forces arrived. But Gabe was interpreting that last part loosely.

If he got a clear shot on Montoya *period*, the SF team's assault wouldn't be necessary.

Once again, Victoria had come through with an awesome piece of intel and they'd been able to make it here within hours of her showing them the location on a satellite map. Without her, Montoya might have slipped away and disappeared off the radar for good.

Lying prone beside Gabe, propped up on his elbows, Colebrook peered through his spotting scope. "He's moving. Five-hundred-twenty yards."

"Got him." Gabe adjusted his aim, tracked Montoya's movement through the high-powered scope. The cabin gave him just enough protection that Gabe didn't have a clear shot, only the back of Montoya's right arm and leg visible as he dug.

Gabe zeroed in on him and waited.

Waiting was his specialty. He could wait hours in this position without moving. Days, if necessary. This asshole had zero idea what was going on as he dug up what appeared to be a duffel full of what was no doubt cash, tossed it aside and moved a dozen paces to the right to dig again.

"Damn. How much cash you think they've got buried out here?" Colebrook murmured.

"Dunno." *Don't care.* One way or another, Montoya wasn't walking out of here tonight.

His target was currently more than five football field lengths away but Gabe had made shots at more than twice that distance. The angle was perfect. The air was dry and the wind light. All he needed was for Montoya to move a couple more steps to his right.

"SF team's in position at the south end of the valley," Colebrook murmured.

Gabe noted it but didn't respond, all his attention on the crosshairs of his rifle as he cradled the buttstock snug against his shoulder.

Montoya took a step to his right.

Gabe's breathing was slow and steady, his heart rate calm, finger curled around the trigger. He blocked out all thoughts of Oceane and his hatred for the piece of shit in his crosshairs, pretended this was just like every other target, even though it wasn't.

Montoya took another step to the right. He bent to adjust something on the shovel, then turned and began carrying one of the bags back toward the rock formation where he'd parked his vehicle. One might even argue he was about to make his escape.

It was goddamn perfect.

"Be advised, target is moving back toward vehicle," Colebrook said over their comms.

"Copy that," Taggart replied, then added, "He doesn't leave here."

Oh, he won't. Gabe remained locked on his unsuspecting target, mentally coaxing him along. *One more step. Just take one more step for me.*

Montoya did.

He straightened and turned slightly, unknowingly facing Gabe. Giving him a full center mass target.

Gabe adjusted his aim ever so slightly. Exhaled, letting the air out of his lungs. And then he squeezed the trigger.

The rifle's report echoed throughout the desolate landscape an instant before the bullet found its mark. Montoya jerked and collapsed to the ground as it tore through his body. Hitting him in the lower part of his thoracic spine rather than through the heart or lungs.

"Hit, lower center mass," Colebrook said.

Gabe paused only long enough to watch Montoya flop painfully to his belly and begin dragging himself across the ground toward cover, his paralyzed legs trailing behind him.

Colebrook immediately began issuing adjustments for another shot.

Gabe wouldn't be taking one.

Coming up on his knees, he began packing away the rifle, aware of Colebrook's stare on him.

"What are you doing?" his teammate finally asked.

"Leaving."

"But... You're not going to finish him off?"

"Can't."

"Can't?" He sounded confused.

"Weapon malfunctioned. Must have jammed or something." He took the scope off, tucked it into its case.

It took Colebrook a moment to catch on. "God, I *hate* it when that happens."

"Me too." Standing, he slung the rifle over his shoulder, pausing to look down into the valley below. At this distance Montoya was nothing but a tiny black insect inching across the ground.

A mortally wounded and paralyzed insect who wouldn't last much longer. Maybe ten minutes, tops. Barely enough time for the Mexicans to reach him.

But in those final few minutes while his heart continued beating, Montoya would suffer. And hopefully he was as terrified right now as his victims had been.

He wouldn't suffer as much as he deserved to, not after all the atrocities he'd committed, but shattering his spine and making him slowly bleed out before the Mexican SF team could move in was better than nothing.

It was the best Gabe could do.

He didn't say a word as he turned away and headed down the ridge to where Taggart and the others waited. Colebrook scrambled to catch up with him.

Gabe didn't care what consequences he would face for his actions, though he doubted they would be that bad. His conscience was clear.

The monster responsible for destroying Oceane's life was gone. That was all that mattered.

All he cared about was that he had just given the woman he'd fallen in love with the chance to find some peace now that Montoya had been given what he deserved.

Chapter Twenty-Two

"**Y**ou ready?"

Oceane glanced up into Gabe's face as they stood next to the SUV he'd borrowed from headquarters twenty minutes before. She reached for his hand, something catching in her chest when he immediately curled his fingers around hers in a solid grip. "Yes. Thank you for doing this."

Her father and *el Escorpion* were both gone, no longer threats to her. And a few hours ago, thanks to Victoria's keen insight, Montoya had been killed by Mexican forces. Or at least that was the story.

Oceane eyed Gabe. He had called her himself to tell her the news, on his way to the airport in Chihuahua. She had flown back here to Veracruz with most of his team, except for Taggart and Colebrook, who had been with him, and Brock, who had been sent back to D.C. on a transport. Victoria was with him but leaving D.C. in the morning. So Oceane had lost someone else today as well.

Gabe scanned the quiet cemetery. Still on guard even though the men hunting her were all gone. It was deserted at this hour, the moonlight transforming the sad and somber place into something totally magical. Palm trees swayed in the warm breeze, the heady scent of jasmine and gardenia perfuming the air.

This was the most beautiful cemetery in Veracruz. Oceane had come here many times with her mother to visit her grandparents' graves over the years.

Now she had come to say goodbye to her mother.

"It's just over here," Oceane told him, leading him toward the third row on the left.

The beautifully maintained grass was soft beneath the soles of her shoes. She felt as if she was in a dream as she walked toward the graves of her family. Her heart drummed in her ears, a sense of dread coiling inside her. She'd wanted to come here for months. Had hated not being able to be here to lay her mother to rest.

When the new white marble headstone came into view she faltered and let go of Gabe's hand. Her entire body was numb, the pain in her chest eclipsing everything as she stopped in front of the grave and saw her mother's name on the stone.

Anya Marie St. Fleur, beloved mother and friend.

Pain knifed through her. A white-hot blade slicing through her chest.

She made a choked sound and dropped to her knees in front of the stone, lifting a trembling hand to touch the letters engraved in the cold marble. She had thought she had done her grieving for her mother. But seeing this made it so final. Brought all those horrific memories back.

Her mother had deceived her for years, yet Oceane had long since forgiven her. She had loved her mother more than anyone in this world. The thought of going the rest of her life without ever seeing her mother again was too heavy a burden to carry.

Tears spilled down her face as the sobs wracked her. Everything hit her at once. All the fear. The violence. The loss. And somehow, she had to find the strength to move past it, figure out a way to go on and live her life.

But not here in Veracruz, or even in Mexico. There were too many painful memories here. She needed to start over somewhere else. Wished it could be in the U.S.

Warmth registered through the haze of pain. She slowly became aware that Gabe was hunkered down behind her, both his arms wrapped around her. Supporting her. Comforting and sheltering her. She turned into him and let the grief pour out of her along with the tears, sheltered in his solid embrace.

When she'd finally calmed she sagged against him and stayed like that for a time, staring at the headstone. "At least he made sure her final wishes were carried out," she said, referring to her father. Why had her mother given Oceane his surname, rather than her own? Maybe because she thought it would offer some sort of protection throughout her life. Oceane still didn't know what she felt about him, it was all so mixed up and contradictory.

Maybe it always would be. Everything about him confused her. Even her feelings about his death. She wouldn't be attending his funeral, however. Forgiveness only went so far.

Gabe didn't say anything, just stroked a soothing hand over her hair. His quiet, solid presence eased her.

She had thought a lot about what she would say to her mother if she ever got the chance to come here. She said it now, the Spanish words flowing from her, gradually easing the ache in her chest. "I love you. I'll always love you and carry you in my heart. But I'm going to find a way to let the past go now and start living my life. I know you would want that and be proud of me."

She got up, Gabe helping her, and set the single pink rose on top of the headstone. Her mother's favorite. "I have to go now. Love you." Before she could start crying again, she turned away and walked toward the SUV.

Gabe stood at the door when she climbed in. When she straightened from doing up her seatbelt, he was there, taking her face in his hands, his pale gaze searching hers. She wasn't sure what he saw, or what he was looking for, but then he bent his head ˈand kissed her and she stopped thinking altogether.

His thumb moved softly over her cheek as he straightened, then he shut the door and went around to the driver's side. He held her hand as he drove her to the hotel where she was booked in under an alias and walked her up to her room. He checked it before allowing her inside.

"You okay?" he asked her quietly when he shut the door behind her.

"I don't know," she answered honestly. "A lot has happened. I'm not sure what I feel right now."

He stood beside the door, hands in his pockets. "I can understand that."

She turned to face him fully, studied him. He wore a pair of well-worn jeans and a navy blue T-shirt that hugged his muscles. His dark blond hair was cut short, a few days' worth of stubble on his face.

He was breathtaking. Ruggedly masculine in a way that made her insides go haywire. Always so quiet and contained. But those pale blue eyes of his told a different story. He hid his emotions well, far better than her, but now that she knew him she could read him a little.

And right now, she saw the secret in his eyes along with the masculine hunger when he looked at her.

She didn't see the point in dancing around her suspicions now, and she wanted to know the answer to the question burning brightest inside her. So she asked him straight out. "You killed Montoya, didn't you?"

Shock flared in the depths of his eyes, his face going slack with surprise for an instant before he put his calm mask back in place. "What? Why would you think that?"

Too late. He'd already given himself away.

Holding his gaze, she walked toward him, stopped inches away. Close enough that she had to tilt her head back to look into his eyes. "Thank you."

He stared at her for a heartbeat, then looked away. Not answering, but not denying it either.

"How did he die?"

His gaze came back to hers. Stayed. Almost as if he was trying to decide whether or not she could handle it.

So she pushed. "Was it fast?"

He shook his head slightly. "No. Not fast. I made sure."

It probably meant there was something seriously wrong with her, but his answer, knowing he would do that for her, was the most amazing demonstration of devotion he could ever have given her. And there was no holding her feelings back for him even a moment longer.

"Gabe." She stepped up against him, wrapped her arms around his broad back. "I love you."

She caught his quiet, indrawn breath, the slight jerk of surprise an instant before his heavy arms came around her. "What?"

She squeezed him tighter. "I don't want to hide it anymore. I love you. Have for a while now."

His hand slid into her hair, tugged her head back. When she looked up, she caught her breath at the raging hunger burning in those piercing blue eyes.

She gasped into his mouth as it closed over hers. Forceful. Dominant. Branding her along with the heat of his hands as he popped her off her feet and carried her to the wide bed behind her.

Their clothes came off in a flurry of motion, ended up scattered on the floor. Then they were naked and he was pressing her down into the bed, his hard, hot body blanketing hers, his hips wedged between her open thighs.

Yes. Please. Need you.

"I'm here. Right here," he said, and she realized she must have said the words aloud. "And I'm not going anywhere."

The rush of sensation and emotion were almost too much. Even the lightest brush of his hands and mouth made her burn, her skin sensitized to the slightest touch. He left no doubt as to how much he wanted her, or that he was in charge. The way he held her, positioned and pinned her made her crazy with yearning.

She was moaning, babbling to him in Spanish without realizing it, pleasure swamping her as he stroked and kissed her all over. Neither of her previous lovers had come anywhere close to this. They were fumbling boys compared to him. Gabe was all powerful, hungry man as he held her exactly where he wanted her and asserted his mastery over her body.

His hands held her hips steady as his lips released her throbbing nipple and laid a burning trail of kisses down the center of her body. Down her stomach. Her abdomen. To the secret place between her thighs.

Oceane bit her lip, her fingers tangled in his short hair, her whole body alive and aching for fulfillment.

He had her twisting, panting, her fingers clenched around his hair as his lips and tongue caressed the sensitive folds, swirled around the taut bud at the top of her sex. She made an incoherent sound and gave herself over to the sensation. To him. He built her pleasure with slow precision, licking and sucking until she thought she would go mad.

And when she was right there on the edge of release, he finally slid a condom on and stretched out on top of her, stared down into her face as he slid deep inside her.

She cried out his name, her soul quivering at the rightness of it. His mouth muffled it, his tongue twining with hers as he stretched her, filled her, making the ache inside her worse.

All too soon he stopped, withdrew and rolled her onto her knees. "Hold on," he whispered, taking her hands and curling them into the bedding.

She did as he said, holding her breath. Waiting to see what he would do. Then she felt the pressure once more, the heat as he positioned himself and surged deep. Her cry of surrender echoed in her ears as she shuddered in his hold.

He was all around her. Inside her. His hot, hard body curved around her back. One wonderfully strong arm banded around her waist, the other reaching down to slide his hand between her legs to stroke her swollen, sensitive nub.

"Gabe, oh, please…" she gasped out, heart hammering, the pleasure building and building. Wonderful and terrifying at the same time.

His low, sexy voice spoke against her ear. Telling her how beautiful she was. How good she felt. Praising her. Melting all the remaining cold inside her and replacing it with a warm glow that suffused her whole body.

Then he said the best part.

"*Te amo*," he whispered against her neck, his hips surging slow and steady, making her lose her mind as he caressed between her thighs, the dual caresses igniting nerve endings she hadn't even known existed until now.

Release crashed through her. Her cries rang unchecked in the silence, the pleasure shattering. He followed a moment later with a raw groan against her shoulder, his arms locked tight around her.

She drifted, languorous and sated as he eased her onto her side, withdrew and left the bed. Water ran in the bathroom, then he came back and tucked his body around hers, holding her close.

Sighing in contentment, she ran her fingers up and down his corded forearm, savoring the feel of him wrapped around her like a blanket. "Did you mean it?

That last part?" She had to know in case it had merely been in the throes of passion. A phrase she had never understood until a few minutes ago.

He kissed her shoulder. "Yeah. I meant it."

She smiled in the dimness. "I was hoping so."

He exhaled, his breath stirring the curls at her nape. "What are we gonna do about this?"

"Well." She wiggled closer, caught his hand and pulled it up to her mouth to kiss it. "I talked to one of my marshals. Given the events of the past twenty-four hours, there's no real reason for me to stay in WITSEC anymore."

He stilled, even his breathing halting. "Yeah?"

She nodded. "But I don't want to stay to Mexico. I want to start over somewhere in the States. I don't know whether I can get citizenship or not."

"They'll give it to you," he said, sounding sure of it. "What about Virginia? Would you live there?"

Now she stilled. Was he saying what she thought he was?

She rolled to face him, his features just visible in the dim lighting. "I haven't seen much of it, to be honest. Is it nice there?"

He grinned at her attempt at humor. "I'll show you any part of it you want if it means you'll consider moving there."

"I've never been to Oregon, either. I hear Bend is beautiful."

He grinned, his teeth gleaming in the light coming through the window. "It's pretty there too. We could go there for a holiday when we get back to the States, and I'll introduce you to my mom and cousins."

Her heart rolled over in her chest. He had utterly captured her heart. "I would love that."

He gathered her closer. "Then we'll go. But in the meantime, I think you should stay with me at my place."

"I would love to stay with you, Gabe," she whispered against his lips, then kissed him.

But he pulled back, a worried frown creasing his forehead. "What about Ruiz?" His fingers stroked lightly up and down her spine. "If he's still alive, would it be safe for you?"

She snuggled closer, laid her cheek on his shoulder. "He's no threat to me now. And I'm not a threat to him either." He was safely behind bars. Would die there someday. Then all the monsters from her past would finally be gone.

****

Carlos Ruiz's heart rate kicked up a notch as he read the newspaper article the guard had just given him. Nieto was dead. Apparently so was *el Escorpion*. And Montoya too.

Carlos wasn't exactly broken up about losing the man who had taken over his operations, but he sure as hell was happy about the first two being dead. Besides, there were dozens of men who would kill for the chance to take over his territory. It was just a matter of working his connections to find someone strong enough to do the job. Now that the head of the cartel was gone, it was the perfect time for someone with aspirations to take everything over, make it his own.

He couldn't help but gloat a little. He may never get out of here alive, but he was still alive where the others were dead and he had decades left with which to savor his victory over his rivals. Make plans. Put them into action through his asset here in the prison.

"Ruiz. Breakfast."

He got up stiffly from his bunk and crossed to the slot where the tray waited. He took it, along with the cup of lukewarm coffee. The slot slammed shut once more as he limped back to his bed.

Coffee in hand, he sipped at it while he read the remainder of the article. Interesting. A DEA agent had been taken prisoner and freed during the operation that had led to Nieto's death. What had really happened though? Mexican officials were taking full credit for the killings, but Carlos was willing to bet the Americans had been involved somewhat.

He forked up a bite of eggs, then a gooey bit of grits—like cornmeal, but not nearly as appetizing—and swallowed. The food was tasteless but he no longer cared as long as it filled his belly.

Something hard met his tongue on his next mouthful of grits.

Pulse tripping, he pulled out the capsule and cracked it open. The tiny paper was rolled up tight, smaller than usual. He opened it, frowned at the two hastily scrawled words written there.

It's over.

It could mean any number of things. That Nieto was no longer enjoying his takeover of Carlos's territory. The end of the *Veneno* cartel in its current form with *el Escorpion's* death. Montoya no longer being in control of Ruiz's remaining organization.

At any rate, the message unnecessary and unhelpful since he'd just read about it in the paper.

Rolling it back up, he tucked it inside the capsule, sealed it, then swallowed it with a mouthful of coffee. Maybe it was because the coffee was stone cold now, but it tasted far more bitter than usual.

He set the newspaper clipping aside and resumed eating the rest of his breakfast, contemplating what message he should send to his remaining network now. He had to swallow twice to get the next bite of eggs down, as if something was stuck in his throat.

No. As if something was cutting off his airway.

He dropped his fork, shoved the plate away and bent over, grabbing his throat as he began to choke. What the hell? Was he having a heart attack? It felt like there was an elephant sitting on his chest.

He fell off his bunk, managed to crawl to the door. His lungs weren't working. It was like they were paralyzed. His face was heating, eyes bulging as he gasped for air.

He flung out an arm, managed to bang it against the steel door to draw the guard's attention.

And then it hit him.

It's over.

The capsule. They'd fucking poisoned him.

But how? *Who?*

He shook his head, his body bucking on the concrete floor as he fought for air. There was none. And no one came to help him.

His heart stopped.

His mouth opened, his bulging eyes fixed on the concrete ceiling above him as the darkness took over, leaving him with one final, haunting thought.

Who the fuck had done this to him?

Chapter Twenty-Three

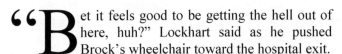

"**B**et it feels good to be getting the hell out of here, huh?" Lockhart said as he pushed Brock's wheelchair toward the hospital exit. "You have no idea." He'd only been in three days up here in D.C., two before his shoulder surgery and one after, but they had felt like an eternity without Tori.

He hadn't even been able to tell her goodbye. They'd given him something before loading him on the transport back to D.C. with her. When he'd woken up, he had been in his hospital room and she had been gone.

He'd never known pain like that. The kind that made it feel like his chest was being split open from the inside.

And he loved how everyone including the medical staff kept telling him to rest, when it seemed like someone was in his room every fucking ten minutes to poke or prod him for something. Blood sample. Blood pressure. Body temp. Giving him a shot of something.

You're just a grumpy asshole because Tori's gone. You should have told her everything when you had the chance.

It hurt too much to think about, so he shoved it aside. He'd have plenty of time to wallow in his own self-pity once he got home.

"Okay, this is us," Lockhart said, hitting the keyfob and sliding the side door of the vehicle open.

Brock stared at it in horror. "A minivan?" He cranked his head around to stare up at Lockhart. "Since when do you drive a minivan?"

"Ha. This is Taggart's wife's ride. You think I'd ever own one of these?" He snorted, insulted. "Please. Taggart was busy with something and I didn't want you to be stuck in here a moment longer than you had to be, so I said I'm come over and take you home. You're welcome." He pushed Brock over to it. "We thought this would make it easier for you to get in and out. You know, being that you're a fucking cripple and all."

Brock shot him a mock glare. "My legs work just fine. And this cripple can take you any day of the week, so you remember that."

"Sure." Lockhart set the brakes on the chair. "Climb in, Cap."

He did, wincing as he pulled the seatbelt over his chest. His right arm was still bound to his chest with a sling to take the strain off his newly repaired shoulder, but the left side didn't feel so great either. Thankfully the doc thought Brock would likely be able to return to his duties as FAST Bravo's team leader once he was all healed up. As to when that would be, it all depended on how rehab went.

"Say cheese."

Brock whipped his head around. "Wha—"

Lockhart snapped a picture of him with his phone and tucked it into his back pocket, grinning.

He shook his head. "Maka put you up to this, didn't he?"

"He sure as shit did. And I'm getting a twelve-pack of beer for it, so it's totally worth it."

Brock couldn't help but chuckle, then regretted it. "Ow. Fuck. Maka's not even here and he's making me laugh."

"Laughter's the best medicine, haven't you heard?"

"Not when you have cracked ribs."

"Yeah, okay. Maybe not then." He hit the keyfob again, stood there grinning like an idiot as the side panel door slid closed. "You gotta admit, this is pretty handy."

Brock snorted and didn't bother answering, anxious to get home to his own bed where he could actually get more than twenty minutes' sleep at once. If he could stop thinking about Tori and what had happened long enough to actually stay asleep.

But once he walked into his place, an invisible weight settled on his chest. He was tired, sore as hell and generally in a piss-poor mood, but on top of all that, a wave of loneliness hit him.

The last time he'd been here, he'd been getting ready to meet Tori. He glanced at the couch, remembered the sight of her naked and trusting there up until things went wrong.

She was long gone now, having left two days ago to start her new life somewhere on the other side of the country. But it was like her ghost still lingered here, haunting him with her memory.

His body would heal, but his heart never would.

He loved her. Wished the hell he had told her before he'd been put on that transport. Now he had to find her. Find a way to be with her. Because that was the only way he would ever be whole again.

"Okay, man, you need anything else?" Lockhart asked, standing with hands on hips in the kitchen. "Taggart's gonna pop over in a bit, bring some food with him."

"Nah, I'm good. Thanks for everything."

"Hey, no worries. You got anything here to snack on while you wait?" He opened the fridge, looked around. "Want some cheese and crackers?"

"Sure, that sounds good." Truth was, he didn't want to be alone just yet. He'd have plenty of that in the weeks ahead while he was recovering. He was too sore to sleep right now anyway.

Lockhart had just put the plate of cheese, crackers and pickles onto the table for them when Brock's phone buzzed. He fished it out, some part of him hoping against hope that it might be Tori. But of course, it wasn't. He hid his disappointment. "Taggart's here. Can you let him in?"

"Sure." Lockhart walked over to the keypad by the front door and hit the button, then waited to let their commander in.

"Loved the shot of you in the minivan," Taggart said as he walked in with armfuls of grocery bags.

Brock threw a disbelieving look at Lockhart. "You texted everyone?"

"Yep. It was part of the deal." He took the bags from Taggart, put them on the counter.

Taggart chuckled as he walked over and sank down on the sofa across from Brock, handing him a stack of mail. "Grabbed this for you on my way up."

"Thanks." There was junk mail, some bills, and a small package without a return address. He didn't recognize the writing.

"Good to be home?" Taggart asked as Lockhart put the groceries away for Brock.

Sure. "Yeah."

"You've got at least a week's worth of food there, plus one of Abby's lasagnas and a loaf of her homemade garlic cheese bread. Piper sent a bunch of baking."

Okay, that made being here on his own slightly less depressing. "I don't know how Maka and Colebrook aren't six hundred pounds each," Brock muttered. "I'll text them to say thanks." Overcome by curiosity, Brock ripped open one end of the padded envelope. His heart stuttered, seemed to stop a moment when he saw the flash of light blue.

He opened it wider. When he saw the contents, he sucked in a painful breath.

Tori. She had sent him the blue scarf she had worn to the hotel. The one she'd tied his hands to the headboard with. And there were two of the candles he'd brought as well.

He reached for the folded note she had enclosed, his fingers slightly unsteady as he opened it.

You will always be my light in the darkness. I want to be yours as well. T

Fuck. Him.

He sat there staring at it, realized belatedly that both Taggart and Lockhart were watching him curiously. He tucked the note away, set the envelope inside, his chest full of lead. This couldn't be the end. He had to find her. Figure out how to make it work between them. There had to be a way. He couldn't accept the alternative.

The way Taggart was watching him made Brock's nape tingle. "What?" he asked. "Something up?"

"Yeah." He waved Lockhart over, waited until he'd sat next to Brock before continuing. "Two things. One, Ruiz is dead."

Brock's eyes widened. "You're shitting me." No way it was from natural causes.

"Nope. Guards found him dead in his cell this morning. Looks like a heart attack, but we won't know until we get the coroner's report after the autopsy."

Brock looked at Lockhart. "No way it was a heart attack." He looked back at Taggart. "So then…they're all gone." The threat to Tori was over. "Does Victoria know?"

"I imagine she'll be told soon."

God, with Ruiz gone, she was no longer under any serious threat that Brock could think of. The chances of anyone trying to hunt her down and going after her to avenge Ruiz's memory were nil. Her demons had all been sent back to hell where they belonged. Now she could move on. Because she was finally safe. Free.

Damn, he wished he could be the one to tell her that. To tell her so many things he—

"And two," Taggart said, bringing Brock out of his thoughts, "is we've got a big fucking problem on our hands."

"Why?" Lockhart said, frowning.

"The cartel's still functioning as if nothing's happened."

"What, you mean financially? That's not so weird, it could just be the accountants or whatever moving money around. It'll take a few more days for us to see the disruptions kick in," Brock said.

Taggart shook his head. "Under normal circumstances I would agree with you. But the reason I couldn't pick you up this morning is because I was called into an emergency meeting."

Brock went to lean forward and brace his elbows on his knees, winced and sat up, putting his left hand to his healing ribs. God, he was glad the bastard who had done this to him was dead. "And?"

"*El Escorpion* is still active."

Brock shook his head. "That's impossible. Nieto gave Oceane Diaz's name, and he checked out with the DEA as being the head. Now he's dead."

"Nope. There's been new activity within the cartel over their network in the past few hours. Chatter about new operations, issued in exactly the same way that *el Escorpion* always has." He paused a moment, letting the gravity of it hit home. "*El Escorpion* is still active, and it's too soon for anyone to have replaced Diaz yet, which means he was never the head of the cartel."

Brock stared at him in stunned silence. If Diaz wasn't *el Escorpion*, then who the hell was?

****

Maria Diaz splashed more cold water on her face, then patted it with a towel and straightened to look in the mirror over the sink as the train swayed from side to side. Her eyes were red-rimmed and puffy, swollen as her heart was swollen.

Her son was dead. The government had somehow identified Fernando and tracked him to the village where they'd shot him down like a dog in the street.

Through the wall of the connecting stateroom, the sound of muffled sobbing reached her. Maria sighed and closed her eyes a moment. Poor Sophia.

Quietly she eased the door open and stepped inside. Sophia was lying on her side on the bed, curled up in the fetal position, the heartbreaking sounds of her grief making more tears prick Maria's eyes. She sat on the edge of the bed and set a gentle hand on her daughter-in-law's shuddering back. "I know, *cariña*. I know it hurts."

Sophia didn't move, only began to cry harder.

Maria drew in a bracing breath. "He was a good man, and you were a good wife to him. He loved you and the children more than anything." She sat there stroking Sophia's back for long minutes. "It's going to be hard, but we must be strong. For the children. We don't want to upset them. As far as they're concerned, their father is only away on business. They'll learn the truth soon enough."

"My heart is b-broken," Sophia sobbed.

"I know, dear one. Mine too." But she still had work to do, and it couldn't wait, even for a broken heart.

She waited another minute, and when Sophia continued to weep inconsolably, lost her patience. "I'll go to the children," she said as she stood and headed for the door. "You can come join us when you've composed yourself again."

She found her grandchildren in the car where she'd left them with their books. Putting on a smile, she sat between them on the luxuriously padded bench as the Panamanian scenery flashed past out the window and put an arm around each of them. "Should we play a card game?"

"Oh, yes," Isa cried, setting down her book and reaching for the deck of cards on the table in front of her.

Everyone thought Fernando had been the head of the cartel. She mentally snorted at the thought. The men in charge of the investigation were all so fucking stupid. No one would ever suspect a seventy-two-year-old woman of being capable of running such a formidable organization.

She hadn't survived, risked and sacrificed so much all these years—sacrifices that now included her only child—just to surrender now. No. Fernando's death had to mean something. Had to be worth it for his children, or Maria couldn't live with it.

"All right, seven cards each. No peeking," she said as she dealt the deck for a game of rummy. "We'll play for the gummy bears I put in my purse."

Her grandson gave her a gap-toothed smile, his eyes an exact mirror of his father's as they sparkled up at her. And for a moment her heart clenched. "You know the best games, *Abuelita*."

Maria smiled, a steely resolve pushing the grief back down into the box she would keep it in. That was how one survived. "I do." She played them well, too.

Because she was the master of them all.

Chapter Twenty-Four

Bellingham, WA
Two weeks later

Victoria stopped in the act of transferring her second load of laundry from the washer to the dryer and turned her head toward the door, listening. She thought she'd heard something—

A knock sounded at the back door.

She frowned, tossed the damp sweater she was holding into the dryer and headed down the stairs. Was it her neighbor? Sometimes the elderly lady next door came to bring her something. Cookies, cut flowers from her garden.

But when she rounded the corner of the downstairs hallway and reached the mudroom, she froze at the sight of a man's silhouette outlined there. Fear punched through her for a second, followed closely by a painful swell of hope. Brock?

No, the build wasn't right. Too short. Not broad enough through the shoulders.

"Who is it?" she called out, already turning toward the hall and the front door if she needed to escape.

"Bill Carruthers. U.S. Marshals."

Marshals? Instant suspicion made her pause. "Where's Tony?" Her WITSEC handler. He was the only one she kept in contact with. The only one who had ever visited her here.

"On another assignment. Check your phone. He left you a message a couple hours ago, telling you to expect me."

Damn, she'd left her phone charging in her office. She'd left it there this morning after plotting out the last bit of her novel and hadn't checked it since. "Hang on," she told Carruthers through the door, not caring if it was rude to leave him standing on the stoop, and rushed to her office, keeping one eye on the front door. WITSEC said she was safe here under her new alias, but she wasn't taking any chances.

Sure enough, there was a message from Tony, saying his boss would be stopping by to talk to her.

She unlocked the back door, gave Carruthers—a fortyish man in jeans and a button down—a rueful smile as he held up his ID for her to check. "Sorry about that. Can't be too careful. Old habits die hard, and all that."

"That's the truth," he said with an easy grin as he stepped inside and looked around. "Nice place."

She shut the door behind him. "I like it. It's homey." She had fallen a little in love with the green heritage Victorian the moment Tony had driven up to it. As far as starting her life over, this was a beautiful home to begin it in. Even if she had a gaping hole in her heart—and her life—without Brock.

All Tony had been able to tell her was that Brock had been discharged after his shoulder surgery a little over a week ago. She thought of him constantly, had reached for her phone so many times to call him, only to realize she couldn't. For her safety. And to keep from hurting him more by not letting him go.

Carruthers gestured to the hallway. "Can we sit down for a few minutes?"

"Oh, sure. Right this way." She led him through to her living room, just off the kitchen, and gestured to the couch, the only piece of furniture in the room so far. "Sorry about the lack of furniture. I'm still getting set up." She sat on the hearth in front of the wood burning fireplace opposite him.

He sank onto the couch, rested his forearms on his knees and studied her. "You settling in okay? I know it's not an easy adjustment."

"I'm fine. Fairhaven's the most beautiful spot in Bellingham. Lots of little shops and cafes for me to explore, and I like walking along the beach. I'm going to be volunteering at the library to get my feet wet while I work on my next book, starting this coming weekend." She didn't know why she was babbling, except his visit made her nervous. "But you didn't come here to ask me that."

A faint smile tugged at his mouth at her astuteness. "No. I didn't."

"So what is it?"

"I have good news and bad news."

She expelled a breath. She'd had enough bad news to last her three lifetimes. The last news she had received from Tony was that both Montoya and Ruiz were dead. She preferred that kind of news. "Okay. I'll take the bad news first."

"Thought you might."

Her pulse thudded as she watched him, worry creeping into her brain. *Please let Brock be okay. Please let Brock be okay.*

"Fernando Diaz wasn't *el Escorpion.*"

The unease fell away, replaced by shock. "He wasn't?"

284

Carruthers shook his head. "No. And as of this moment, we have no idea who is. The head of the cartel is still out there, very much alive, and running business as usual."

"That's the bad news?"

"Yes."

Okay. It didn't sound so terrible to her. Unless she was missing something. "So what's the good news?"

He studied her for a long moment, until she had to stem the urge to fidget. "We've analyzed your case to death over the past couple of weeks. Going over intel, combing through recent chatter. Looking for possible connections to existing cartel members, trying to figure out the threat level against you."

"And?"

"And we can't find one."

She blinked. "Pardon?"

One side of his mouth twitched in amusement. "As far as we can see, there's no longer any credible threat against you from anyone inside the cartel. And though *el Escorpion* might not have been captured, again, as far as we can tell, whoever it is has no reason to target you now that Ruiz, Nieto and Montoya are all dead."

Blood pulsed in her ears, disbelief holding her immobile. "So you're saying...what exactly?"

"I'm saying that the risk to your safety is over. You don't need to be in the program anymore."

WITSEC. She could leave without worrying? Stop looking over her shoulder all the time? Reclaim what remained of her real life? Could this actually be happening?

"So I'm...free?" she asked, needing him to spell it out.

He nodded, his eyes kind as he smiled at her. "You're free. Tony wanted to be the one to tell you, but since he couldn't, I told him I'd come in his place. Hope you don't mind."

"No, of course I don't mind…" She stood, raked her hands through her hair and faced him, a tremulous smile quivering on her lips. "So that's it. Once I'm out I can leave here anytime and go anywhere I want." *See anyone I want.*

Brock. *Oh God, Brock…* A twisting sensation squeezed her heart.

"Anywhere you want. Although I would stay out of Mexico if I were you, just to play it safe."

She snorted. "If I never stepped foot on Mexican soil again, it would be too soon."

Carruthers got to his feet. "Something else you should know."

There was more? She wasn't sure if she could take more.

"Oceane Nieto is out of the program too."

Her eyes widened. But it made sense if Ruiz, Montoya and Nieto were all gone. "She is? Do you know where she went?"

"She's still in the D.C. area, I believe. Last I heard, government's fast tracking her citizenship." He opened his mouth to say something else, stopped when his phone rang. He pulled it from his pocket, glanced at her. "Sorry, I have to take this." He started for the hallway, finger hovering over the accept button. "Tony will call you when he's able to, probably sometime tonight. You can let him know what you decide if you've made up your mind by then."

Oh, she'd made it up already. She had lined up a life for herself here, but it meant nothing without Brock, and she could write her book anywhere. All she needed was *him*. "Sure. Thank you."

"You're welcome."

The moment she let him out and locked the door behind him, she spun back around and let out a laugh of pure joy. "I'm free." It sounded so strange. Seemed surreal after everything she'd been through.

She couldn't wait to tell Brock. Couldn't wait to simply hear his voice again. She missed him so much it hurt.

Racing to her office, she grabbed her phone and dialed his number with a shaking hand, heart thudding as she waited for him to answer.

"The number you have called is no longer in service," an automated voice said instead.

Her heart sank. Dammit! Of course he had changed his number. His old phone had either been lost or destroyed when he'd been taken prisoner. Who else did she know that might know how to reach him?

Thinking fast, from memory she dialed the number of one of the marshals from her former security detail. Moments later, the same message sounded in her ear.

"Shit," she breathed, then raced for the front door. Maybe Carruthers could—

She ripped it open just in time to see him driving down the street, phone to his ear. Her shoulders sagged.

No.

Disheartened but determined, she went back inside, dialing Tony. "It's Tori," she told his voicemail. "Call me back as soon as you get this. I need a favor."

Ending the call, she headed for the kitchen and the bottle of wine she had been saving for this weekend, impatient as hell and having no choice but to wait. Her mind was made up. The moment she was free to leave, she was out of here.

And as soon as she left, she was going to Brock

Chapter Twenty-Five

Nighttime was so quiet out here. Every little sound was heightened.

Instead of the usual rush of traffic in the street out in front of his condo, there was only the chirp of crickets in the air as Brock sat at the end of the dock and stared out at the lake, his bare feet dangling inches above the water. Moonlight rippled on the dark surface, and when he tipped his head back, the sky was a midnight blue velvet blanket, punctuated by a million diamond-bright stars.

Out here his nearest neighbor was a mile down the lake, and they only visited on weekends and in the summer. He had absolute privacy here. All the time and peace he could ever want.

Except peace kept eluding him. He wasn't sure if he would ever find it again.

He closed his eyes, inhaled a deep breath, thankful that his ribs no longer hurt. His repaired shoulder still bothered him, but not as bad as it had for the first week or two. The stitches in his face were gone as well, leaving an angry red scar that slashed over his nose and upper cheek.

He hadn't been to Oregon since his SF days, back when he'd done his winter mountaineering training on Mount Hood. He'd never been to Bend before. One of Lockhart's cousins had set Brock up at this cabin out on the lake for some R&R. The guy had offered Brock a job with a private security startup that he ran if things didn't pan out the way Brock hoped with his recovery.

Brock wasn't ready to contemplate that yet. He was too busy torturing himself with thoughts of Tori.

He thought of her constantly. How was she? Was she settling in okay in her new town? She would be lonely. Probably not sleeping.

He missed her so damn much. Wanted to see her. Be with her. As long as it wouldn't compromise her safety. At one point he'd even considered trying to break into the WITSEC files to find her location, and managed to talk himself down before he'd done something stupid that would end his career.

He'd been talking with his WITSEC contacts to see if anything could be done about their situation. So far, the threat to her safety was still considered credible enough that Brock hadn't tried to find her. Though he wasn't sure how much longer he could hold off.

He'd arrived here four days ago after finishing off the latest round of physio appointments for his shoulder. The left one was okay now. The right one had limited range of motion and was still sore, would probably take a good six months to fully heal.

Right now, he was in wait and see mode. If it turned out he couldn't meet the physical requirements to keep him with FAST Bravo, Taggart had hinted that his job as team commander might be open for Brock to apply for someday soon.

Right now, he didn't want to think about any of that. For the moment he couldn't go back to rejoin the team as an operator and staying at home all by himself had made him nuts, so he was here taking advantage of the downtime. Today it had been warm enough out for a short swim in the lake. Not far, just enough to stretch his muscles and give his shoulder a gentle workout without pushing too hard. He had hoped it would exhaust him enough to help him sleep.

No such luck. So here he was, sitting on this dock.

A sound carried from behind him, out on the road.

He looked over his shoulder, searching for the source. He caught a flash of a vehicle's headlights on the road out front of the cabin. Then they disappeared and it was only the moonlight and crickets again.

He turned back to stare out at the water, a slight breeze picking up. Taggart had called to check in on him earlier, said something cryptic about a surprise arriving tonight, but nothing had shown up at the cabin door.

Now it was almost midnight. He should be inside trying to sleep, but he slept for shit these days and the thought of lying in bed staring up at the ceiling and trying not to think about either Tori or what had happened to him was about as appealing as having pins stuck in his eyes.

Something moved behind him. He snapped his head around, all his senses on alert. Then it became clearer.

Footsteps. Coming from near the cabin.

He jumped up and started down the dock, cursing himself for not bringing his pistol out here with him. The likelihood of anyone coming after him here was almost zero, but he still felt half-naked without his weapon.

"Brock?"

He stopped dead at the sound of that voice calling for him. For a moment he was convinced he was hearing things. Or maybe dreaming.

Then a silhouette with slender curves appeared around the side of the cabin and stepped into the moonlight.

His heart seized.

Tori.

She stopped when she saw him, a joyous smile breaking over her face. "Oh, you're here," she breathed and hurried toward him, her dark brown hair flowing behind her. "I thought I had the wrong place."

Brock wasn't even aware of his feet moving. One second he was staring at her like she was a ghost. The next he was running at her, his feet thudding on the wooden dock, his heart racing like it was about to explode.

She met him partway, a laugh spilling out of her as she flung herself into his waiting arms, the most beautiful sound he'd ever heard.

Brock groaned and locked her to him, lifting her off the ground. His throat thickened as he buried his face in her hair. His shoulder protested her weight but he didn't care if it hurt. He didn't ever want to let go of her.

"God, what are you doing here?" he rasped out, so grateful to see her that he nearly sank to his knees.

Her arms tightened around him fiercely. "I'm out of WITSEC."

"What?" He pulled back to stare down at her, keeping her dangling off the ground, hardly able to believe this was really happening. That she was here. That he was actually able to touch her again.

Her teeth flashed white in the moonlight as she smiled up at him. "I heard about Ruiz and Montoya. And that *el Escorpion* is still out there. It took a while, but the Marshals service finally decided there was no longer any credible threat against me, so I made the call and I'm officially out of the program. I tried contacting you but I didn't have a new number for you. I was in Bellingham, Washington, so as soon as I got the all clear and found out you were this close, I hopped in the car and drove straight here."

God, he couldn't stop drinking in the sight of her. "How did you find me?"

"They put me in touch with Taggart when I left the program. He had Lockhart call me and give me the address." She tilted her head to the side. "You don't mind, do you?"

"Are you kidding me?" he said on a laugh and crushed her to him once more. "Oh, God, I missed you." It meant so much to him that she would come here to be with him. Because he loved her, but also because she was a fellow survivor and understood what he'd been through. Understood what it was like for him now, trying to deal with the aftermath.

"I missed you more." When he set her down she took his face in her hands and peered up into his eyes. "Your stitches are out."

He couldn't let go of her. Felt like he should pinch himself. "Yeah. I look like I went through a windshield or something."

"No. You were too perfect before. And you'll always be gorgeous to me, no matter what." She lifted up on tiptoe and kissed him. Smiled. Then it faded. She traced a finger beneath one of his eyes. "You haven't been sleeping."

"No. I…can't. Not most nights."

She nodded. "It's hard. But it will get better once your subconscious starts to believe you're safe. Baby steps." She flashed another smile that had his heart knocking against his ribs. "And maybe you'll sleep better with me beside you."

Brock plunged his hand into her hair and kissed her until she moaned and grabbed hold of his shoulders for support. The hunger roaring through him was unlike anything he'd ever felt before.

Deeper. More primal. Because there was a darkness inside him now that hadn't existed before. A constant battle to fight off the sense of helplessness he had been forced to feel during his captivity. The fight to regain his power as a man.

He tried to rein it in, not wanting to frighten her or stir any bad memories but it was so damn hard to think straight with the taste and scent of her making his head spin.

He couldn't stop. Needed to imprint himself on her in every way. He never should have let her go in the first place. Should have sacrificed whatever it took to be with her.

"I can't let you go," he rasped out against the side of her neck, one hand buried in her hair, the other gripping her hip tight. Tighter than he should.

"Shh," she soothed, kissing his temple as she stroked his hair. "I know. It's okay."

But she didn't know. Couldn't know or understand the dark need spiraling out of control inside him. The one that made him want to strip her right here and now and take her the way he'd imagined for so many months.

Pinning her. Dominating her.

"Brock," she whispered, moaned when he nibbled and nipped at the side of her neck, pulled her pelvis tight to his erection and rocked into her.

Her hands slid under the hem of his shirt to touch his abdomen. The instant her palms made contact with his bare skin, a wave of lust crashed over him, so strong it stole his breath.

He should slow down. Carry her into the cabin, his shoulder be damned, build a fire and lay her down in front of it, make love to her there. Make it romantic, show her how much she meant to him.

That she was *everything* to him.

But he was starving for her. And if he didn't get inside her soon he might actually die right here on this dock. "Need you," he muttered, nipping the tender spot where her neck and shoulder met. "Need you so much, angel."

She gasped and arched into him. "Need you too."

Holding her close he spun them around, searching for the deck chairs. They were a few yards away, and they had long cushions on them.

He lifted her off her feet with his good arm around her waist and carried her over, his mouth on hers. As soon as her feet touched the dock he reached down and grabbed the cushions, jerking them off onto the wooden planks into a low stack.

He pulled her down on top of them, stretched her out on her back and began taking her clothes off. She sat up and helped, carefully peeled his shirt off. He hid a wince as his right shoulder pulled but he didn't care about the pain as he sat back on his heels to drink in the sight of her.

She was gorgeous in the moonlight, all that golden skin, her entire body bared to his ravenous gaze. He'd never felt this desperate, this possessive. He wanted to mark her. Claim her in a way that no one ever had or would. She was *his* and *only* his.

He wanted her to feel that inside and out. "Should never have let you go," he muttered. "Ever."

Her dark eyes gazed up at him, soft with trust, full of arousal. She lifted a hand to cup his cheek, as though she sensed his inner battle. "I'm here now. Don't stop," she whispered.

He groaned and surged forward to take her mouth again, covering her with his body. Adjusting his weight on his left arm to take the strain off his healing shoulder. "Can't slow down," he bit out between kisses.

She answered by winding her legs around his hips. Something inside him snapped. He stopped thinking, stopped fighting the need lashing him and set about claiming his woman.

He cupped her breasts in his hands and sucked on the taut peaks, reveled in her sighs, the sexy movements she made as he teased one, then the other, before moving down the center of her body. He pushed her knees apart, exposing her glistening folds to his gaze. With a sound somewhere between a moan and a growl, he knelt, gripped her hips hard and buried his face between her legs.

Her choked cry spurred him on even more, the desperate bite of her fingers in his scalp pushing him to make her beg. He focused on making her insane, loving every twist of her hips as he licked and sucked at her softest flesh, drove his tongue into her warmth, his cock throbbing, desperate for the moment when he slid deep inside her.

Only when she was gasping, begging did he ease off and surge up to cover her once more with his weight. Her eyes were heavy-lidded, glazed with pleasure as she gazed up at him.

And then she slowly raised her hands over her head. Surrendering full control of her body to him.

The gesture made his heart explode with tenderness.

He laced his fingers through hers, squeezed in reassurance. She relaxed underneath him, rolled her hips as she held his gaze. Her willingness to surrender control to him turned him inside out, symbolized not only her absolute trust in him, but saying that she was his.

He couldn't wait a second longer to be inside her.

Unable to hold back, he pulled his wallet out of his back pocket, slid a condom on. Settling most of his weight on his left forearm, he ignored the twinge in his right shoulder and slid home with a single thrust.

Making her his once more.

VICTORIA SUCKED IN a sharp breath as Brock pushed deep inside her, her eyes sliding closed against the burn of tears. Not from pain. From being connected with him as intimately as she could. From feeling like she belonged to him.

But there was also pleasure. So much pleasure, emotional and physical as he pinned her beneath him and took her the way he needed to. The way she wanted him to.

He moaned her name, his muscles bunching beneath her hands, her thighs as she twined them around his hips. "Love you," he gasped out. "Love you so goddamn much."

Her heart split wide open. She had dreamed of hearing those words from him for so long, hadn't dared to let herself hope she ever would, before. "Sweetheart, I love you too," she answered, emotion clogging her throat.

He growled and pinned her harder. Even then there was no fear, no pain. She stared up into his beautiful, scarred face, half in shadow and half in moonlight and fell impossibly more in love with him.

Wrapping her arms around him, she cradled him close as he pumped in and out, the almost feral sounds coming out of him sending a thrill through her. He was working up to an explosion and she didn't want to miss a moment of it.

"Can't stop," he ground out, bowing his head to press his forehead to hers.

Rather than answer verbally, Victoria smoothed a hand down his back and squeezed him with her core. He gave a deep, sensual groan, his face twisting with the strain of trying to hold back. She didn't want him to hold back with her. Not now. Not ever again.

Raising her head, she kissed the side of his flexed jaw. Flicked her tongue over the corner of his mouth.

Brock buried a hand in her hair and fused their lips together, his tongue plunging deep along with the motion of his hips. Two more thrusts and he went rigid in her arms, his head falling back on his shoulders as his release hit.

His raw, sensual moans filled the night as his big body shuddered against hers. Finally, he sagged onto his left arm and dropped his head to her shoulder, breathing hard.

She slid her hand through his hair, ran the other over his broad back. "You okay?"

He lifted up slightly to look down at her, his eyes worried. "I was going to ask you that."

God, she loved this man. "More than okay. What about your shoulder?"

His grin flashed in the moonlight as he chuckled softly. "I'll live." He withdrew gently, leaned to the side to grab his shirt, cleaned himself up.

She shivered lightly in the cool night air, her body aching with unfulfilled need.

"You cold?"

"A little." Mostly dying of sexual frustration.

He grabbed a blanket that had fallen from one of the deck chairs and spread it over them. "Well I'm about to make you hot," he murmured, giving her a toe-curling kiss before disappearing under the blanket, tugging the top of it over her shoulders to keep the cool air out.

She bit her lip against a smile as his mouth trailed across her breast, his tongue finding a sensitive nipple. He whispered something and kept going, sucking and stroking his tongue across both sensitive peaks before moving lower.

By the time he reached where she needed him most her thighs were trembling, stomach muscles pulled taut, her entire body screaming with need and anticipation. She couldn't help but cry out when he dragged his tongue across her swollen flesh, slow and tender.

His hands gripped her hips, holding her steady as he teased and stroked, quickly zeroing in on the exact spot on her clit that made her mindless. When she whimpered and pushed against his mouth he eased a hand between her thighs and slid a finger into her, curving it to slide over the hidden sweet spot inside her.

Over and over he stroked, licked, sucked. In no rush now, determined to take his time and make her lose her mind.

It felt like her bones were dissolving. The pleasure swelled higher, faster, until she was teetering on the brink. He slowed his hand, kept the sweet caress of his tongue steady.

Too much.

She sobbed out his name as she started coming, her whole body shaking. She was soaring, his grip on her hips the only thing keeping her from flying apart.

Gasping, weak, she sank back against the cushions at last, her heart racing. Sweat beaded her skin as he eased his way back up her body, trailing tender kisses in his wake.

Moments later Brock's head popped out from under the blanket. He came up on his knees and braced his hands on either side of her head to peer down at her, so gorgeous even with the scar he took her breath away. "Hi."

She smiled up at him. "Hi. I can't move."

He grinned. "I'm glad to hear that."

She managed to summon the strength to lift a hand and trace her fingers down the length of his nose, over his sensuous lips. "So how long are you staying here?"

"Depends. How long do you want to stay?"

"Hmmm, I don't know. Forever?"

A deep chuckle reverberated in his chest. "It's tempting, but this is a little isolated, even for me." He paused, grew serious. "How did you make out in Bellingham?"

"I was okay. Signed up to volunteer at the local library. And I started my new book."

"You did?"

"Mmhmm. Outline's all done and I've got the first three chapters written."

"I'm glad you decided to do it."

"Me too." She'd never imagined feeling this way about anyone. Willing to put her life into his hands. Willing to do anything to protect him. "You know what name I chose for my new identity, when I was in WITSEC?" she said, changing the subject.

He propped his chin in his left hand, watching her. "What?"

"Tori Hamilton."

He stilled, staring down at her in surprise.

"I wanted to take a piece of you with me. That was my solution."

He cupped the side of her face with his free hand, turned it so that she looked into his eyes. "Then I say we make it official."

She blinked, unsure she'd heard him right. "What?"

"I want to make you mine forever." His gray eyes were steady, full of a tender possessiveness and pride that stole her breath. "Marry me, Tori."

He was serious. A tremulous smile tugged at her lips, the sting of tears blurring her vision. "Yes. Yes, I'll marry you."

His answering smile lit up his stormy gray eyes, filled her heart to bursting. "God, I love you." He leaned over her to kiss her tenderly, lingered there for a long moment before sitting up and pushing to his feet. "We'll pick out a ring when we get back to Virginia. Unless you want me to surprise you?"

"I'd love that."

"Done."

Before she could say anything else he reached down to grab her hand and haul her to her feet. She squeaked and grabbed the blanket, wrapping it around her naked body as she glanced around, her face heating.

He laughed. "Too late for modesty now. I'm sure everyone within a five-mile radius heard you when you came."

She gasped, clutched the blanket around her. "They did not."

His grin was boyish, making her heart turn over. Her future husband. It was too incredible to believe yet.

"Come on." He wound a strong arm around her shoulders, drew her into his body. "I can't carry you just yet, so you'll have to walk into the cabin with me. I'll build us a fire and make us a bed in front of it. Sound good?"

"Sounds dreamy."

"Yeah. I hope you don't plan on sleeping much tonight," he added with a wicked smile that made her toes curl. "Although you might be the cure I needed for my insomnia."

Much later, as she lay curled up in his arms in front of the dying fire on the bed he'd made for them, she noticed a change in his breathing. It was deeper. Steadier.

Lifting her head from his chest to look up at him, she found him fast asleep.

His face was so peaceful in the glow of the embers, his body relaxed. Because he instinctively knew he was safe here with her on a deep, subconscious level.

Victoria smiled to herself in the dying light of the fire. From now on they would always be there for each other. Ready to chase away the darkness and slay any demons that came back to haunt them. They were both survivors. Starting tonight, they would face the future together, side by side.

Snuggling in closer to the man she was going to spend the rest of her life with, she closed her eyes with a sigh and followed him into sleep. Sheltered in his loving, protective arms, where the specters from her past could no longer hurt her.

—The End—

Dear reader,

Thank you for reading *Fast Vengeance*. I hope you enjoyed it. If you'd like to stay in touch with me and be the first to learn about new releases you can:

- Join my newsletter at:
  http://kayleacross.com/v2/newsletter/
- Find me on Facebook:
  https://www.facebook.com/KayleaCrossAuthor/
- Follow me on Twitter:
  https://twitter.com/kayleacross
- Follow me on Instagram:
  https://www.instagram.com/kaylea_cross_author/

Also, please consider leaving a review at your favorite online book retailer. It helps other readers discover new books.

Happy reading,
Kaylea

Excerpt from
Guarded
Hostage Rescue Team Series

By Kaylea Cross
Copyright © 2018 Kaylea Cross

Chapter One

S tretched out on her belly on a wooded ridge overlooking the valley floor, Briar stared through her
night vision riflescope at the log cabin below. The
scent of the forest surrounded her. Damp and earthy and
fresh after a hard rain that had just eased to a light shower
a few minutes ago. "I count five heat signatures in the
house," she murmured, careful not to let her voice carry.

"I'm seeing the same." Lying in supported prone position beside her, her boss Alex Rycroft studied the small
screen in his hands. The image showed an infrared feed
from a drone circling the area high above. "Command,
can you confirm?" he asked quietly.

The answer came through their earpieces a moment
later. "Affirmative. Five tangos in target location."

Even though it was damp and cold, Briar was loving
every second of this. It had been too damn long since
she'd been out in the field. Even longer since she'd acted
as a sniper.

A health scare during an op more than a year ago was
to blame. She had been hit with some kind of Taser that
had triggered cardiac arrest due to an undiagnosed ar-
rhythmia she hadn't been aware of. Since then she'd
mostly been working as an analyst.

It felt good to be back in her element, though she
wasn't used to having a spotter with her. Back when she'd
been a Valkyrie she'd always worked alone. Working
with Rycroft was awesome, however. He was former SF

and had more experience than anyone she'd worked with before. Tonight they were providing recon and acting as overwatch if a tactical team was called in for a direct assault on the target.

The feel of the sniper rifle in her hands soothed her and gave her a sense of calm. She was good at this. It was what she did best, actually. When she got home, she would have to hit the range with Matt and get her fix. Because after this op, her sniping days were pretty much over.

"There should be more of them," Rycroft murmured to her.

Briar never took her eyes from the scope, the cold and damp after being camped out in the rain for the past two days barely registering. Learning how to ignore physical discomfort was one of the first things that had been drilled into her in the Valkyrie Program.

That, and to never trust or rely on anyone but herself.

Reversing that ingrained programming had proven hardest for her since joining the civilian world. She still struggled with trusting people, letting them in. Sometimes it even came up with her husband, Matt, who thankfully still wanted to keep her around.

Briar focused on the cabin, analyzing it. "Think anyone's in a cellar under there maybe?" There wouldn't be a basement; the structure was too old and crudely built to have one. But an old storage cellar was a possibility.

"Maybe."

So far the five people in the cabin hadn't come back out. She did another slow sweep of the area, making sure she hadn't missed anything. This right-wing group had gained support and attention in recent months. They were reportedly planning a major attack on a soft, civilian target in NYC. Fucking hateful cowards.

A flash of movement caught her attention.

"Wait, I've got movement in the trees to the northeast." She zeroed in on it. As she watched, adjusting the scope's focus, three more figures emerged from the tree line to the right of the cabin. All men, and all dressed in tactical gear they'd probably bought at the nearest surplus store.

They didn't move like amateurs, though. They moved slowly, appeared to be alert and cautious as they scanned the area, each of them holding what looked like M4s. "Bodyguards?" she murmured.

"Could be." A pause as Rycroft switched frequencies. "Get me an overhead visual," he said to the drone pilot.

"Roger that," came the response.

"You recognize any of them?" Rycroft asked her.

"No." None of them matched the pictures she'd memorized of the group's leader and other key members. Three of who were already inside the cabin. The NSA, FBI and DHS wanted them all captured.

While Rycroft watched his screen, Briar kept her attention on the men emerging from the trees. The group's leader was supposed to be here, yet he wasn't one of the five men in the cabin. She'd watched each one arrive, and he hadn't shown. These three newcomers moved like they were disciplined and had some kind of tactical training. Not a total surprise, since many members of the group were reported to be former military.

But none of them knew she and Rycroft were up here, watching. None of them knew they were in her crosshairs, or that she could kill any one of them with a squeeze of the trigger. She had used this weapon for more than a decade. It was calibrated specifically for her frame and preferences, so perfect it was like an extension of her body.

"Someone's coming out the front door," she said.

A man stepped out onto the front porch seconds later, holding a flat object in his hands. He shook it out, reached up and attached it to something sticking out of the front wall.

A freaking Nazi flag to mark their repulsive club-house.

"Lovely," she muttered under her breath.

"Looks like they're rolling out the old welcome mat for someone special," Rycroft said.

The leader. He had to be either on his way, or nearby. She scanned the trees again. Why couldn't she see him? "The detail's stopped moving." The three men in front of the tree line all stood several paces apart, maintaining a secure perimeter. "Waiting for someone."

She adjusted her aim, centering her crosshairs on the middle guy. This had to be it. All the NSA's intel said Dempsey would be here tonight, to plan the upcoming attack with the other high-ranking members. Home grown terrorists, every single one of them.

"I'm alerting the team." Rycroft contacted the commander of the FBI tactical team back at the command post fifteen miles away. An FBI SWAT team, not the Hostage Rescue Team. That was her sexy Matt's territory, and God she loved that about him. "Your boys ready to go?"

"Affirmative. Everyone's on board, helo's ready to launch."

"Might have found what we're looking for. Stand by." Then to her, "They're at a field five miles from here. Be here in a few minutes if we pull the trigger on this thing."

Oh, how she loved to pull the trigger.

Briar listened with half an ear, more interested in who the guard detail was waiting for. She didn't have to wait long to find out.

More figures appeared through the dense forest of trees. Two big men. A third trailing a few steps behind them, moving without as much caution. "You seeing this?" she whispered to Rycroft.

"Trees are too thick for the drone." He picked up his spotter scope instead, located the men. "Can you ID any of the newcomers?"

"Not the first two." The third man finally came into view, and a flash of elation hit her. "It's Dempsey." There was no mistaking that bearded face.

She adjusted her grip on her weapon, snugged her right cheek against the buttstock, her index finger on the trigger guard. She centered her crosshairs over his chest and waited.

The difference was still jarring. In her former life she would already have put a bullet through him and be packing up to move out of the area. But the rules were different now. She could only fire under direct orders from Rycroft or if someone posed a direct threat to her or someone else on their team.

She couldn't help it if she hoped this asshole gave her a reason to fire. One less twisted human cockroach for the world to worry about.

Rycroft contacted the team commander again. "Target confirmed. Move in."

"Roger that," the commander responded. "ETA four minutes."

Briar kept careful watch as the security detail escorted Dempsey to the cabin. The guy on the porch was there to meet him. His four buddies inside came out to greet their leader with Nazi salutes.

Her lip curled in disgust. Too bad the NSA wanted these guys alive, for questioning and prosecution. She would rather end this a different way. But that was just her, because she was savage when it came to stuff like this. Luckily, Matt loved that about her.

Everything moved fast from that point. Onboard the incoming helo, the SWAT team leader conversed with Rycroft. She and Rycroft provided eyes for them on their final approach to the LZ.

Moments later the sound of aircraft engines broke the quiet. The sky was dark overhead, the thick cloud cover blocking the moon. Perfect conditions for an assault.

Through her scope, she spotted the two helos the instant they punched through the cloud deck and dropped into the clearing. The men outside the cabin barely had time to react before the SWAT teams began swarming out of the aircraft.

Dempsey ran into the cabin with three of his guards, while the others scattered like roaches behind cover. A few of the dumbasses fired at the SWAT team.

Briar's pulse remained calm, her breathing slow and steady as she watched the assault, ready to fire the instant she got the command. She kept her eyes on one of the bodyguards who managed to slip around the far right side of the cabin and take shelter behind an old stone shed.

"Target right, two o'clock. Six-hundred-eight yards," Rycroft murmured, his voice as calm as if he was commenting on the weather.

"On him."

The man raised his rifle to his shoulder and took aim at the assault team, clearly thinking he was safe behind cover. But he wasn't. From here she had a perfect view of the side of his head.

She honed in on his ear, adjusted the scope's reticle. Curved her finger around the trigger. And waited.

An ounce or two more pressure...

Just out of her view, one of the SWAT members engaged a bodyguard. The man behind the shed shifted. She waited for Rycroft's command.

"Fire," he said.

She squeezed the trigger. The butt kicked into her shoulder, her body absorbing the force of the recoil as the report echoed through the woods. Less than a heartbeat later, her bullet struck the target. His head exploded like a melon and he slumped over, dead before he even hit the ground.

She pulled back the bolt and pushed it forward in one smooth, automatic motion, clearing the chamber and loading the next round.

"Good hit," Rycroft murmured. "Target, eleven o'clock. Six-hundred-two yards."

She shifted the barrel slightly left, found the man he was looking at. "Got him."

But she never got the chance to fire another round.

After a brief exchange of fire between SWAT and the neo-Nazi fucktards, it was over.

"HVT in custody, cabin clear. Sweeping rear area now," the team leader said.

Good deal. Keeping watch just in case, Briar never took her eye from her scope as she scanned the area, looking for more threats they might have missed.

She and Rycroft kept watch until SWAT was done securing the area. Agents loaded the prisoners onto the helos and took off, leaving the scene for the mop-up crews to deal with.

Pushing back into a kneeling position, Rycroft looked over at her, his grin barely visible in the near darkness. "Guess that means the fun's over. Ready to get out of here?"

"Yeah."

They gathered up their gear and hiked back to the dirt bikes they'd hidden before riding out to the closest road where a pickup waited for them. The driver took them to the command center.

After finishing their reports—the part Briar hated but was grudgingly accepting more and more—she and Rycroft each got a hot shower and a mug of coffee, which she declined. Rycroft raised an eyebrow at her in surprise but didn't say anything as she climbed into the SUV. He drove them to the airport where a small private plane awaited them.

She spent the hour-long flight dozing on and off, woke when they came in for their final approach. Yawning, she stretched her arms over her head. Rycroft looked totally alert, as if he'd never slept at all. He was a handsome, well-built man, even in his fifties. Not that he was anywhere near as gorgeous as Matt. But still. "For a retired guy, you sure don't need much sleep," she told him.

He grinned, his silver eyes glinting. "It's called parenting. Only the strong survive."

She huffed out a laugh and followed him off the plane to the small terminal building where an excited squeal startled her. She stopped, watched as a little purple blur streaked around the corner and came at them.

Rycroft dropped his bags, a huge smile lighting his face as he crouched down and held his arms open. "There's my girl," he said, catching Sarah as the raven-haired toddler launched herself into her father's arms.

A bittersweet, poignant pang hit Briar in the center of her chest as she watched them. The deep, incredible bond between them was undeniable, even though they weren't related by blood.

The scene made her think of Matt. He had always wanted to be a father, and she had no doubt he would be amazing at it. She wanted a family too, but deep inside she worried she wasn't cut out for it. She wasn't exactly maternal. Or normal, for that matter. Kids were fragile and impressionable. She didn't want to ruin one.

Then Grace came around the corner, smiling fondly at her daughter and husband. "She insisted we come to get you," she said to him as she walked up to hug him.

"I'm glad. This is a nice surprise." Still holding Sarah, he leaned down to kiss the crown of his wife's head, the pigtailed toddler snuggled up in his strong arms.

The picture they presented made Briar miss Matt even more.

Sarah made eye contact with Briar over her father's broad shoulder, grinned. "Hi Briar."

Briar couldn't help but grin back. She wasn't that comfortable around kids or babies, but this one seemed to like her well enough, so maybe there was still hope for her. "Hey, Sarah-Grace."

Rycroft glanced back at her, jerked his head toward the exit. "Come on, we'll give you a lift."

"Thanks, but I've already got a cab coming. You guys go ahead."

He raised an eyebrow. "You sure?"

She nodded. "And maybe get that baby some pancakes on the way home."

Sarah's head popped off her father's shoulder, her black eyes lighting up. "Pancakes? I *love* pancakes."

Rycroft shot Briar a wry look. "Thanks a lot." He shifted Sarah into his left arm and reached down to pick up his bags while Grace wound an arm around his waist. "See you Monday."

"Yeah." Briar waited a moment, giving them some space because being too close to their family unit felt like an intrusion for some reason, then headed for the front doors.

While waiting for her cab, she pulled out her phone to call Matt, then held off. He was on an op in Colorado. She didn't want to take the chance of distracting him in any way right now.

But she was sure looking forward to this particular reunion. She couldn't wait to see the look on his face when she told him her news…

(Coming July 2018…)

About the Author

NY Times and USA Today Bestselling author Kaylea Cross writes edge-of-your-seat military romantic suspense. Her work has won many awards, including the Daphne du Maurier Award of Excellence, and has been nominated multiple times for the National Readers' Choice Awards. A Registered Massage Therapist by trade, Kaylea is also an avid gardener, artist, Civil War buff, Special Ops aficionado, belly dance enthusiast and former nationally-carded softball pitcher. She lives in Vancouver, BC with her husband and family.

You can visit Kaylea at www.kayleacross.com. If you would like to be notified of future releases, please join her newsletter: http://kayleacross.com/v2/newsletter/

Complete Booklist

ROMANTIC SUSPENSE

DEA FAST Series
Falling Fast
Fast Kill
Stand Fast
Strike Fast
Fast Fury
Fast Justice
Fast Vengeance

Colebrook Siblings Trilogy
Brody's Vow
Wyatt's Stand
Easton's Claim

Hostage Rescue Team Series
Marked
Targeted
Hunted
Disavowed
Avenged
Exposed
Seized
Wanted
Betrayed
Reclaimed
Shattered

Titanium Security Series
Ignited
Singed
Burned

Extinguished
Rekindled
Blindsided: A Titanium Christmas novella

Bagram Special Ops Series
Deadly Descent
Tactical Strike
Lethal Pursuit
Danger Close
Collateral Damage
Never Surrender (a MacKenzie Family novella)

Suspense Series
Out of Her League
Cover of Darkness
No Turning Back
Relentless
Absolution

PARANORMAL ROMANCE
Empowered Series
Darkest Caress

HISTORICAL ROMANCE
The Vacant Chair

EROTIC ROMANCE (writing as *Callie Croix*)
Deacon's Touch
Dillon's Claim
No Holds Barred
Touch Me
Let Me In
Covert Seduction

Made in the USA
Middletown, DE
26 May 2018